ISOLATION

THE DR SINCLAIR INVESTIGATIONS:
BOOK ONE

SJ GARDINER

ISOLATION PRESS

DEDICATION

To Mum, my first and best fan
I owe you everything

CHAPTER ONE

Bugger off, death—you're not taking this one. Dr Julia Sinclair snapped on latex gloves, then peeled away the pus-soaked dressing to reveal one of the nastiest wound infections she'd seen so far during her Infectious Diseases training.

"Bet that hurts like a bitch."

"Too bloody right." Brad Delaney's flushed cheeks contrasted with the white bed linen and made him look younger than twenty-four. Pain shadowed his eyes. "I look like a shark's been chewing on me. Did the surgeon cock it up and send you to cover his arse?"

She adopted her best reassure-the-patient face and kept her voice light and unworried. "Your appendix burst on the operating table. He had to open you up to wash all the crap out—if you'll excuse the technical term. Standard antibiotics aren't clearing the infection, so he asked for my advice. I'll be gentle, but I need to examine your abdomen. Okay?"

A tingle of adrenaline crept up the back of her neck. Did getting goosebumps from the challenge of a patient's life-threatening infection make her heartless? Maybe. But hell, she needed a distraction.

"Whatever it takes to get me out of here," he said. "Alive."

She palpated the reddened skin around his surgical incisions. Heat burned through her gloves.

Brad flinched.

"Sorry." Julia grabbed a swab kit off the side-table, opened the plastic packet and showed him the oversized cotton bud. "I need to collect some pus from deep inside your wound. We'll analyse it in the lab to find out what bugs are causing your infection."

His eyes widened, but he nodded.

"Brace yourself. This'll be cold." She wiped a saline-moistened gauze pad over his abdomen to clear the surface gunk, then grabbed a pair of forceps to loosen a staple from his surgical wound. Purulent discharge oozed across his skin. The stench of decay caught in the back of her throat. Lucky she'd missed lunch.

"Gross," Gabriel Flynn said in an almost-too-loud whisper. The new Infection Control Nurse leant forward with a dressing pad and mopped the stream of pus before it slimed onto the sheets.

"A little decorum, please."

"Sorry, doc." He tilted his head to one side. "My mouth gets me into so much trouble."

With his spiky blond hair and purple paisley shirt, Gabriel reminded her of a cheeky parrot. She couldn't help the twitch of her lips, but Brad's infection was no laughing matter. Calling it gross was like saying Perth summers were a little warm.

After giving Gabriel the evil eye, she resurrected her there's-nothing-wrong-with-a-little-pus expression and faced Brad again. "Ignore Gabriel. It's his first day here and I'm still house-training him."

"Hope he's quick with the sick bowl." Sweat beaded on Brad's forehead. He swallowed.

"Almost finished, then I'll get you something for the nausea."

Julia probed the incision with the swab, then smeared some discharge onto a glass slide. She slid the swab into its gel-filled holder, labelled the specimens, and slipped them into a plastic biohazard bag.

"Let me clean that up and cover your wound with a fresh dressing." Gabriel discarded the rubbish into a bag, then opened a new dressing pack.

While he poured a sachet of pink chlorhexidine disinfectant into a plastic bowl, Julia removed her gloves. She edged between the privacy curtains around the bed, then washed her hands at the sink near the door of the four-bed room. By the time she returned to her patient's bedside, Gabriel had secured the clean dressing and was drawing the sheet over Brad's abdomen.

"Thanks, Brad," she said. "I'll leave a note in your chart for your doctors and see you again tomorrow morning. Don't worry. We'll beat this bug."

Brad grimaced. "I'd try escaping, but in my condition even the old lolly trolley lady would catch me."

She drew open the curtains just as Brad flicked on the television. An ad for the evening news blared out.

"Discovered in Kings Park this afternoon. Don't miss this breaking story on Perth's best news."

She froze, staring at the televised images of blue-overalled police searching the bush in nearby Kings Park.

"It can't be," she whispered.

She'd heard the helicopter earlier in the afternoon, but assumed it was a tourist flight or maybe a medevac chopper rushing a patient to hospital. The news camera scanned the city skyline, swept over Kings Park, then zoomed closer like a wedge-tailed eagle swooping in for the kill. A clearing deep in the bush. Men in plain clothes stared at the ground.

A grave.

Gabriel's hand on her forearm jolted her back to life. Blood thundered in her ears, drowning out his words.

A few moments later, at the surgical ward nurses' station, Julia wrote Brad's details on a pathology request form. She gouged the date into the paper. The one-year anniversary of the day her world had shattered.

"Are you changing his antibiotics?" Gabriel asked.

Julia dragged her mind back to the patient. "I'll get an urgent Gram stain first to see why the standard triple therapy isn't working." She flashed him a smile, hoping it looked more real than it felt. "Jumping the queue is one of the few perks of working in the lab, but don't abuse the privilege. Stroppy scientists can make our lives miserable."

"Yes, mistress." Gabriel bowed his head. "Anything you say."

"Better believe it. While the boss is on holiday for the next two weeks, I don't want any mutinies ruining my chance at the Senior Registrar job."

The new post in Infectious Diseases and Clinical Microbiology had generated a lot of interest amongst her fellow Infectious Diseases trainees. If someone else landed the job, she'd have to move interstate or overseas. How could she leave Perth without knowing the truth?

She signed the request form and slipped it into the outer pocket of the biohazard bag. An arm wrapped around her waist. Warm breath caressed the side of her neck.

"Who's the toy boy?" A sultry whisper. "Should I be jealous?"

"Valerie, please. Not in front of the children." Julia spun around and hugged her best friend for a moment. "Meet my new Infection Control lackey, oops, I mean nurse, Gabriel Flynn. He's from south of the river. And Gabriel, I forget Valerie's exact title, but she's in charge of this surgical ward and if you really want to piss her off, call her Matron Cavanaugh."

Valerie poked out her tongue, an act at odds with her dark-haired elegance.

"That's the same face she pulled when we met in primary school," Julia said to Gabriel. "I hope she'll grow up one day."

Valerie zapped Gabriel with a high-voltage smile. "I know all Julia's dirty little secrets. Buy me a drink or three sometime if you want to know where the bodies are buried." She stroked his upper arm. "Are you wearing body armour, or are those muscles I can feel?"

"Stop groping the poor guy," Julia said, more sharply than she intended.

"Oh, sweetie, you know I didn't mean actual bodies." Valerie draped her arm around Julia's shoulders and pulled her close.

"Forget it." She shrugged off Valerie's arm before the comfort shattered her veneer of control. "I have to get this swab back to the lab."

"Talking about bodies, did you hear the news?" Gabriel shifted his weight from one foot to the other, as if too excited to keep still. "They found a body in Kings Park. I wonder if it's one of those missing girls."

Valerie gasped.

"Come on, Gabriel. We can't stand around gossiping or there'll be another dead body to deal with." Julia shooed him towards the exit. "Yours."

"I'm off-duty in five minutes," Valerie said. "I'll give you a lift home."

"No, I'll be fine." She squeezed the letter dangling from her necklace until the bar of the "T" dug into her palm.

"Nonsense. I'm not letting you go home alone, not when . . . You shouldn't be alone tonight. Car park, basement level, ten minutes or else."

"Yes, Matron." Julia's nerves unravelled a fraction. "What would I do without you? See you in ten."

"My idea of ten minutes or yours?" Valerie pointed to Gabriel's watch. "Vital equipment. In case nobody warned you, your main job is keeping her on time and making sure she remembers to go home."

"Thanks, Valerie. There goes my reputation for punctuality."

Julia escaped the surgical ward, with Valerie's laughter trailing behind her. Gabriel walked by her side. Please don't let him ask.

He darted glances at her.

"Is there something I should know about those missing girls?" he asked a few moments later.

"Secret women's business. I'd tell you, but then I'd have to lobotomise you and completely erase your memory."

"Okay, okay. I'll butt out."

She faked a laugh. "So, how'd you like your first day at Perth General Hospital?"

"Hmm, let me think. A puke-inducing wound, the promise of some juicy gossip about my new boss, and I've even been fondled. More excitement than I've had in months. Absolute heaven."

They continued in silence through hospital-green corridors and down a flight of stairs until they reached the Clinical Microbiology laboratory in the Department of Pathology. The lab was tucked away in the old part of the hospital, where the architecture was more haunted asylum than high-tech scientific institute. She led Gabriel to the bacteriology section, her far-from-fragrant home away from home while she completed her Infectious Diseases studies.

Gabriel pinched his nose. "Does it always smell like a urinal?"

"Sometimes it's more eau de rubbish dump. You'll get used to it."

"I can't wait."

"Working evening shifts again?" she asked the scientist who hunched over a computer keyboard, both index fingers in full-flight. "Bet your wife loves that. Who did you annoy this time?"

"Nobody. I volunteered." He swivelled away from the keyboard. "Anything to get me away from home while the twins are teething. What's your excuse?"

"Saving lives, avoiding domestic chaos, the usual. Would you do a quick Gram stain for me? Please?"

"Sure, if you'll phone this urgent CSF result through to Emergency." He handed her a request form with some numbers written on the back.

She scanned the form. "Champagne tap. Someone's been practising."

"What's a champagne tap?" Gabriel asked.

"If there are no red blood cells in the cerebrospinal fluid, the person who did the lumbar puncture didn't cause any bleeding. Once upon a time, they'd score a bottle of champagne—or cheap bubbly, more likely."

By the time she'd phoned the result to the registrar in the Emergency Department, the Gram stain was ready. She sat at the double-header microscope and adjusted the fine focus to find lots of white blood cells and grapelike clusters of dark blue bacteria.

"Shit. Staph infection. No wonder triple therapy isn't working."

Gabriel peered down the other pair of eye-pieces. "Pink and blue blobs."

"You'll never have to do any lab work, but learning some basic microbiology will help you." Julia used the pointer, an arrow-shaped orange light, to show him the significant features. "The big blobs are white blood cells, a sign of the body fighting infection. Those small, round, blue ones clumped together like bunches of grapes are staphylococci."

"Cool."

"I'll phone it through to the ward and add fluclox to cover the staph. Go home, Gabriel. This should only take a minute."

Right. She could've discovered a cure for the common cold in less time than it actually took. The surgical Resident Medical Officer had already left for the day, and the nurse refused to take a phone order. At last, she tracked down the evening shift RMO and told him to prescribe the antibiotic and give the first dose.

⸺◈⸺

Twenty minutes later, Julia threw open the stairwell door to the gloomy carpark basement and hesitated. How could it get so cold in summer? She rubbed her goose-bumped arms. If it weren't for the petrol fumes and tyres squealing on the floor above, she'd swear she was in a subterranean crypt. The oppressive darkness triggered her childhood nightmare of being trapped underground, buried alive.

Don't be ridiculous. She stepped forward. The heavy door slammed shut behind her.

"Fabulous security, slackers." Her voice echoed. She glared at the far corner where the security camera's red light winked in lazy insolence. "Ever considered getting off your arse and changing a light globe down here?"

A total waste of breath, but it made her feel a little better.

"Valerie? Where are you?"

No reply.

Once her eyes acclimatised to the dark, she walked along the rows of cars. On her third circuit, she spotted the battered Toyota dwarfed between two four-wheel-drive tanks. The "This Bitch Bites" sticker on the rear window warned misguided tailgaters. She peered inside. Empty. Valerie was never late. Payback?

Julia returned to the stairwell. She propped the door open with her body, then hunted through her briefcase until she unearthed her mobile phone. No text messages or missed calls. She hit Valerie's number, and waited for her excuse.

It rang and rang and rang. No answer, no diversion to voicemail. Odd.

She moved the phone away from her ear and strained to hear if Madonna's "Like a Virgin" tinkled somewhere in the car park.

Nothing. She ended the call.

An emergency on the ward? A lost child or a wandering patient? The distraction of a well-muscled thigh? Maybe she'd lost her phone and gone searching for help. Classic Valerie trouble-shooting. Why do it yourself when you could charm a susceptible man into doing it for you?

She phoned the ward clerk. "Is Valerie still there?"

"She left about twenty minutes ago. Tried her mobile? It's surgically attached to her hand."

"Thanks."

Maybe Valerie was in one of the hospital's many black holes where mobile phone reception mysteriously vanished. Julia scribbled a note and left it under one of the Toyota's windscreen wipers. She'd call her again from home, or better still, a well-lit and crowded bar. Not a night for being alone.

Julia rushed to the stairwell and raced up the stairs, eager to escape the gloom before she scared herself to death.

Her mobile beeped as soon as she hit daylight. A text from Valerie: Tied up. V.

Not even close to an apology. Knowing Valerie, she really might be tied up—and enjoying it. Julia's shoulders relaxed. Nothing drastic had happened to her dearest friend.

If only she could say the same for her sister.

Twelve long months of waiting for Tess to walk through the door. Twelve long months of hoping to hear her sister's voice on the phone.

Twelve long months of hell.

Chapter Two

Gatecrashing a homicide investigation probably wasn't what his therapist had in mind for his first trip out of the office. Tough. Detective Sergeant Nick Randall had been confined to desk duties for an eternity. Another day driving a desk? His head would explode.

He dragged on a pair of paper booties, then followed the trail of blue and white crime scene tape deep into the bush. Being a Monday, there weren't many day-trippers around to gawp at all the police activity in Kings Park. Traffic buzzed on the nearby freeway overpass, drivers rushing across the Narrows Bridge over the Swan River, eager to get home after a hard day's work. He should be amongst them, but had detoured after hearing the news. Forget beer o'clock. A task force could be his best way back to the Major Crime Squad.

Sweat trickled down his spine. The Fremantle Doctor must be late. That cool sea breeze made summers bearable. He swatted a suicidal blowfly and pressed on. With each step, civilisation faded. It made perfect sense in a sick and twisted way. Why drive out to the country or up into the Darling Ranges to dump a corpse when natural bush sat right next to the city? A killer's paradise.

Several minutes later, he reached the edge of a small clearing and stopped to soak in the crime scene atmosphere, the first he'd attended in far too long. His heart rate kicked up. He felt more alive than he had in months. A news helicopter swooped past, the downdraft thrashing the leaves overhead. Most action focussed on the far side of the clearing under a massive ghost gum with a smooth, white trunk and branches that could snap and fall with deadly force.

A stocky guy with close-cropped grey hair waved to him. "Hey, Nick. Someone's dying to meet you." Detective Inspector George Jaworski's booming laugh ricocheted through the ghost gums, startling the kookaburras into competition.

"Time for a new joke book, boss." Nick strode along the path marked by metal plates until he stood by the gravesite.

"About bloody time they let you out." George slapped him on the back, then turned to the forensics officer with a camera. "Remember Nick Randall, mate? Hope the trick cyclists didn't bugger him up too much."

Nick's shoulders tightened. So much for confidentiality. "Like I needed more doctors."

"Been hitting the bleach?" George ruffled Nick's hair.

"Surf trip down south."

"Shark bait," the forensics officer said with a shudder.

"Look at him. Bikini bait, more like. Enough buggerising about." George gestured at the disturbed ground. "Look like any of your missing persons?"

Nick crouched beside the remains. The stench of decomposition reminded him to breathe through his mouth. Leaf litter and grey sand covered most of the body. Smaller bones were scattered about, suggesting animal activity. Hungry cats, perhaps. What a gross idea. Metal glinted in the sand. A ring encircling a bony finger. Clumps of dried flesh clung to the larger bones. No sign of any clothing. Hang on. Something rubbery?

He glanced up. "Okay to clear some of this dirt?"

"Knock yourself out."

Nick pulled on a latex glove, then brushed some sand away, careful not to disturb the body. "Breast implant. Looks like the vic's a female. Serial number could help with her ID."

He stood up, wiped the sand off his gloved hands. The forensics officer snapped another shot.

George nodded. "Knew you were a boob man."

"Beware jumping to conclusions, gentlemen." A young Indian woman in blue overalls approached them, a fishing tackle box held in one elegant hand. "Have you not considered gender reassignment surgery?"

"G'day, doc. Thought we'd start without you. Meet my former DS, Nick Randall. He's taking it easy with some old missing persons cases." George welcomed her with a grin. "Dr Indira Singh is the new forensic pathologist, a vast improvement on the cranky old sod we used to get."

The pathologist opened her tackle box to reveal a medical kit. After donning latex gloves, she picked up a stethoscope. She bent over the body as if searching for the heart.

"I too have my feeble jokes." She smiled, straightened up, and put her stethoscope back in the tackle box. "This person is most definitely dead, as you can see for yourselves."

"How long has she—or he—been here?" George dragged out the emphasis on "he".

"You know better than to ask me to speculate on such a matter, Detective Inspector." Dr Singh squatted to examine the body, directing her attention to the pelvic bones. "Judging by the angle of the pubic rami, 'she' is the correct pronoun, Detective Inspector. Considerable decomposition has occurred. It has been very hot and dry. I would suggest more than a month, but there are many factors to consider. If we find evidence of insect activity, the forensic entomologist will be of most use."

"I don't remember any missing women with breast implants, but I'll check the records," Nick said. "Maybe she's from interstate."

Dr Singh rubbed her lower back, then took a brush from her medical kit. She flicked more sand away from the victim's breast area. "I am not a 'boob man' and I hesitate to claim any expertise in cosmetic surgery, but I am not familiar with this model of implant."

"Foreign?" Nick asked.

"Perhaps that is the case. I hope to schedule the autopsy for tomorrow morning. I'll determine the serial number and pass it on to you then."

"Thank you, doctor." Autopsy? Great. The price he had to pay if he wanted to get back into the Major Crime Squad.

"Back up a second there, mate." George scowled. "I'll go to the autopsy and will call you with the serial number so you can check it on your computer."

Dr Singh cleared her throat. "Excuse me, gentlemen. I wish to examine this woman's body in situ and in relative peace, so please take your pissing contest elsewhere."

A smile dimpled one of her cheeks.

"Sorry, doctor. Of course." Nick crossed the clearing to the shelter of another ghost gum.

"Back in a tick," George said to Dr Singh, then followed him.

Nick spun around. "For fuck's sake, boss. I can handle an autopsy."

"I never said you couldn't, but this is a homicide investigation. In case you've forgotten, you're not an active member of Major Crimes."

"I passed my psych eval. I'm cleared for normal duties. What else do I have to do?"

George raised his hands, palms forward. "Give it time. They're being extra cautious. If I hadn't stopped you, you could've broken that doctor's jaw."

"Bastard deserved it. How did he miss that injury?" The question still haunted him. Almost as often as "Why had he gone to work and left her alone?"

"Look, I'm sorry about your fiancée, and if you need to talk . . ."

"Yeah, I know, but I'm all talked out." Nick blinked away the image of Kym's face, distorted by agony. "I'd rather bury myself in work."

"Denial. That's the spirit. Go back to the old orifice. Hit the Missing Persons database. I need someone I can trust working on the ID of this body." George's tone left no room for disagreement. "I'll square it with your boss."

More bloody paperwork. Nick counted silently to ten. Better make that one hundred if he wanted to regain his position in the Major Crime Squad.

CHAPTER THREE

JULIA PEERED THROUGH HER hair at the alarm clock. Only six thirty, far too early to get up on a Tuesday, especially when she wasn't due at work until nine. She stretched her legs, then froze. Her left foot was touching something hairy and warm—another leg, if she wasn't mistaken. Pretty sure it wasn't one of hers. She rolled over and studied the sleeping beauty beside her.

Spot diagnosis? She'd lost her mind.

After missing her lift from Valerie, she'd passed the Subiaco Hotel on her walk home. There he'd been, her ex. He'd dragged her into an enthusiastic hug and wouldn't let her go until she agreed to just one drink. Better than going home alone to an empty house. Trust Leon to lure her away from her worries about patients and skeletons, distracting her with soft words and broad shoulders. Alcohol never improved her judgement.

That, and temporary hormonal insanity.

She edged the sheet down his back. Anatomy had always been her favourite subject at uni. Just a peek. Even asleep, he looked fitter than she remembered. What was his secret? She spent too much time with sick people. One healthy, naked man and she couldn't resist a perve.

Eyes only. Hands off.

Much safer to study her bedroom. Apart from the scattered clothes trailing from the door towards the bed, it wasn't too messy. Polished jarrah timber floors shone in the early morning sun. Oscar, her grey and white cat, gave her the evil eye from his perch on the bedside table, his displeasure obvious in every twitch of his tail. How dare she stay out late, bringing home some stranger to sleep on his bed?

She slid out of bed and tiptoed to the kitchen to battle with the Whiskas can. The smell of tuna made her gag. She left Oscar snuffling at his food bowl, and retreated to the bathroom for a long, cool shower.

Afterwards, she wrapped herself in a towel and returned to the bedroom. A groan from the bed reminded her she wasn't alone.

"Why is it so bright in here?" Leon hid his face in the pillow, leaving some of his best assets exposed.

She tossed the cat's ball at him. It bounced off his bare buttock and badoinged across the floor. "Have you had butt implants?"

"Show some respect. I'm dying here." The pillow muffled his voice. He rolled over and sat up ever so slowly. Both hands held his head steady, as if to stop it from falling off.

"You big sook."

"She'll kill me."

Her stomach dropped, a rollercoaster of disbelief. "She'll kill you?"

"My fiancée." Leon grimaced. "Nobody saw us together, did they?"

Fiancée? Dead man talking.

"You're a hopeless tart. I knew that and yet here you are. Naked. In my bed. Again. How could I be so stupid?"

"You looked so tense. I thought you needed stress relief."

"Great. Leon and his magic, stress-relieving penis."

"Don't be like that, babe." He tried his little-boy-lost smile. It failed. "Don't babe me. Try that on your fiancée."

"She'll kill me. Lucky she's away this week. Did I enjoy myself?"

"How much did you drink last night?"

"Out of practice. She won't let me touch alcohol." He circled his fingertips over the sides of his forehead. Maybe his brain was in danger of leaking out of his skull.

Good. "Don't worry. Your virtue is intact."

"But . . ." He lifted the sheet and glanced down at his naked body, then at the trail of clothes across the floor.

"Nothing happened. I came out of the bathroom, ready for action, and found you snoring your head off. A lucky escape. For me."

"Did you spike my drink?"

"I'm not that desperate."

"I do hate to disappoint . . ."

"I'll survive. Now, get your almost-married naked body out of my bed."

A languid stretch while he examined the surroundings. "Punching bag in the bedroom? That's strangely arousing." He crossed the floor and faked slow-motion punches at the bag. "Had it for long?"

"Valerie gave it to me last Christmas. It had your face taped to it."

"Ouch, guess I deserved that."

His hangover apparently forgotten, he threw more power into his punches and picked up speed. Muscles rippled beneath his skin.

His bare skin. Why wasn't nude boxing an Olympic sport?

"Put some clothes on before one of us gets hurt." She forced herself to look away. "Let's go out for breakfast."

"But what if someone sees us together?"

He was the one in a so-called committed relationship. She shook her head. Maybe she should be committed.

Julia lost her appetite when she saw Tuesday's *West Australian* newspaper. The skeleton in Kings Park dominated the front page. A full-page story inside speculated on the victim's identity. Her last photo of Tess smiled up at her, breaking her heart all over again.

No identification yet, or the police family liaison officer would've called with an update. How long would she have to wait this time?

She abandoned Leon mid-breakfast and rushed to the hospital. She logged on to the laboratory computer system to check and release the morning's lab reports. The occasional case generated a phone call or required an explanatory comment, but most were straightforward. So far, no hassles. Typical. Just when she needed to be too busy to think, work slackened off.

Her firefighter calendar caught her eye—another gift from Valerie, of course. Mr December 2019 was a few days overdue. That took ten seconds to fix. Hell, last December . . . She had to escape her thoughts.

She dashed into the bacteriology lab. "Any positive blood cultures for me to sort out?"

A machine monitored blood culture bottles continuously, triggering an alarm if it detected bacterial growth. Patients with bacteria circulating in their bloodstreams needed urgent antibiotic treatment.

"Nope." The morning shift scientist stacked agar plates into the incubator.

"Just my luck. A severe shortage of sick people." She ignored his raised eyebrows. "Is anything growing on Brad Delaney's wound swab?"

"Yes, a heavy growth of *Staph aureus*. I left the plates on the bench." The scientist slammed the incubator door. A dank odour wafted through the lab.

Julia opened one of the blood agar plates to find the familiar yellow colonies that gave the bacteria its name. Golden staph. Lots of people carried it on their skin or in their noses with no problems, but in an open wound it could be a cold-blooded killer.

"Glad I started him on fluclox last night," she said. "That should cover it. I'll let the team know." If nothing else, she had her job under control.

She returned to her office and pulled up Brad's latest blood results on her computer. Had he responded to the change in antibiotics? She scrolled down the screen. Oh, no, his latest white cell count had soared even higher and his other inflammatory markers had also skyrocketed.

Hang on. They'd moved him overnight to the High Dependency Unit, the HDU, one step down from the Intensive Care Unit. A sure sign his condition had deteriorated. Poor Brad. That'd teach her to wish she was busy.

⋅⋅⋅◆⋅⋅⋅

Several minutes later, Julia entered the HDU. The high-tech unit looked after those patients not quite sick enough for the Intensive Care Unit, but requiring more care than the general wards could provide. She approached the nurse in charge, a no-nonsense woman who'd been a nurse since the days when doctors were gods and matrons ruled the hospital.

"How's Brad Delaney?" she asked.

The woman pulled a face that suggested Julia should look for herself and not ask stupid questions of nurses who have better things to do. "Not that flash. Spiking fevers up to thirty-nine degrees. His IV site's a right mess."

Julia hurried to Brad's bedside. He blinked at her, bemused. She lifted the sheet off his left arm. Her breath caught in her throat. His entire arm was swollen. Florid inflammation spread from his intravenous line insertion site. A septic pool festered under the clear dressing on his forearm. A right mess, indeed.

She turned back to the nurse. "That line needs changing ASAP, and please send the tip to the lab for culture."

The fluclox hadn't touched his infection. Was it a resistant strain? She took his medical chart from the nurses' desk and flicked through it. Methicillin-resistant *Staphylococcus aureus*, or MRSA, was uncommon in Western Australia—one, if not the only, advantage of its geographical isolation. The bacteria had earned its name by being untreatable with most common antibiotics. As a precaution, patients and hospital staff who had been in hospitals either interstate or overseas were screened for MRSA and isolated from other patients until their swabs were cleared.

Brad had never been in hospital before. Had he travelled? Nothing about it in his chart. Had he caught it in Perth General Hospital from another patient? Or worse, from a staff member?

The surgical registrar entered the unit and ambled over to Brad's bedside. The wrinkles in his scrubs matched the creases in his face. He must've collapsed onto an on-call bed after a hard night's operating. After pulling on some sterile gloves, he removed the dressing from Brad's surgical wound.

Brad pushed the registrar's hands away.

Julia grabbed Brad's hands and held them out of the way. So hot and sweaty. "Sorry, Brad. This won't take long."

A blocked drain stench filled the air. Inflamed redness spread across Brad's whole lower abdomen, most severe around the stabs used for the laparoscopy and the slash where the surgeon had opened him up to wash out the peritoneal cavity. Thick, yellow discharge drained from all the wounds.

The registrar palpated Brad's abdomen, making him curse. "Tight as a drum. I'll have to take him back to theatre." He dragged his gloves off, then flicked them into the bin. "Do you know the sensitivities yet?"

"Not until tomorrow morning. Fluclox isn't working. Let's change it to vancomycin in case it's MRSA. Keep the Gram-negative and anaerobe cover going." She altered the antibiotic order on the medication chart. "We'd better get a set of blood cultures before the first dose of vanc, and move him to a single room. He has to be in isolation."

The nurse had her hands on her hips and her attitude set on stubborn. "We'll have to special him if he's in a single room. I don't have enough staff."

Having one nurse dedicated to the care of one patient meant the other nurses had to pick up extra work—never a popular suggestion.

"I could close the unit to new admissions if you'd prefer." Julia's voice sharpened. She was in no mood for a nursing mutiny.

The registrar raised his hands in surrender. "Leave me out of this. I'm just the guy with the knife."

"I suppose I could call in an agency nurse."

"Whatever it takes." Julia turned back to Brad. "We'll give you a different antibiotic straight away. You need another operation today. The surgeon will let you know more about that soon. Brad? Do you understand?"

His eyes flickered shut. He mumbled something.

Bugger. "Where's the vanc? I'll give him the first dose now."

She had to get on top of the infection fast. Brad had to survive.

⁂

After confirming Brad's operation was organised, Julia paged Gabriel. If it was an MRSA wound infection, they had to check everyone Brad had been in contact with since his admission to hospital. An uncontrolled outbreak the second the boss went on holiday? That whooshing sound was her promotion flying out the window.

She tracked him down to the nurses' station on the third-floor surgical ward, where he and the ward clerk were chatting like a couple of manic schoolgirls.

"We've got a problem. Where's Valerie?" she asked. "Saves me repeating myself."

"No idea." Gabriel gestured towards a couple of nurses near a drug trolley. "They were complaining about her being late."

Miss Punctuality, late? Julia's spidey senses sparked to full alert. "Has anyone phoned her?"

The ward clerk nodded. "No answer at home, and her mobile's off."

Julia phoned Valerie's home number and mobile herself. No answer. There must be some rational explanation for Valerie's absence, but why hadn't she let someone know she'd be late?

Had Martin MacDougall tempted her away for the night? Maybe they'd overslept. Julia scanned the operating theatre list on the ward clerk's desk. Martin's second case had finished already, but that didn't mean he was the one operating. Someone could be covering his list at short notice.

She swapped the theatre list for the ward clerk's list of current inpatients to see which of them had come in contact with Brad Delaney. How far back to look? He would've gone straight to theatre from Emergency. Hell, what if one of the theatre staff was the source of Brad's infection?

"Gabriel, that patient we saw yesterday might have MRSA. Would you start a list of ward contacts while I pop down to theatre?" Too easy for people to ignore phone calls and emails. The direct approach worked best.

"Love to. Even if it's not MRSA, it'll be a good practice run for me." He pulled a notebook from his pocket with a flourish. "Fire away."

"Thanks. Make a list of all the patients who shared Brad Delaney's room since his admission. Also, get a copy of the nurses' roster and crosscheck with his medical record to see who looked after him. Note doctors and other staff too. Any questions, page me. I won't be long."

———◦———

Julia drummed her fingers on the reception desk, waiting for the theatre nurse manager to reappear. Her gaze drifted to the whiteboard with the morning's list of operations. Like most doctors, surgeons had their own language full of acronyms—some were familiar, others stretched her imagination.

Wait a minute. Martin was operating. Valerie couldn't be with him. What case was he up to? His lap chole had gone to recovery, so he'd removed a gall bladder already. Next on the list was "Ex lap" . . . hmm, exploratory laparotomy. Cut someone open, find the problem, fix it. If only her job was that straightforward. Scalpel envy.

"Here you go." The nurse manager handed over a list of all the theatre staff who'd worked last Friday. "Some people float between rooms, so if you want to know exactly who worked in what theatre and when, you'll have to check the op notes and ask around. I don't have time to do it for you."

"Thanks, that's all I need . . . although while I'm here, how's theatre three going?"

The nurse manager pushed a microphone towards Julia. "Hit three and ask."

She did. "Dr Sinclair here. Could you ask Martin to call me between cases? Or if he's nearly finished, I'll wait at the reception desk."

Voices mumbled, then the nurse came back on the line. "He said to tell you he's elbow-deep in this patient and running way behind schedule. He wants to talk to you about this case anyway, so you should get changed and come on in."

More mumbling. "Unless you're scared of a little blood, he said."

Cheeky sod. She dealt with worse bodily fluids every day. "See you soon."

"Do you know how to—"

"I remember."

In the operating suite change-room, she slipped into a set of surgical scrubs and pulled a pair of booties over her shoes. Dressed for action, she left through the door that led into the clean area. Cutting through the anaesthetics bay, she cleaned her hands with hand sanitiser, then put on a cap and mask. No need to scrub in, so she skipped the gloves. She entered theatre three, then joined the anaesthetist at the head of the operating table.

Martin glanced at her. The skin around his denim-blue eyes crinkled. "Just in time for the good bit."

He diathermied a small bleeder. The stench of sizzling flesh penetrated Julia's mask. A quick dab with gauze to confirm the bleeding had stopped, then Martin reached into the open abdominal wound and pulled out the patient's spleen.

"Get a load of this." His bloody gloved fingers exposed the tear in the spleen. "Almost ripped in half."

"What happened?"

"Trail bike flipped upside down. Handle-bar skewered him."

"Ouch. Vaccinated?"

"No time. Too unstable. Leave a consult in the chart for you?"

"Sure, I'll see him when he wakes up." She'd have to warn the patient of the increased risks of infection post-splenectomy.

"I'd hate him to die of overwhelming sepsis after my excellent surgery."

"Such modesty."

Martin bowed, then turned his attention back to the patient, checking for any more bleeding from the operative site.

"Perfect. See? Magic hands."

"I've heard. That's why I wanted to talk to you." Beside her, the anaesthetist chuckled. Julia's cheeks flamed. "That's not what I meant."

"What did you and Valerie get up to last night?" Martin picked up a suture needle.

Her heart skipped a beat. "Valerie stood me up. I assumed you'd distracted her. When did you see her last?"

"Yesterday, just after lunch. Why?"

"She hasn't come to work today and I can't get hold of her. Did she mention anything to you?"

He sutured his patient's surgical incision. His movements were so calm, his demeanour so unruffled, she itched to slap him.

"She wanted to go away for a couple of days, but . . . uh, I couldn't. Maybe she's buggered off without me."

"Where to?" Better she escaped for a break than—oh, no. She couldn't bear the alternative.

"Somewhere down south."

The door flew open.

Simon Bailey, an anaesthetics registrar, crossed the room with a feline grace that belied his weightlifter build. "Heard you had an interesting case, Martin. Need a hand?"

"Can you protect me from Julia? She thinks I'm hiding Valerie." He finished suturing and stepped back from the operating table.

"Watch her right hook," Simon said. "Saw her at the hospital gym. Punching bag never had a chance."

"How come I haven't seen you there?" Martin asked her.

"Too crowded." Too much testosterone and too many eyes.

"I had no one to spot me last time I lifted." Simon nudged her shoulder. "Attendance has dropped off since you left."

Martin laughed. "I bet. Do you spar somewhere else? I'd pay to watch—"

"Boys! Valerie's missing. Don't you care?"

"Of course I do." Martin gestured for her to follow him into the scrub room. He tore off his mask and removed his gloves. "I'd help look for her, but this patient jumped the queue and I'm way behind with my morning list."

The scrub nurse peered around the corner of the door. "Room four are screaming for you, Martin, and you haven't done your op notes in here yet." She held the door open, waiting.

"Let me know when you find her." He flashed Julia a smile, then returned to the operating theatre.

Simon moved closer. "Are you okay? You look like you need that drink I owe you."

His heavy-lidded gaze reminded Julia of her cat watching a mouse. Concern for Valerie must've kicked her imagination into overdrive.

"What drink?"

"Surgical Christmas party?"

"It's not like me to forget a drink, but that was a whole year ago." That was the week Tess disappeared. Her vision shimmered.

"She'll be fine. Valerie's a survivor."

"What if she's had an accident or is too sick to get to the phone or . . . I have to check her house."

"Come on, I'll give you a lift." Simon grabbed her elbow and steered her towards the change-rooms. "See you on the other side."

"It's okay. If she hasn't turned up, I'll duck out at lunchtime."

"I've got a free hour now."

She pulled away and rubbed her arm as if his fingers had branded her skin. "No, I have to get back to work. Thanks, anyway."

"Do it your own way." He held his hands up in surrender. "It wouldn't kill you to let someone help you for a change."

"You sound just like my mother." Or Valerie.

Where could she be?

Chapter Four

Dr Indira Singh adjusted the overhead microphone. The morning meeting with the coroner and her fellow forensic pathologists had finished at last. She prepared for her first autopsy of the day, that of the corpse discovered in Kings Park.

The mortuary technician had already weighed the body and positioned it on the autopsy table. She waited for him to finish clattering the instruments on the metal side-table before she turned on the microphone. Behind her, the door creaked open. She turned around as Detective Inspector George Jaworski strolled into the small room, a room that felt even smaller with his presence.

"G'day, doc." His deep voice echoed in the starkly furnished space. "Ready for action?"

"Your timing is impeccable."

"Bet you say that to all the guys." He inhaled deeply. "Dry decomp. Not bad. I like to get my nose settled in as soon as possible."

"A wise move, Detective Inspector, utilising how the sense of smell fatigues rapidly."

He grimaced. "Doesn't always work. Call me George and I'll let you in on a little secret."

"Do tell, George."

"Whenever the body needs the dirty room, I make sure I'm busy elsewhere and send one of the young guys along."

"I wonder if I could do the same." She glanced at the corpse. "No, I owe it to the victims to look after them, regardless of their physical condition. Now, are we waiting for anyone else to join us? Detective Sergeant Randall perhaps?"

"Nope. He's busy with paperwork. Let's get cracking."

"Cracking? I promise to be more careful than that."

He snorted. "I'll shut up and let you get to work."

"Thank you, George." She turned to the mortuary technician. "Are the X-rays ready?"

"I'll check." He left the room.

"Such a degree of decomposition complicates the post-mortem examination," she said. "Our forensic anthropologist will examine the body later today, but I thought it important to ascertain the serial numbers of the breast implants so we can identify this woman as expeditiously as possible."

Someone must miss her.

The technician re-entered the room. "There's a hold-up with the X-rays, but they'll be here by the time you finish the external exam. Crime scene guys should be here any second."

"Well, let's get cracking." She clicked on the microphone and began her introductory spiel.

She would do her absolute best to return this woman to her family and loved ones. Shame she hadn't been discovered earlier, but it was fortunate they had found her at all. Unlike so many others.

⊙

Julia leant forward on the hard plastic chair, nerves buzzing like high-voltage wires. Her shirt clung to her back. The air-conditioning barely dented the late afternoon heat. By the time she'd caught up with the lab work, Valerie still hadn't reappeared or returned her calls. Her local cop shop had shut for the day, so she'd driven into the city to her closest 24-hour police station, Curtin House in Beaufort Street.

Another glance at her watch. Still Tuesday. Only five minutes had passed since the last time she checked. Would this police officer ever appear?

A faint whiff of stale cigarette smoke hung in the waiting room air, defying the No Smoking sign on the wall. Inane mobile phone conversations added to the pollution. A poster telling her to lock her car and not to leave valuables in it held her attention for a few seconds. What was the point of worrying about a few trinkets when her best friend was missing? Valerie. Missing. She squeezed her eyes shut.

Despair drilled deeper into her bones.

"Miss Sinclair?"

Julia felt rather than heard her name, like the seductive heat of a vodka shot. She opened her eyes and looked towards the doorway. Holy crap. A tall, blond man walked towards her, faded jeans moulded to his long legs. He could be Mr January in the police calendar. Hell, he should be the whole twelve months. She stood up and smoothed her skirt with sweaty palms.

"I'm Detective Sergeant Nick Randall." His green eyes held her gaze.

"Yes?"

He raised one eyebrow, and she noticed a scar sliced through it. "You want to report someone missing?"

How could she succumb to lust when her best friend was missing, or worse? She nodded, not trusting her voice to cooperate or her libido to behave.

"Sorry about the delay. Come through to the interview rooms. It's cooler upstairs."

He ushered her into a lift, up a few floors, down a long corridor and into an interview room, then he left her alone. Soft blue paint on the walls, a couple of faux leather armchairs, and a coffee table. Not at all what she'd expected. Where was the metal cage with harsh lighting and the stench of fear soaked into the brick-work? Maybe she watched too many crime shows on TV.

She settled into the chair opposite the door. Her heart raced. The police had come to her home when Tess vanished. One endless year ago, but the memories cut deep.

Moments later, the police officer returned. He placed two glasses of water on the table, then sat opposite her. "Okay. I'll need to enter details on the computer later, but first, tell me why you're here."

"Right, where do I start? I saw Valerie at work late yesterday afternoon. We both work at the Perth General Hospital. We've known each other for years. She offered me a lift home, but I was late and when I got to her car, she was nowhere to be seen. I got a text saying she was tied up, but nothing specific." Her words stumbled over one another. She yanked at the neck of her T-shirt. Not enough air. "I've kept trying to contact her, but have had no luck. She didn't turn up to work this morning. Her car's still in the hospital car park, in the same bay as yesterday. I went to her house and found today's newspaper lying on the front verge, the letterbox full of mail. She hasn't been home since yesterday. Nobody at the hospital knows where she is. And she wouldn't take time off work without notifying anyone."

She sagged into the chair and drew in a lungful of oxygen. Blurting it all out made the reality sink in. Tess, all over again. She pressed her fingers to the letter on her necklace, the one she'd bought for her sister's birthday.

"Does she have a husband? A boyfriend?"

"Yes, a boyfriend, but he denies knowing where she is. I doubt his wife would let him go away with Valerie." Her smile froze halfway to her cheeks. "Wives are funny that way."

"What's his name?" He flipped open a notebook.

"Martin MacDougall, a surgeon at our hospital."

"Who else might know where she is? Family? Neighbours?"

"Her parents live in the eastern states, somewhere in country Victoria." She broke eye contact and stared at the table. They'd be heartbroken. "She doesn't have much to do with her neighbours."

"Anyone else we should talk to?"

"Her ex-husband, Richard Cavanaugh. She kicked him out last year after one punch too many. They're not divorced yet. For some bizarre reason, he thinks she'll take him back if he hangs around often enough." She crossed her legs and whacked her shin on the coffee table. "Ouch."

"She's only been missing for one night."

"A lot can happen in one night."

"Yes." His answer, harsh and raw. He rubbed his right hand over the scar on his forehead, masking his expression.

"A year ago, my sister disappeared."

"Sinclair? I thought the name was familiar." He flicked through some pages of his notebook. "Tess Sinclair's your sister?"

"Yes." Her voice quavered. "Why have you got her name in your notebook? Is it her? The body in Kings Park?"

"How old is your sister?" His expression gave nothing away.

"She's sixteen . . . she was sixteen when she disappeared. By now, she'd be seventeen." Julia could feel each heartbeat thump in her throat. She could see each flicker of the fluorescent light. She could hear the clock ticking slower and slower, taunting her.

"We don't have a firm identification yet, but . . ." He paused as if deciding how to break her heart. "Did your sister ever have surgery?"

"She had her appendix out when she was ten." Why wouldn't he tell her? She wanted to rip the pen from his hand.

"Nothing cosmetic?"

"Definitely not. Does that mean it's not her?"

"Yes."

Julia slumped forward. She rested her elbows on her knees and cradled her head in her hands. The surge of adrenaline left her shaky. She concentrated on each breath until her shoulders unknotted and her vision cleared.

She had to thrust aside her concern for Tess. Her sister would haunt her nightmares forever, but now she had to focus on Valerie. Valerie had helped her survive those black days. She couldn't, wouldn't abandon her.

"What else do you need from me?"

"Do you have a key to her house?"

"No, Martin might have one. I'll ask him."

"Leave that to me."

She hesitated, unsure if she could face the empty house. "Could I go with you? I'd know if anything was out of place."

"Possibly, but only after we've examined the place first. If anything goes wrong, the boss will have my . . ."

"Balls for breakfast?"

"Exactly," he said, with a laugh in his voice. "I didn't realise you knew him. Now, let's get these details on the computer."

He stood and guided her to an open-plan office around the corner. Straightaway, his phone rang.

"Nick Randall. Yes. Send her up to my desk." He turned back to Julia. "Info on another case. Should only take a minute." He opened a file on his computer. "Let's start with Valerie's full name, address and date of birth."

Moments later, he glanced towards the doorway and raised a hand in greeting. Footsteps tapped towards them.

"Julia?"

She spun around. Indira Singh stood behind her, immaculately dressed in a sapphire blue silk suit. They'd bonded over cocktails at the last College of Pathologists' annual dinner.

"Hope you're not wearing that to a crime scene," Julia said.

Indira laughed. "No, I'm on my way to court. No exposure to body fluids, I hope. Why are you here?"

"A friend of mine is missing, Valerie Cavanaugh."

"I'm so sorry to hear that." The pathologist glanced at her watch. "I wish I had more time, but I must be incredibly rude and pass some information to Detective Sergeant Randall, then rush away."

"Pretend I'm not here," Julia said.

"No. Listen in. You may be able to help the detective." Indira handed a piece of paper to Nick Randall. "This is the breast implant information. I've emailed the serial number to the manufacturer and will forward any news to you. Now this is where Julia may assist us. I also found a surgical plate in the victim's forearm. X-ray examination revealed inflammatory changes consistent with infection around the plate."

"Any chance of cultures?" Julia asked.

Indira shook her head. "Decomposition is too advanced, I fear."

"Ribosomal RNA might identify the bacteria involved, but I don't know how that could help identify your victim."

Nick cleared his throat. "You lost me at inflammatory."

"I'll leave you to explain, Julia. I must dash." Indira left.

"Sorry. I'm training in Infectious Diseases and get a bit carried away with work jargon. The victim has an infected metal plate in her arm."

"How would they treat that?"

"She'd need intravenous antibiotics and surgery to remove the plate."

"She'd have to go to a hospital for that?"

"Very likely. A GP or an emergency department doctor might have seen her first, but orthopaedic surgeons and infectious disease specialists would treat her."

"But if the plate's still there, does that mean she hasn't been treated?"

"Well, yes, but she could be on a waiting list for consultation and missed her appointment. I could check hospital records."

"Thanks, but no. Back to Valerie." He turned back to the computer.

"Was that about the Kings Park body?"

"I can't discuss other investigations."

"With my contacts, I could find out who your mystery patient is like that." She clicked her fingers.

"I don't mean to be rude, but you're here about your missing friend. Date of birth?"

While the detective filled in the blanks for the computer record, she wondered where else she could look for Valerie. By the time she finished her statement, Martin should be home from work. She had to talk to him again. The decision to take action, any action, anaesthetised her pain.

———◦———

An hour later, Julia drove through Perth's leafy western suburbs, past homes with ever-increasing price tags and onwards to the edge of the Indian Ocean. With the sun dropping into the sea with a fiery flourish, the day's heat eased a few degrees. A perfect evening for a drive in an Audi TT convertible with the top down. Shame she only had her antique A3.

The house, in the suburb of City Beach, stood a couple of streets back from the Indian Ocean, a hint of salty coolness in the surrounding air. She knocked on Martin's front door. No doubt the second storey showcased highly prized—and highly priced—ocean views. She vaguely recalled hearing about a mountain of old money, but couldn't remember if it came from Martin's family or his wife's.

She scanned the minimalist garden. A low box hedge along the front border, pruned with military precision. The soft green lawn revived memories of running barefoot through sprinklers on a hot summer afternoon. A childhood treat lost to water restrictions.

At last, a bleary-eyed woman opened the door. Dressed in a red batik sarong and a torn white T-shirt, she clutched the doorframe like a clinging vine. Her feet were bare, and she sure was suffering from a bad hair day. Had she just tumbled out of bed?

"What do you want?" Slurring her words, the woman shielded her eyes from the twilight as if she confronted the midday sun.

Julia wasn't convinced the feral wreck could be Martin's wife. Not the man who made surgical scrubs look like designer wear. "Is this Martin MacDougall's house?"

"Yes, I'm Rachel, his wife. Who are you?" she asked in a couldn't-care-less monotone. She swung on the door handle with one hand while the other had a death-grip on the frame.

"I'm Dr Julia Sinclair. I want to discuss a patient with Martin for a case presentation I'm doing tomorrow." She held up a folder she'd brought as a ruse. "The hospital told me he'd left early, and as I was coming over this way . . ."

"He's not here yet." Rachel shoved the door closed.

Julia grabbed the edge of it and stuck her foot in the doorway. "Can I come in for a few minutes and wait for him?"

"Oh, I suppose so. Do whatever you like. Your sort always does."

Rachel let go of the door and ambled up the hallway, not seeming to care if Julia followed or not. She dragged her hand along the wall for physical, or perhaps moral, support. When she reached a lounge room, she collapsed onto a white leather armchair.

Julia sat on the matching sofa. Everything in the room was white, painfully white. She should have left her sunglasses on. Lucky Rachel's sarong was red; otherwise, she'd have faded into nothingness.

A grandfather clock ticked the silence away. What was taking Martin so long? He'd left the hospital well before her, according to the switchboard. If anything had happened to Valerie, he'd be the prime suspect. She couldn't imagine him hurting her, though. Did he have an alibi for Monday night?

"I tried to catch him at the hospital yesterday afternoon too, but he'd already left," Julia said. "I wish I worked his hours."

"I don't know who's been feeding you lies at that bloody hospital, but he's never home early."

"It was a nurse, Valerie Cavanaugh."

The previously listless woman sprang out of the armchair like a snake uncoiling, ready to strike. "How dare you mention that husband-stealing bitch in my house? Get out. Out." Her face twisted; her words snarled.

Not such a secret affair. "She's missing. I wondered . . ."

"I hope the bitch is dead." Rachel collapsed into the chair again.

Her eyes closed. As if all her energy had drained away. A bizarre contrast. What was wrong with her?

"When did Martin get home last night?"

"How the hell would I know? He treats this place like a bloody hotel." She jumped up and loomed over Julia, spitting words like shrapnel. "Maybe he came home and maybe he didn't. Maybe he was at your place, bitch."

Julia slid to one side, then tried to stand. Rachel shoved her back onto the sofa and continued to rant.

"I know your game. You're here to check out the house, thinking you can get Martin to ditch me and you can move in. I'm phoning the hospital to complain about you."

"No, I'm here—"

"Forget it. You haven't got a hope in hell. All this is in my name. He'll never leave me." Rachel gestured towards the door. "Keep your filthy hands off my husband and fuck off out of my life."

Julia escaped out the front door while Rachel hurled obscenities after her. Poor Martin. He was heading straight for a nuclear explosion.

Chapter Five

Back in her office on Wednesday morning, Julia checked Brad's results on the computer. She had to keep her mind occupied so she wouldn't obsess about Valerie. Valerie, who still hadn't returned her phone calls, whose house stayed empty and lifeless. Work, Julia. She focussed on the screen.

Shit. Methicillin-resistant *Staph aureus*. Very resistant too, more so than the usual Western Australian community-acquired strains. He must've been in contact with a carrier, either in the hospital or before admission.

She scrolled down the list of antibiotic sensitivities. Hang on; the bug was too resistant. The scientist must have entered the wrong result code. She rushed into the lab, ready to deliver a tongue-lashing.

"Who's on swabs today?" she asked.

"What now?" Lorena scowled at her. "Whatever it was, my evil twin did it. I've been slaving over hot plates since six this morning. I need coffee."

Coffee? Julia smothered a yawn. Bloody nuisance phone calls had interrupted her few hours of sleep. Every time, she expected to hear Valerie's voice. Every time, nothing but dead air.

"You should've had your coffee before entering those results. Have you heard of vancomycin-resistant *Staph aureus* being isolated in Australia?"

Lorena stomped over to the corner bench and snatched up an agar plate. She thrust it at Julia. "Look for yourself. I'm out of here."

"Not so fast." Julia opened the plate. Sure enough, the bug grew right up to the vancomycin disc.

"What's up?" Gabriel peered over her shoulder.

"Remember Brad?" She showed him the agar plate. "If this really is staph, and these results are correct, he's going to be world-famous—and not in a good way."

"I haven't got a clue what's going on," Gabriel said. "Enlighten me."

"Vancomycin-resistant MRSA is the Hannibal Lecter version of MRSA. VRSA. It's rare, it scares the crap out of us, and we sure as hell don't want it lurking in our hospitals."

"Ooh, nasty." Gabriel shuddered.

She turned back to Lorena. "Confirm it's a *Staph aureus*, repeat the sensitivities and set up every E-test we've got. Please. Call it MRSA for now. Don't report the vancomycin result yet."

She reviewed Brad's other specimens on the computer and could barely believe what she found. His intravenous line was infected, and the blood cultures had flagged as positive overnight. The infection had spread through his bloodstream. And they'd transferred him to the Intensive Care Unit.

What a disaster. Any staff or patient contact could have caught the staph and spread it further. The last thing the hospital needed was an outbreak of antibiotic-resistant bacteria. Any cockups? There went her future in Infectious Diseases.

And Brad could die.

Her heart and conscience pulled in opposite directions. She couldn't delegate the MRSA or VRSA problem. Her search for Valerie had to wait. She had to trust the police. Hell, like she had with Tess? She groaned. No bloody choice.

"Let's go to ICU." She rubbed the side of her neck. Her muscles were tight as steel rods under her skin.

"Absolutely," Gabriel said. "My first ever contact tracing exercise and I'm going to end up in all the medical journals. So, how far do we go with screening?"

"We'll get swabs from all staff contacts and any patients who shared a room with him."

"No new admissions to those rooms until we say they're clear?"

"Yes. Bed control will love us. Wait until we talk to the surgeons about their swabs. I can hear their moans already."

Time to unleash the inner bitch. Make them wash their hands like good little boys and girls. One corner of her mouth twitched.

Gabriel frowned. "I don't see what's so funny."

"We'd get more cooperation if we had an appropriate uniform. Perhaps something in black leather with studs and chains."

"I love that idea," he said. "Can I go home to change? I've got a riding crop somewhere . . ."

"Settle down, cowboy. We don't want to scare the patients. Just the doctors and nurses."

⸻ ⬥ ⸻

At Curtin House on Wednesday morning, Nick Randall's attempts to identify the Kings Park body had stalled. All the reported local missing women were too tall, too short, too young, too old, or just plain not even missing anymore. The best chance of identification rested on the breast implants and the fractured arm. A quick result could smooth his path back into the Squad.

After the morning briefing, he'd hustled back to his office, determined to prove himself. He had circulated her description through the National Police Reference System. The police media unit already struggled with a tidal wave of phone calls from the concerned public. The crime scene examiners were flat out working their magic on anything and everything found at the burial site, but that all took time.

If only this was television, they'd have wrapped up the case by now. His sisters were addicted to those crime shows. A bloody fingerprint here, a swabbed epithelial there, whack it in a machine, press go and the killer's name pops up on a screen within seconds. Nothing like real life. Nothing even remotely resembling real life.

What else could he do? More bloody phone calls. Perfect.

What about Valerie Cavanaugh? He'd checked her house on the way home. Nothing suspicious. Crime scene techs had gone over her car. He'd sent one of the young Ds from Wembley station to check security footage at the hospital. A dud camera and poor lighting in the staff car park ruined that idea, but she had swiped her ID card to enter the back door of the Emergency Department at about half past five.

Her doctor boyfriend hadn't returned Nick's call, despite the urgent message he'd left on the guy's mobile the night before. Time to visit the hospital to catch the elusive Dr MacDougall in person?

The hospital.

Fuck.

His first trip to a hospital since the accident. Plenty of reasons to stay in the office. Paper to shuffle, phone calls to make, thumbs to twiddle. He should work on the Kings Park case. Keep George from going ballistic.

As much as he hated hospitals, he had to escape his desk before the paperwork nailed him into a coffin and started digging his grave.

⋅◆⋅

Nick parked out the front of the Perth General Hospital, near the Emergency Department. He got out of the car and glanced up. Just a six-storey building full of sick people. How scary could it be?

He could do it. So long as he didn't bump into that prick doctor who'd sent Kym home. No guarantee he wouldn't hit him this time, despite hours of anger management counselling.

Focus. Maybe someone from the Emergency Department saw Valerie Cavanaugh leaving there on Monday night. If not, he could page Dr MacDougall from their extension. Busy surgeon or not, he'd have to answer a call from Emergency.

Striding past the department's triage desk, he entered the main treatment area. The antiseptic scent washed over him, awakening memories. Trolleys clattered, machines beeped, patients moaned. His chest tightened. Keep it together. He forced himself back to the present.

An elderly woman grabbed his arm and spoke to him. Nick had to lean in to hear her. Turned out she thought he was her husband come to take her home. He searched for someone to help. At last, a familiar face.

"Dan," he called, catching the attention of a male nurse—an old schoolmate he hadn't seen for months. "Can you help us out here?"

"Yeah, dead boring today." Dan took the old woman's arm. "Come on, love. He's too young for you." He led her to a nearby cubicle, then returned. "Fancy a cuppa?"

Nick followed him to the staff tea room. Full of old magazines and newspapers, it looked as if a small newsagency had exploded.

Dan sniffed the milk carton, then screwed up his face and tossed the carton in the bin. The filter coffee pot sat empty; dregs crusted in the bottom.

"I'll skip the coffee, thanks," Nick said.

"Wise decision. So, what's up?"

"Do you know Valerie Cavanaugh? She's a nurse on the surgical ward."

"Yeah, she used to work down here. Brown hair, legs that go on forever. What's she done?" Dan threw a pile of magazines into the corner and sprawled across a beaten-up sofa.

"She's missing."

"No shit." His cheeks paled. "Since when?"

Nick sank into a scruffy armchair. "She went through here about five thirty on Monday night."

"Missing? I can't believe it." Dan stared at the ceiling. The ceiling stared back. He jumped to his feet. "Let me check the database. We had a big MVA come in about then."

Dan darted out of the room. Nick followed him to a computer in the treatment area and watched over his shoulder as he scrolled for details of the motor vehicle accident.

"There." Dan tapped the screen. "The MVA arrived at five thirty p.m. I waited outside for a few minutes before the ambulance arrived. Yeah, I remember now. I did see her."

"Which way did she go?"

"Towards the staff car park." He gestured to the right. "It's quicker than going through the other wards."

"Anyone with her? Following her?"

"Sorry, mate. I was more interested in the ambulance."

"Anyone else around who might've seen something?"

More sky-gazing. "An orderly was having a smoke outside. Angelo Velutti."

Nick wrote the name in his notebook. "Where would I find him?"

Siren wailing, lights flashing, an ambulance squealed to a stop in front of the Emergency Department. Dan dashed to the rear of the ambulance, dragged open the doors and helped the paramedic haul out the trolley.

Nick followed. His pulse hammered in his throat.

The patient writhed and struggled against the restraints that held her on the trolley. Long, blood-streaked blonde hair obscured her face. Guttural moans, muttered curses. She freed one arm. Her elbow lashed out, crushed the paramedic's groin. He doubled over, gasping, tears streaming down his contorted cheeks.

Nick winced in sympathy.

Another nurse scurried over and helped the injured paramedic to a chair. Dan reached across the trolley and grabbed the patient's free arm. She snatched it back, threw herself away from him. The trolley wobbled. Dan struggled to hold it, to stop it tipping over.

Nick lunged forward and shoved the patient back onto the trolley. He gripped her arm tight.

Dan grinned. "If you ever want to have children, do not let go of that arm until the ambo's strapped her down."

The coppery scent of blood invaded his senses. Blood, so much blood. Just like the car crash. His vision blurred. He blinked a few times as if that would clear the blood-soaked memories from his mind.

"Okay. I've got her now." The paramedic tucked the patient's arm under the blanket and refastened the strap to hold her in place.

Nick walked back to the counter and took a deep breath. The adrenaline spike ebbed, leaving him drained.

"Try the orderlies' call room, just around the corner from here," Dan said.

"Sorry? Oh, yeah, the orderly. Thanks, mate." Nick handed him a business card. "Think of anything else, give me a bell. One last question. How do I page a doctor from here?"

"Grab a phone and dial one for the switchboard."

Nick followed those instructions. "I need to speak to Dr Martin MacDougall."

"I'll page him for you. Please hold."

He waited, listening to a recorded voice recite the unending list of hospital services, none of which he ever wanted to need.

At last, another female voice said, "He's busy operating. Can I take a message?"

"Tried that already. When will he finish operating?"

"Not before lunchtime."

Crap. He couldn't hang around the hospital that long. How about that orderly?

Fifteen minutes later, a dark-haired man, complete with Elvis sideburns, shoved past Nick and entered the orderlies' call room.

"About bloody time, Angelo," the supervisor said. "What've you done this time? Cops are after you." He gestured towards Nick, who had stepped into the doorway behind Angelo.

Angelo Velutti spun around. He thrust out his chin. "What?"

"Detective Sergeant Nick Randall. I have a few questions about Monday night." He held out his hand.

The orderly ignored it, patting his pocket instead. "Let's go outside for a smoke."

"No bloody way." The supervisor stood. "You can use my office, so I know when you're free for another job." He ushered them into a smaller room next door, grabbed the racing guide off the table, and left.

Nick took the chair closest to the door and gestured towards the one behind the desk. "Did you work the evening shift on Monday?"

"Yeah. So?" The orderly leant back in the chair and swung his feet onto the desk.

"Do you know a nurse called Valerie Cavanaugh?"

"What's her problem this time?" Angelo sneered. "Stuck-up cow. Spreads her legs for the doctors, from what I hear. Wouldn't know a real man if he bit her on the arse."

"Settle, petal. I only asked if you knew her. I didn't want a character assassination."

"If that bitch has complained about me again . . ." He thumped his feet back onto the floor, leant forward, and assailed Nick with a gust of foul breath.

Nick leant back. "Listen for a minute," he said. A short-fused temper and Valerie had made a complaint against him? Worth exploring. "She was reported missing yesterday. Did you see her on Monday night?"

"Missing? You should've said." His hands remained clenched, but the redness of his cheeks faded.

"You didn't give me a chance. Did you see her on Monday night?"

"Yeah, I reckon I did. Outside Emergency. During smoko." Angelo slouched again, a picture of relaxed innocence.

"Anyone with her?"

"Don't think so."

"Anyone following her?"

"No. I watched her all the way." Angelo leered, a full betcha-wish-you'd-been-there leer. "Didn't see anyone blocking my view."

"Did she talk to anyone?"

"Nope."

"If you think of anything later on, call me." Nick handed him a card. Angelo didn't take it, so he left it on the desk. "Thanks for your cooperation."

Nick left the office, glad to escape the cigarette fumes. When he turned to thank the supervisor, he saw Angelo flick the card into the bin. The orderly smirked at him.

After his initial over-reaction, Angelo had been far too casual, as if accustomed to police enquiries. A criminal record? Who could he talk to about Valerie's complaint?

His mobile rang. He flipped it open. George. Bloody typical. The moment he escaped the paperwork, the boss found him and reeled him back in.

He answered and got slammed by George's booming voice.

"Imagine my surprise when I ring Missing Persons to see if they have any likely candidates for corpse of the day and, bugger me, I find myself referred to you, but you're out on enquiries. Location unknown."

He held the phone a safe distance from his ear. "I can explain, boss."

George steamrollered over him. "You, the very person I put in charge of identifying Monday's body. And have you done that yet? Not that I can bloody see."

"I didn't realise I was officially back in Major Crimes."

"Don't get smart with me, sunshine. I gave you a job, a relatively simple task, but a vitally important one and you swan off on a completely unrelated matter." A deep sigh gusted down the phone line. "I thought you were working on old cases, not chasing nurses who've been missing five minutes."

"Finished?" Nick asked. "The Kings Park skeleton doesn't match the description of any local missing persons. The interstate guys are checking their books. Dr Singh is following up on the breast implants and the bone surgery. I've had every concerned parent on the phone. Every serial confessor, every psychic, every nosy bugger and his wife hounding me for information."

"Yeah, well, remember who you want to work for," George said, sounding a fraction less homicidal.

"Sure, boss. Now back up a minute and tell me why you called. Something about a corpse . . ."

"Shit."

Nick could hear the rasp of George rubbing his hand over his head, a sure sign of stress. "Boss?"

"We've got another one. Could be your missing nurse."

Fuck. "I'll bring a photo. Where is she?"

Let them try to kick him off this investigation.

Chapter Six

Abandoning his hospital enquiries, Nick rushed through the money-laden western suburbs to Swanbourne Beach. He pulled into the car park and got out of his car. A light sea breeze eased the sting of the summer sun. He sucked in a lungful of salt air and gazed across the glare of white sand, tempted by the cool blue water. Too flat to surf. If only he could dive in, forget about death.

Usually, mobs of seagulls filled the air with their screeches, but not this morning. Even the rhythmic crashing of the waves seemed subdued.

Deathly quiet.

Off to the right, the blue-overalled forensic team gathered potential clues. Several uniformed police deterred rubberneckers and deflected beach-goers. Leather-skinned sunbathers had slunk further down the beach. Public nudity and police didn't mix. No press had arrived. Yet.

In the distance, the unmistakable bulk of Detective Inspector George Jaworski sheltered in the shade of a red and white striped beach umbrella. Nick put on a pair of blue paper overalls and disposable booties, then followed the metal plates that marked a path through the scrub-covered sand dunes.

George glowered and thrust his hand out for the photograph. "Don't think I don't know what you're up to. You're here to deliver a photo, and that's all. Got it?"

"Sure, boss. Whatever you say." Like hell.

Nearby, a shallow grave hid in the dip between two sand dunes. The naked woman sprawled in front of them, her hands crossed modestly over her groin. Her long, brown hair straggled about her face, blood-streaked and tangled. When the wind changed, a whiff of vomit added to the sensory overload.

The sight of the dead woman jettisoned him nine months into the past. He closed his eyes, reliving the moment he had walked into their bedroom. Kym's body contorted on the floor; her lifeless eyes fixed on him. Accusing eyes. Even though she'd been driving, he blamed himself for her death. Guilty for not driving. Guilty for not insisting she stay in hospital when that prick doctor sent her home with an undiagnosed head injury.

Guilty for working all night while she died alone.

"She your missing nurse?"

He spotted the concern in George's eyes. How long would it take before everyone stopped expecting him to crack? He shut down his emotions, buried his memories deep and concentrated on the job.

"Sure looks like her. Any ID with the body?"

"Not that we've discovered." George gestured towards the forensic team spread throughout the dunes and across the sand. "Dogs beat us to the grave. Maybe they carried something off."

"Has the pathologist been yet?"

"Yeah, the charming Dr Singh. She had to dash off to a nasty case, a possible cot death. Gave me the usual guff about waiting until she gets the body on the slab before giving anything away. She was kind enough to suggest the victim wasn't killed here, probably somewhere indoors, away from these bloody blowflies." George waved his hand in front of his face. The great Australian salute.

Nick crouched beside the body. A large bruise distorted her right cheekbone, as if someone had backhanded her. Adhesive marks on her cheeks, consistent with a gag of some description. Abrasions encircled both wrists and ankles. Hands and feet were swollen, engorged with blood. Restraints. Her fingernails were torn and bloody. Had she scratched her killer?

Someone had slashed her abdomen with one long wound down the midline, two angled cuts on the right side of her belly. Gaping wounds crusted with bloodstained sand. A semi-circle had been carved beneath each breast, with a straight line running up to and through the nipple. Both groins were slashed too; must be superficial or she would've bled out from her femorals quick smart. He'd seen that once on a motorcyclist who'd hit a tree at high speed.

The killer certainly had a penchant for patterns. He could check the interstate crime databases for similar signatures. He closed his eyes as if that would erase the image from his mind. No chance.

The police photographer hovered overhead, impatient. Nick straightened and got out of his way. The photographer continued recording the crime scene, his camera flashing away as if he were at some gruesome fashion shoot.

"Thanks for the photo, mate." George glanced at it again, then shoved it into a folder. "I'll let you get back to work now."

Nick noticed some activity near the edge of the car park and distracted George. "What's going on over there?"

They crossed the sand. The forensic scientist had marked a footprint in a patch of wet sand near a dripping tap. He was making a cast from it for later comparison with various types of shoes.

"Only a partial," he said. "Deep impression, either a big bastard or someone carrying a heavy weight." He carried on with his task.

"Who found her?" Nick asked.

"The old guy with the beagle sitting on the sand down there. Looks like a stunned mullet. Says the dog sniffed her out."

"If he was hoping for a perve on the nude beach, he got more than he bargained for."

"Yeah. I'd better chat to him. Call me if anything turns up on the other case."

"I'll contact her next of kin to confirm ID."

George's eyes narrowed. "Will you now?"

"Makes sense. I've got all the details. How much longer before they move the body?"

"Soon enough. Meat wagon is here already. I'll get someone to call you when the mortuary's ready for a viewing."

Hang on a minute. Too easy. He waited for the list of restrictions, but none came. "Thanks, boss. Appreciate it."

"You'd better. I'm sticking my knackers on the chopping block for you. If anyone even breaks a fingernail in your presence, you'll be out on your arse. Clear?"

"Crystal." Great. Which did they expect him to do? Burst into tears or beat someone up? Make up their bloody minds.

Another shark-like smile. "And since you're so keen to be involved in this case, you can come to the autopsy too. Dr Singh said she'd expedite it, maybe later today, but more likely tomorrow morning."

Autopsy? Crap. Let the nightmares begin.

⟡

Julia swiped her ID card to enter the Intensive Care Unit. Gabriel shadowed her. A central raised platform loomed straight in front: the nurses' station with its bank of computer monitors. Four beds lined either side of the main room, each surrounded by an array of equipment, from drip-stands to ventilators. Bed-head monitors flashed and squiggled vital statistics. The swoosh of ventilators provided soothing background music to the chaotic calm of the ICU.

On spotting Julia's approach, the Nurse Unit Manager hid behind her clipboard. "Whatever you've got to say, I don't want to hear it."

"Brad Delaney definitely has MRSA." Julia didn't want to mention the possibility of anything worse. Hell, she didn't even want to think about it. "Hope he's in isolation."

"Nobody ever brings me good news." The NUM checked her bed list. "Phew. Yes, room nine around the corner, one of our isolation rooms."

"Excellent. So long as they've followed the MRSA policy since his transfer." She turned to Gabriel. "Will you check while I talk to the doctors? You know the drill—gowns, gloves, handwashing, cattle prod for any infringements."

"With pleasure." He scurried away to room nine.

Julia strode towards the back of the ICU and into the staff tea room, lured by the scent of coffee. Full of doctors, just as she'd expected.

"Fancy some of my homemade spicy pear cake?" Phil, one of the ICU consultants, handed her a plate. He studied her face. "Late night? Coffee. Stat."

"Some nocturnal masturbator abused my phones last night." Every call had been an electric shock to her shattered nervous system, but she hadn't dared leave the landline off the hook or turn off her mobile. What if Valerie rang?

The early morning sight in the bathroom mirror had made her want a head transplant. Bags under her eyes? Try man-sized suitcases.

"Aha, the nocturnal masturbator." Phil turned to one of the junior doctors. "It wasn't you, was it?"

An exaggerated eye-roll. "Wish I had enough energy."

Julia poured a mug of industrial-strength black coffee. She inhaled deeply, willing the caffeine straight into her sleep-deprived brain, then ate some cake for a sugar hit. "Divine. Ever considered giving up your day job?"

"No bloody way. With three kids under six and a fourth on the way, I come here for a rest. Too bloody fertile, that's my problem." Phil settled his feet on the coffee table, exposing his Snoopy socks. "Hey, trade you cake for babysitting."

She clutched her heart. "Me and a roomful of ankle-biters? I'd rather let your new residents practise procedures on me."

"That can be arranged." He twirled a fake moustache. "What's the latest on Brad Delaney?"

"We've confirmed MRSA." She mentally crossed her fingers while she underplayed the truth. The vancomycin resistance must be a mistake. "How's he going?"

"The surgical registrar drained a shitload of pus. Hypotensive post-op, so we've had him on a dopamine infusion. Temp's still spiking. And, just for fun, there's a new heart murmur."

Had the infection settled on his heart valve?

"MRSA endocarditis. Just what we need."

Endocarditis was dangerous enough without it being due to antibiotic-resistant bacteria. Life-threatening. How do you tell a 24-year-old guy he might die from having his appendix out?

"He's having a trans-oesophageal echo later," Phil said.

By passing a tube down his oesophagus, they could examine his heart valve. She'd wait for the result before seeing Brad. No point in both of them worrying.

"He's not responding to vanc as quickly as I'd like." Should she mention the possibility of VRSA? Lab error or real threat, she had to treat it. "I'll see if the pharmacy has any linezolid or daptomycin. If he needs a long course, I'd prefer daptomycin, but I'll take whatever's in stock for now."

"Something you're not telling me?" Phil asked.

She faked a smile. "Just being super-cautious with the boss away."

"I see. Don't want to mess up your chance at the new job."

"Exactly. How did you know?"

"Better keep my patients alive. I'm on the interview panel for new positions."

"Great, no pressure then."

She concentrated on her cake and life-giving coffee. Mid-swallow, her pager vibrated against her waistband. She glanced at the message screen. Nick Randall. Her throat clamped tight. He'd promised her an update at lunchtime. Why call her two hours early? She forced another sip of coffee to clear her throat, then raced into an empty office to grab a phone.

"Julia Sinclair speaking." Her hands trembled, as did her voice.

Silence for a moment, then Nick spoke with an uncomfortable formality. "Dr Sinclair, bad news, I'm afraid."

"You've found Valerie." The room darkened as fog engulfed her.

"A body fitting her description was found at Swanbourne Beach early this morning."

"A body . . ." No, it couldn't be Valerie. "The beach? Are you sure? Can I see her?" Valerie didn't even like the beach.

"With her parents being so far away, her ex is the closest next of kin, but he's in the middle of some surgery on a dog . . ." His voice faded away as if his resolve had faltered.

"Where is she?"

"They're taking her to the State Mortuary. Was she wearing any jewellery when you saw her last?"

Her mind blanked. "Um, she would've had earrings on. Why can't I remember which ones?"

"Can you hang on a minute? I've got another call."

Silence. She crushed her sister's necklace into her palm while staring into nothingness.

"She's at the mortuary now," he said a few minutes later. "Could you recognise the earrings?"

"I've been there . . ." She remembered another viewing not long after Tess disappeared. A false alarm. She had to know for sure. "I used to work near there. Half an hour suit you?"

"I'll bring over the earrings."

"No, I need to see her. Half an hour." She put the phone down before he could answer.

How could she survive this? She'd seen dead bodies before—too many—but never one of her friends, never someone so close to her heart.

Chapter Seven

Dazed, Julia wandered back to her office. Her mind ricocheted from thought to thought. Was Valerie really dead? Who killed her? Martin must be the prime suspect. Richard couldn't be discounted, with his track record of violence against her. Maybe some complete stranger snatched her from the car park. And why the beach? Martin lived on the coast, close to Swanbourne Beach.

"Hello. Anybody home?" A distant voice penetrated the fog. Gabriel looked down at her, frowning.

"Standing there long?" she asked, her voice flat.

"Long enough to wonder if you're stroking out." He pulled up a chair and peered at her. "Are you okay?"

"Just some personal stuff." Tears burned at the back of her eyes. She had to stay in control.

"Maybe it'll help to talk about it."

"It's nothing. Really." She rubbed the side of her head. "Bit of a headache."

"You look exhausted."

"A bloody prank caller kept me up half the night. Think I'll go home for a couple of hours."

"I'll give you a lift."

"No."

Gabriel winced like a spanked puppy that wasn't sure what it had done wrong. "I just want to help."

"Sorry. Carry on with the contact tracing. Got your preliminary list?"

Focus on some mindless routine tasks.

"Back in a tick." He whirled away to the office next door and returned seconds later with a computer printout. "Here we go."

She scanned his list of patients and hospital staff. The words blurred. "Swab the patients first. They'll be more cooperative. You'll be fine with the nurses, too. Doctors can get a bit bolshie—especially surgeons—so leave them to me if they give you any trouble."

"What about request forms? Can I sign them or do you have to?"

"You can sign for any Infection Control specimens." She slid open a desk drawer and grabbed a pad of request forms. "Fill these in, tick the patient or staff box. That'll remind you which sites to swab—usually nose, throat, any wounds. Grab a box of swabs from our storeroom. Have I forgotten anything?"

"Nothing comes to mind. Go, have a break."

"Thanks. Call me on my mobile if you have any questions."

Questions, questions, questions. One overruled all the others. Was Valerie really dead? She reached under her desk for her handbag.

Martin rushed through the doorway. "What the hell did you say to Rachel?"

She jumped. Gabriel almost levitated off his chair.

"Gabriel, could you give us some privacy?" Her stomach spiralled towards the floor. "Please?"

He slunk out of the room.

Martin slammed the door behind him, then leant over her. The flare of red across his cheeks contrasted with the chips of glacier ice in his eyes. "What were you thinking? She's so bloody fragile."

"I wanted to let you know the police would contact you about . . . Valerie." She couldn't tell him yet. Not until she knew for sure.

"She accused me of spending Monday night with Valerie. Some friend you are."

"Well, where were you?"

"I crashed at Simon's place. We tried to drink his cellar dry."

"Rachel already knew about you and Valerie."

"No way."

"When I mentioned Valerie, she self-destructed." Julia remembered the crazed expression on Rachel's face. She rubbed goosebumps on her arms. Had her blood frozen?

"You're shaking. What's wrong?" He touched her shoulder.

"They found a body on Swanbourne Beach." The words escaped before she could stop them.

All colour drained from his face. "No. Please, no."

"It might not be her. The police have contacted Richard to identify the body, but he's been held up."

"That bastard. Why?"

"He's her next of kin. They're still married."

"I wish she'd divorced him."

"Why? You're still married." She slung her bag over one shoulder and edged past Martin. "This isn't helping. I have to go."

"Where? The mortuary?"

She nodded. "They've asked me to look at some jewellery."

"I'll drive you."

She hesitated. "Okay."

Not her wisest decision, but she couldn't face going alone.

⬥

Twenty minutes later, Julia and Martin parked near the State Mortuary. Martin had said nothing during the drive over. She'd been too lost in her own misery to say more than a few words herself. A brief musing on how close Kings Park was, and how many undiscovered bodies could be buried there.

She walked along the driveway, hesitation in every step. A funeral director's van drove past. Delivery or takeaway? Hysterical giggles threatened to erupt.

They reached the entrance and Martin pressed the buzzer, then stepped back and waited, silent, arms folded across his chest. A few minutes later, Nick Randall came outside.

She smoothed down her skirt, drying her palms. "I'll identify the body."

"No, I'll bring out the jewellery. Richard Cavanaugh is coming later." Nick looked behind her. "Unless you're Richard?"

"Martin MacDougall."

"So, Dr Sinclair told you?"

"Sorry," she said. "He caught me as I was leaving."

"We want to know if Valerie's dead." Martin placed an arm around her shoulder. "And that bastard shouldn't be allowed anywhere near her."

"Richard Cavanaugh is legally her next of kin."

"We're not even sure it is Valerie," Julia said. "Let me see her."

Martin's fingers dug into her shoulder. "I'll wait out here."

"Okay, just Dr Sinclair," Nick said. "Take your time."

"I know the way." She rushed inside before she could chicken out, then stopped in the first viewing room.

Her heart banged against her ribs. Through the viewing window, she saw a mortuary trolley, a body covered with a white sheet. An overalled man stood nearby, waiting for a sign, waiting to break her heart.

"Are you sure?" Nick asked. "I can bring the jewellery out."

"I have to see her."

He nodded to the mortuary technician, who drew back the sheet to uncover the face.

Her poor bruised face. How could that lifeless mannequin be Valerie? The hair was the right length and colour, but swollen bruises distorted her features. Maybe it's not her. A second of hope obliterated by bleak reality.

Valerie.

She edged closer, pressed her palms against the windowsill to hold herself up on fragile legs. The scar under her left eye, where Richard's wedding ring had cut her cheek. On a nearby table, an evidence bag showcased her favourite silver earrings, the ones Julia had bought her to celebrate kicking him out of her life.

Nothing to celebrate now.

"Nick Randall, meet Valerie Cavanaugh." Her voice sounded like it came from a stranger. Maybe it was an echo from her hollowed-out chest cavity.

She said a quiet goodbye to her dearest friend. She didn't want to see what other injuries she'd suffered, couldn't bear to know how Valerie had died.

All she wanted was to find the bastard responsible and make him suffer.

One last look to sear the memory into her brain, then she stumbled along the corridor and rushed outside. She blinked at the sun. How could it be so bright when her heart was midnight dark?

Martin stared at her. His shoulders slumped, then he shook his head, denying the reality that must be visible on her face.

Nick walked towards him and broke the news. She followed with her arms wrapped tight around her body, shivering despite the midday heat.

Martin's eyes blanked, and the skin around his mouth tightened.

"Would you like to see her, Dr MacDougall?" Nick asked.

"Don't." She touched Martin's arm gently, as if he might shatter. "Remember Valerie alive."

Martin blinked a few times, cleared his throat. "I assume you still want to talk to me, detective. I have a clinic now. About five?"

If it weren't for the tension vibrating under her fingers, he could've been arranging a golf game.

Nick handed him a business card. "Call me when you're free."

She caught a flicker of movement behind Martin. "Crap."

Richard Cavanaugh charged towards them, his face flushed and his hair dishevelled. Blood-splattered scrubs strained to contain his bulk.

"What the fuck is he doing here?" He crowded Martin, forcing him to stagger backwards a couple of steps.

In a deep, primitive part of her psyche, she ached to join the fight. Whoever killed Valerie deserved more pain and suffering than she could imagine. Her more evolved side waited for one of them to say something incriminating.

Richard's tirade continued. "If you hadn't weaselled your slimy way into her bed, she'd have come back to me."

Nick intercepted him, shielding Martin.

"You deluded prick. She'd never go back to you." Martin's self-control shattered. "That's why you killed her."

"Killed her? Wasn't it an accident?" His gaze darted from Nick to Julia. "I'd never kill her. Tell him, Julia."

"Bullshit. I know what you did to Valerie." Martin's voice caught on her name.

Nick pivoted between them, his hands raised, palms forward.

Richard deflated, his hands shoved in his pockets as if he wanted Martin to hurt him.

"I'm taking Mr Cavanaugh inside now," Nick said, calm and clear. "Take Dr Sinclair home."

Martin didn't respond.

"Come on." She placed one hand on his chest, felt his heart race beneath taut muscles.

One last glare at Richard, then Martin turned away. She watched Richard and Nick disappear into the mortuary.

"I have to check something," she said.

"I'll wait in the car." He scrubbed his hand over his eyes. "I don't trust myself anywhere near that bastard."

"If he killed her, get in the queue." She had to talk to Richard, figure out if he was guilty, but she'd get more out of him without Martin around. "Don't wait. I'll find my own way back."

Chapter Eight

After persuading Martin to leave without her, Julia re-entered the mortuary. She hesitated outside the viewing room, listening to Richard's sobs. Her eyes ached with unshed tears. She couldn't collapse yet, not until she knew Valerie would be looked after.

She walked down the corridor to the forensic pathologists' offices. Nobody home. Most desks were buried under microscopes, textbooks, pathology journals, stacks of slides, and piles of paper. One organised oasis amongst the mess. Must be Indira's.

Where could she be? No conveniently open diary. Court? Crime scene? Middle of another autopsy? A glance at her watch. Lunch? Nausea swept through her at the thought of food. She debated phoning Indira, but heard Richard's voice outside, so she compromised with a Post-it note on the computer screen: Valerie needs you. Call me. Julia.

She followed Richard's voice and found him slumped in one of the waiting room chairs, his arms wrapped around his belly. He stared at the floor, ignoring her approach.

Nick frowned at her. "Why are you still here?"

"Looking for Indira, but she's not in her office."

"Does she know Valerie?"

She searched her memory. "I don't think they've ever met."

"Tough on her to examine someone she knows."

"So Indira will do this autopsy?" Relief battled disgust with herself that she hadn't considered Indira's feelings.

"Not up to me." He stepped aside to let her pass. "You should go home."

"Home? How can you expect me to go home after seeing that?" She wanted to fight, to feel anything other than heart-aching loss.

Nick held his hands up. "I assumed—"

"Some maniac abducted Valerie from the hospital. Somebody must've seen something."

"We're investigating all possibilities." The warm caramel tones of his voice didn't blunt the underlying scalpel-edge of determination. "Leave the police work to us."

"She's . . . she was my best friend. I need to help her." She clenched her hands, arms rigid by her sides.

"Take time to grieve."

"What the hell do you know about grief?"

His eyes narrowed to a flash of green ice. "More than I want to. Leave this to us. Please, take Martin and go." His words snapped, his tone unyielding.

"He's already gone. I'll grab a taxi back to the hospital."

"Can I ask a favour?"

"Okay." She drew out her response.

"Will you drive Richard home? I'll follow and give you a lift from there. I need a couple of minutes to finish up here first."

Hell, a reasonable request. He fought dirty. "Sure."

Nick disappeared into another room. She slid onto the chair next to Richard. He hadn't budged. Anger drained away, leaving only emptiness echoing through her soul.

"Richard, where are your car keys?" She had to nudge him twice to get his attention.

He rummaged in a pocket. When he passed her the keys, she stared at his right hand. Bruised and battered knuckles. Fresh bruises.

"Did you punch Valerie?"

He avoided eye contact. "No. Believe me. Please."

"You need to convince yourself first. What happened?"

He muttered something, shaking his head.

"I didn't catch that," she said.

Richard held out his hands, palms down. "I can't remember. I woke up like this on Tuesday morning. What if I killed her?"

"You blacked out?" So pathetic, but if he killed Valerie, how could she feel sorry for him?

"I wouldn't hurt her."

"Bullshit." She'd held Valerie while she trembled, describing his drunken rage. She'd treated her injuries and begged her to leave him. She'd held him at bay with a cricket bat while Valerie packed her suitcase. "What do you remember?"

"I finished work early, about two, went home. Bumped into my neighbour, Robbo." A burst of harsh laughter. "His wife just dumped him, so we had a few beers. Gets blurry after that."

"You still live near the hospital?" An ugly image formed—an alcohol-fuelled ambush in the hospital car park.

"Yeah."

"Would Robbo remember what happened?"

"You kidding? He's a lightweight. Found him passed out on my back lawn the next morning."

"What's going on here?" Nick asked.

Her cheeks burned. How long had he been standing in the doorway? "Richard lives near the hospital, so I can walk from there. No need to follow us."

"That's odd. I could've sworn someone was interrogating a suspect. I'll need Robbo's full name and contact details, Mr Cavanaugh."

Richard dragged his phone from his pocket, and Julia stood, avoiding Nick's eye. Her friend lay dead a few metres away, and here she was grilling poor Richard. Anything to avoid her own grief. Her vision shimmered.

Late Wednesday afternoon, Nick joined George in his office at Curtin House. A quick glance around the room showed nothing out of place. Not just tidy, more like OCD-serial-killer-obliter-ating-all-evidence tidy.

"Victim's boyfriend is downstairs, boss. Martin Mac-Dougall."

"Lucky the ex has already left the building. No love lost there."

"What did you think?"

"Big bastard with a violent streak and a drinking problem." George laughed. "Didn't know whether to charge him or recruit him."

"I should record you and stick it on the internet. You'd go viral." Nick dropped a folder on the desk, making sure he placed it at an angle. "The ex's mate was just as pissed. He mentioned a couple of other names—details in there—guys who may have dropped in. All the nights blur together. Apparently."

"I'll add them to the list." George straightened the folder.

"Maybe one of them was sober enough to drive to the beach and dump a body."

"Or one of them lied to us."

"Shocking. What about the hospital security tapes?"

"Nothing sus so far."

"There's a hospital orderly worth another chat." Nick checked his notebook. "Angelo Velutti."

"Another chat?"

"I spoke to him at the hospital this morning. He let slip Valerie Cavanaugh made a complaint against him. Bet he's wishing he kept his mouth shut."

"Shit. We've got suspects coming out our ears." George jotted the name on another form. "Now, what about this surgeon? First impression?"

He shrugged. "Seemed genuinely upset, but he'd have to be a talented actor to keep a wife and a mistress sweet. And he's a surgeon. Bound to be handy with a knife."

George stood up, stretched his back, and groaned. "I'm getting too old for these early morning starts. Let's rattle his cage."

⚬

Once settled in the interview room, Nick started the recording, then ran through the formalities.

"Thanks for coming in, Dr MacDougall. Can we call you Martin?" George asked.

"Mister. I'm a surgeon. Shit. What does it matter? Call me whatever you bloody well like." Martin rubbed one hand across his mouth. His fingers trembled. "What happened to Valerie?"

"We believe she was murdered. That's as specific as I care to be at the moment." George sat back and gestured for Nick to continue.

"When did you see Valerie Cavanaugh last?"

"Monday, around lunchtime. In the surgical ward. We discussed a patient. She wanted to chat about something else, but I was late for theatre."

"What's the nature of your relationship?"

"You've been talking to the lovely Julia, so you probably know more about it than I do. I've often wondered about those two." His gaze drifted, unfocussed.

"Your relationship with Valerie Cavanaugh?"

"You mean sex? Yes."

"How long for?"

"Six months."

"What did she have planned for Monday evening?"

"Absolutely no idea."

"What did she want to chat about?"

"We'd had a tiff. Maybe she wanted to apologise." He tried a man-of-the-world smile, but couldn't pull it off.

"What did you fight about?"

"A minor verbal disagreement about a weekend away, that's all. Nothing physical."

"Any witnesses?"

"Plenty. The hospital Happy Hour last Friday night."

George broke in with a question. "What does your wife think of your extracurricular activities?"

Martin tugged his left earlobe. "Nothing, I hope. She has health problems. I'd appreciate it if you'd leave her in blissful ignorance."

"That may not be possible." George smiled his best couldn't-give-a-shit-what-you-think smile. "When did you get home Monday night?"

"Never. I had a few too many wines with Simon Bailey, a friend from work. I crashed at his place for the night."

Nick resumed the interview. "Where were you last night?"

"Home with my wife, but she took a couple of sleeping tablets. No point asking her about it. A cyclone wouldn't have woken her."

"Why don't you want us to talk to your wife?"

"She can't confirm I was with her all night." Martin stared at the table.

What was he hiding? "Who else do you think we should talk to?"

"You've seen her ex. Some of the stories she told me about him . . ."

"Anyone else?"

Martin straightened. "My brother-in-law, Carl. He's an anaesthetics technician at the hospital. He threatened me last week."

"Why would that have anything to do with Valerie?"

"He could've killed Valerie to punish me. Or to frame me. Look at this." He unbuttoned his shirt and revealed several circular bruises on his upper chest. "That body-building bastard poked me. If he can do damage like this with one finger, imagine what he could have done to poor Valerie."

"What happened next?"

Martin buttoned his shirt with exaggerated concentration. "Nothing. I had a long operating list that afternoon." He held up his hands, fingers splayed. "Can't afford to damage my hands."

"Did he mention Valerie? Any threats against her?"

"He said he'd stop me screwing around. That's all."

Interesting. "Full name and contact details?"

Martin dragged an iPhone from his pocket.

Nick jotted down Carl's details, then plied Martin with more questions, reconstructing his week, adding more names to an already long list of interviews. He'd be interested in hearing the brother-in-law's version of events.

With two bodies discovered in one week, he was one of several detectives seconded to the Major Crime Squad. They had nominated him as hospital liaison—George's twisted idea of a stress test.

Whatever it took.

CHAPTER NINE

GUILT FROM NEGLECTING HER patients filtered through Julia's grief and dragged her out of bed on Thursday morning. If her boss hadn't been away, she'd have stayed there for months. Her arms ached from pounding her punching bag and her head ached from self-medicating with a bottle of wine. Hopeless attempts to obliterate her misery. The only way she'd survive the day would be to bury herself in work. Good old head-in-the-sand denial and complete, clinical detachment.

When she reached her office, she found a bottle of spring water, a glass, two Panadols, a Berocca multivitamin, and a note from Gabriel: Sorry about Valerie. Thought you might need these.

A flash of memory struck her. Valerie's favourite hangover cure comprised an enormous glass of freshly squeezed orange juice and a bacon sandwich. If only . . . She shook her head. Don't think about Valerie. She had to wall off that part of her brain and snap-freeze her heart for the rest of the day. Work first, collapse later.

She flicked through a pile of phone messages left next to her computer keyboard. *Call ICU pharmacist about lin-something.* Crap. She'd forgotten to follow-up on the new antibiotics for Brad. She grabbed the phone to call the ICU, but decided to review his results first. If the lab had sorted out those staph sensitivities, she might not need to add anything. VRSA had to be a mistake.

She downed the fizzing Berocca, then eased into the lab.

"Those staph plates are over there." Lorena grimaced at her. Or maybe it was a smile. Too brief to tell.

Julia checked the agar plates, searching for the vancomycin E-test. She shook her head. How the hell could it be so resistant to vancomycin? "Are you absolutely sure this is a *Staph aureus*?"

"Of course, I'm bloody sure."

That was better. Grumpy Lorena, she could cope with. Smiling Lorena freaked her out.

"Is there a spare purity plate to send to the reference lab for typing?"

"All packed and ready to go," Lorena said.

"Something interesting?" Gabriel flashed a smile at Lorena and got a growl in return. "Are you okay?" he whispered to Julia.

She gave a quick nod, then showed him the plates. "See that long paper strip with the numbers on it? It's like the antibiotic discs, but it has different concentrations of vancomycin spread along it."

"Okay, but what does it mean?"

"Hang on." She grabbed a microbiology textbook and flicked to the chapter on sensitivity testing. "Here's a normal *Staph aureus*. See that teardrop-shaped clear area, and how the point of it touches the paper strip?"

"Nifty." Gabriel glanced from the book to the agar plate in Julia's hand. "But why's this teardrop so small?"

"Vancomycin can't kill this bug at safe human doses. Vancomycin-resistant MRSA. The devil itself. If this spreads through the hospital, we're screwed."

Hell, when she'd wanted something to distract her from Valerie's murder, a world-class outbreak wasn't quite what she'd had in mind. Someone had a sick sense of humour.

Lorena engulfed her in a hug. "Sorry for your loss."

"Thanks," she whispered, fighting to maintain control. Unexpected sympathy unsettled her.

"Now, toughen up and go kick some medical arse," Lorena said, then carried on working.

"You scared me for a moment. Thought aliens had taken you over," she said to Lorena, then turned back to Gabriel. "Grab a pad of request forms and as many swabs as you can carry. Meet me on the general surgical ward in half an hour."

"What about ICU?" Gabriel asked.

"I'll do that on my own. I'd rather you didn't see me grovel."

Ten minutes later, Julia approached the ICU nurses' station. The consultant scribbled on a form, then dropped it in the internal mail tray.

"Hi, Phil. How's Brad?" she asked.

"No better. Temp's still spiking. The echo confirmed endocarditis and a possible valve ring abscess."

An abscess around the heart valve could kill him. "Have you spoken to the cardiothoracic surgeons?"

"The senior reg is in there now. They'll discuss him at their meeting this afternoon."

"What about his mental state?"

"Away with the fairies."

Maybe bits of the infected tissue had broken away from the heart valve and spread through his bloodstream to his brain. "Any focal neurological signs?"

Phil shook his head. "He's moving all his limbs. Think it's fever rather than septic emboli causing his confusion."

"Hope you're right. Last thing he needs is a brain full of abscesses." She paused. Had she committed professional suicide with her delay? "We've got another problem. A much larger problem."

"Don't like the sound of that."

"His MRSA is also vancomycin-resistant."

He frowned. "Is that why you wanted another antibiotic added?"

"Yes. Did the pharmacist get hold of some?"

"Wait just one minute." His voice quietened with an undercurrent of rage. He led her away from the nurses' station. "You knew this yesterday, and I'm only hearing about it now?"

A band of guilt compressed her lungs. "We had to confirm the sensitivities."

"As long as he's in ICU, Brad Delaney is my patient, my responsibility. Don't you dare withhold information from me." His cheeks flushed. He held up a hand to stop any response. "Our pharmacist tried contacting you last night to see if it was urgent. They didn't have either linezolid or daptomycin in stock. Couldn't reach you on either number."

"Sorry." She wanted to explain, but she had no excuse. The most important case of her career so far. "I'll sort it out now."

"Don't bother. I had some daptomycin taxied over from Charlie's. He had his first dose last night."

"Thanks. I—"

"Don't thank me. Pull yourself together and do your job." Phil shook his head. "If this bug spreads through the ICU . . ."

"I'll do my best to stop it."

"Better hope your best is good enough. Plenty of competition for the Senior Registrar position."

Reality kicked her in the teeth. She had to fight for her job, show she could control the VRSA outbreak. Without Valerie, without her sister Tess, the job was all she had left.

Time for a swabbing frenzy on the surgical ward. Hell. With every step she took, she'd be reminded of Valerie. Every second, she'd expect her to stroll out of a patient room with her usual welcoming smile. All her staff would know by now. How could she face their grief yet keep her own in check?

Late Thursday morning, Nick stood in the cold mortuary. He'd insisted on sticking to the Cavanaugh case. Look where it got him. He kept his gaze focussed a few centimetres above the victim's body.

On the other side of the metal table, Dr Indira Singh dictated a detailed description of the victim's external appearance. Bruises and abrasions, slices and slashes.

So much suffering. What did the cuts mean? How long had the killer tortured her? Why?

"Heard anything about her parents?" George's whisper drew him back to the autopsy room.

Strange how the presence of death invoked a desire for quiet. "Yes, the Victorian cops notified them last night. Devastated."

"Every parent's nightmare."

Dr Singh measured the dimensions of the wounds, while the crime scene officer snapped close-up photos. Each incision, every bruise. Scrutinised, probed, recorded.

"How intriguing." She straightened up from the autopsy table and rubbed her lower back. "I'll need to confirm my suspicions with a surgical textbook, but these wounds are deliberately and precisely placed. No hesitation marks. If I'm correct, each one corresponds to a surgical procedure."

"A wannabe surgeon or a real one?" Nick asked.

"That I cannot determine. Only the initial surgical incisions have been performed. None of the wounds penetrate deeper than the subcutaneous fat layer. That indicates some level of skill."

"Bloody shame," George said. "Someone playing doctor doesn't narrow our suspect pool."

The pathologist continued her scrutiny of the body.

"What do we have here?" She moved the overhead light to a different angle, slanting the beam across the victim's right arm.

"The medical records didn't mention any recent procedures or history of intravenous drug use. That is correct?"

"As far as we know." Nick edged closer to see what had caught her attention.

She demonstrated her findings. "There is a recent puncture wound overlying the antecubital vein, consistent with an intravenous injection or, possibly, the insertion of an intravenous catheter. Is she left- or right-handed?"

"I'll ask Julia Sinclair about that and any medical history." Nick jotted in his notebook.

"So, more evidence leading to someone with medical knowledge," George said.

"Yes, and access to medical supplies." She moved aside for another photograph. "The toxicology screen will be interesting—when it finally arrives. Laboratory delays have been troublesome of late."

"A vet would use drips too, wouldn't he?" Nick asked.

"Definitely."

"What about the boyfriend's brother-in-law? He's an anaesthetics technician, whatever that is. He could get his hands on the equipment, but would he know what to do with it?"

"Something else you could ask Dr Sinclair." George winked at him. "About bloody time you started noticing girls again."

What? Where did that idea come from? "She reported the victim missing and identified the body. Bit hard without some conversation."

"You could be in with a chance there."

"Pounce while she's grieving?" He shook his head. "Romantic advice from the prehistoric ages."

Dr Singh cleared her throat. "Shall we continue, gentlemen?"

As the pathologist's examination moved down the body, Nick's level of discomfort increased. She collected a swab from the genitals.

"Any semen?" George asked.

"Nothing obvious on the external examination." She handed the swab to the crime scene officer.

He took it to a bench, worked some magic and returned a moment later. "Acid phos negative."

"I'll need to examine these swabs under the microscope to be certain. However, I suspect this killer is too careful."

"Typical," Nick said. "Everyone's a forensic expert. Too much *CSI* on TV."

George gave a mournful sigh. "Yeah, give me the good old days when the crooks were too stupid to clean up after themselves."

The mortuary technician rolled the body over. Purplish discolouration was most marked along the length of her back and her calves, but relatively little along her thighs. Dr Singh frowned while dictating the extent of the lividity.

Why were her thighs spared? Surely if her body stayed flat on its back, the entire length of the legs would show signs of it. Nick tried to imagine how her body had been positioned.

Apart from abrasions across the shoulders, there were no other obvious injuries on her back. More photo flashes, then they turned her over again.

"Ready for the internal examination, gentlemen?" Dr Singh reached for a scalpel.

"Love to stay, but I have to get back to the factory. Briefing time." George patted Nick on the shoulder. "Let me know what else the doc finds, mate."

"You're all heart, boss."

"And when you swing by the hospital to chat up Dr Julia, have a word with the surgeon's brother-in-law." George grinned. "I'd like to surprise him before Dr—sorry, Mr—Martin McSmarmy catches up with him."

"Do you think he's a genuine contender?"

"More likely the doc wanted his own arse out of the hot seat, so he blamed someone else. Catch you later." George left.

The autopsy continued. Nick averted his eyes while a deftly wielded scalpel unzipped the body, but he still heard the ribs crunch during the opening of the chest cavity. According to the continued dictation, examination of the heart and lungs revealed no gross abnormalities. The mortuary technician wrote down the weights of the various organs on a whiteboard. Such a waste. The reduction of a human body to a shopping list of parts.

A foetid stench filled the room. The pathologist had opened the abdominal cavity. She drew his unwilling attention to the rusty brown sludge surrounding slippery loops of bowel.

"There has been a large bleed somewhere." Her gloved hands slid over the internal organs with a gentle deftness. "The intestines appear intact on gross inspection and palpation. Some other organ or major blood vessel has been perforated. I'll have a better idea once I've removed the viscera, but this could be the immediate cause of death."

"Doesn't any of this get to you?"

"Sometimes I am glad I'm a vegetarian. One has to distance one's emotions to a certain extent, but still remember these bodies were once someone's parent or child or lover. For the sake of the dead and the living, someone has to find the answers."

"Like identifying the Kings Park skeleton?"

"That is exactly correct. Her breast implants, the surgery on her fractured forearm. Those factors will help return her to her family. Have you learnt anything about her since I spoke to you on Tuesday?"

Was it really only two days ago? "No match yet. Have you seen anything to link these two cases?"

"Same gender, similar age. Advanced decomposition of the other victim makes the injuries difficult to compare. There were knife-marks on some of her bones, but I've not yet found any in this case." She shrugged, then turned back to the table. "If I do, I will take bone samples from both women for toolmark comparison by the forensic scientists. The investigation of suspects, I will leave for you. This is not an episode of *Silent Witness*."

He watched her manipulate and remove assorted unidentifiable organs. The catalogue on the whiteboard grew. Nick wished he could isolate himself from death again. Keep it distant and impersonal. But he couldn't help imagining Kym lying dead on that same metal table, her life thrown away by a careless doctor who'd missed her brain haemorrhage.

"The bladder appears intact. Wait one moment." She scrutinised another body part. "Penetrating trauma to the uterine wall."

"How'd that happen?" he asked, then regretted the images crowding his mind. He knew the answer. "Sick bastard raped her with a sharp object."

"Whatever he used, it also caused a tear in the inferior vena cava. Massive blood loss would have killed her swiftly."

The technician grabbed the saw and moved to the head of the table. Time for removal of the brain. Nick couldn't watch the scalp being turned down over the face. Too close to his nightmares.

Chapter Ten

After several hours on Valerie's ward, Julia's self-control wavered. If Gabriel gave her those puppy dog eyes one more time, she'd either collapse into his arms sobbing or punch him. Probably both. She had to escape.

"Keep going with the swabs here, Gabriel. I'll take these back to the lab." She bundled the specimen bags into a larger plastic bin-bag.

"Why don't you go home early?"

Home? To wallow in misery? She shook her head. A sliver of pain stabbed behind her right eye. "Too much work to do."

A group of nurses buzzed near the elevator doors. They quietened at her approach. A million questions rose in their eyes. Mouths opened.

She bolted for the stairwell, clattered down two flights of stairs. Her right foot slipped off a step and she stumbled, clutching the handrail. Momentum swung her into the railing and knocked the breath from her lungs. The bag fell from her grasp and flew open. Specimens skittered everywhere.

Running away from nurses? Gutless coward.

She slumped onto the step. A quick check for injuries revealed only a twinge in her ankle. Could've been worse. Once her pulse slowed to a nonlethal rate, she collected the specimens and continued down the stairs at a more sedate pace.

Next level—operating suite. She paused. How had Martin fared with the police? She hadn't seen him on the ward, so maybe he was operating. A detour to theatre wouldn't take long.

She approached the reception desk. Unattended, but the theatre timetable showed Martin's name crossed out, another surgeon in his place. Sick? Grieving? Helping the police with their enquiries?

Had Simon confirmed Martin's alibi for Monday night? Another glance at the list revealed Simon was gassing in theatre three on their last case. She'd wait. If the police wasted time on Martin, the actual killer would remain unpunished.

She paced the hallway outside the theatre change-rooms, unwilling to sit in the waiting room in case she missed him. Ten long minutes passed. Time enough to imagine Valerie's terror, that moment when she knew she would die.

At last, the men's room door opened and Simon strode out. A hint of a smile before a more sombre expression shuttered his face.

"Sorry to hear about Valerie." He searched her eyes. "You okay?"

"I'm faking okay so I don't scare the patients."

"No patients here." His voice softened. "I don't scare that easily."

"I'm practising denial. Don't ruin it for me. Have the police spoken to you?"

He jammed his hands in his pockets. "Police? Only about Martin. Why would they want to speak to me?"

"That's what I meant. He's a suspect, but he'd never hurt Valerie."

"Lovers hurt each other all the time."

"Wasn't he with you all Monday night?"

"That's what I told the police."

Was that a flicker of uncertainty?

"What really happened? Tell. Me. Everything."

He hesitated, maybe to consider the pros and cons of revealing the truth. "Martin came back to my place for a drink after work. He rambled a lot. His wife's not well. Valerie was making too many demands on his time. They'd had an argument. He drank more than was good for him, so I let him sleep on the sofa."

"What else?"

"It's nothing."

"Simon. Don't make me hurt you."

"He arrived later than when he told the police. I don't know why."

"Tell the police." Martin guilty? No way. She couldn't be such a shocking judge of character, could she?

"He wasn't that late. Ten, fifteen minutes. Let's play devil's advocate. Not enough time to abduct Valerie and hide her somewhere. Unless he stashed her in the boot of his car overnight."

"He could've drugged and gagged her." Her heart ached at the thought of Valerie tied up, terrified and alone, struggling for survival.

"One dose of sedation lasting over twelve hours?"

A valid point. "What if he gave her another shot during the night? Where did he park?"

"In my garage. There's an entrance off the laundry." He shook his head. "I'm a light sleeper. I would've heard something."

"Sure?"

He frowned. "Although . . . I felt groggy in the morning."

"Drugged?"

"We're mates. He wouldn't roofie me."

"This is crazy." Wasn't she trying to clear Martin?

Male voices echoed in the hallway. She turned towards them.

Her heart sank. A male nurse from ED and that detective. He had to catch her in another compromising position.

"Dr Sinclair, I didn't expect to find you here," Nick Randall said.

She hoisted her bag of specimens. "I do work here."

Simon edged closer, rested his left hand on her shoulder, and reached out to shake the detective's hand. "Dr Simon Bailey, and you are?"

"Nick Randall." He lifted the ID badge that hung from a lanyard around his neck.

Their handshake lasted a fraction too long.

She evaded Simon's proprietary touch with a sideways step. "If you're looking for Martin, he's not operating right now."

"No, I'm after Carl Bennett, an anaesthetics technician, but I do have a couple of questions for you, Dr Sinclair. If you have the time."

Carl who? And what did he have to do with Valerie? "Simon will find him for you. We can use the waiting room."

The ED nurse wandered off. Simon grunted something, then disappeared back into the men's change-room.

She led Nick to the waiting room opposite the reception desk. Hardly anyone ever used it. Theatre staff discouraged relatives from hanging around the operating suite. Otherwise, they might have to talk to them. A handful of hospital-grey armchairs of the not-too-comfortable variety, a battle-scarred coffee table and a stack of magazines from the last millennium. No TV, no window, no welcome mat.

"Why do you want to see Carl Bennett?" she asked.

"He's helping us with our enquiries." He hauled a notepad out of his back pocket, then sat opposite her. "Why were you talking to Simon Bailey?"

"Confidential medical discussion." Take that.

"Of course. Was Valerie left- or right-handed?"

"Right." She shrank into the chair. "You've been at her autopsy. Was it . . . who . . ."

"Dr Singh took good care of her." He jotted her answer down. "What about her recent medical history?"

"No problems. Fit and healthy." She couldn't help picturing Valerie on the autopsy table, all scooped out. She dug her nails into her palms, half-expecting to see them burst through the back of her hands.

"Any medical procedures? Blood tests?"

She shook her head.

"What about medications?"

"Just the Pill, the occasional painkiller. Nothing illegal." She searched his eyes, but he must have passed Inscrutable Expressions 101 with an A grade. "Too early for tox results, so you must have found injection sites."

No response. Would Indira tell her?

Someone knocked, then flung the door open.

"You the detective looking for me?" A bodybuilder with a blond buzz-cut filled the doorway.

Carl Bennett, no doubt. She'd seen him around the hospital, mainly at the gym, but couldn't imagine what he had to do with Valerie.

Nick stood. "Thanks, Dr Sinclair. This helps a lot."

Carl Bennett gave her a slow top to toe once-over. Had his gaze been any more intense, her breasts would've ignited. She had to brush against him to squeeze her way out. Creep didn't budge.

⚬

Nick settled back into the armchair from hell. Whatever happened to "First, do no harm"? Mustn't apply to hospital furniture. He waited for Carl Bennett, seated in the chair opposite, to finish cracking his knuckles and flexing his pecs. Ice-blue eyes stared back at him. Dead eyes. Julia had better stay away from him.

"What's your relationship with Martin MacDougall?" Nick asked.

"He's married to my baby sister. What's that bastard done?" Carl clenched his hands. "If he's hurt Rachel, I'll kill the prick."

"Relax. This is nothing to do with your sister. Careful with the death threats."

Carl laughed, but his eyes didn't join in.

"Dr MacDougall mentioned a recent confrontation with you. What's your version of events?"

"Did he say I threatened him? Poor little baby." He gave a self-satisfied grin.

"Just tell me what happened."

"He's been screwing around on my sister, and I told him to knock it off."

"Did you threaten him in any way?"

"Not really." Carl dragged the last word out.

"He mentioned you said he'd be sorry. What did you mean?"

Another crack of the knuckles. "Nothing specific. Bastard could get me sacked if I hit him. Just wanted to give him a fright."

"Did you approach Valerie Cavanaugh?"

"Why would I do anything to her? She's as much a victim as my sister is."

"Interesting choice of word. Victim. Why do you say that?"

He shrugged. "Playing doctors and nurses? She won't last."

"Maybe she's a serious threat to your sister's marriage."

Carl jerked backwards, scraping his chair along the lino floor. "I've done nothing to Martin or his bloody girlfriend. Sweet fuck all. You ask her."

"Where were you Monday night?"

"Working out."

"What gym?"

"At home."

"Was anyone with you?"

"No."

"Did you see Valerie Cavanaugh on Monday?"

"Don't think so. I don't have much to do with the ward nurses."

"What time did you leave the hospital that night?"

"Shit, I don't know. Fiveish."

"What time did you see Valerie Cavanaugh?"

"Fucked if I know. What's it got to do with me?"

"We found her body yesterday."

Carl slammed his fist on the coffee table. "Martin. That slimy prick. Dobbing me in to save his own hairy arse."

"We take all allegations seriously."

"Why would I kill her?" Carl shook his head. "I could understand it if Martin was dead, but Valerie? You must be bloody joking." His harsh laughter boomed around the room.

"Ruin Martin's life? Frame him for murder?" Nick watched Carl's responses. If he were guilty, would he be able to cover up so convincingly?

"Pig's arse. If I wanted to sort out Martin bloody MacDougall, he'd be too busy spitting out broken teeth to talk to you."

Carl gripped both arms of the chair and pushed hard. The metal buckled until the right side snapped clean off.

Roid rage?

"Bit of a temper you've got there, mate. Pull your head in and tell me what really happened on Monday night. Or should we take this back to the station?"

"I told you the truth already." He chewed one thumbnail, spat the unwanted bit onto the floor. "I don't want to get her in trouble."

"Who?"

"Shit." Carl rubbed his hands down his thighs. "Ask my sister Rachel what that bastard does to her behind closed doors."

He crossed his arms and refused to say another word.

CHAPTER ELEVEN

ON FRIDAY MORNING, JULIA raced to the lab to check the VRSA screening progress. Thursday had disappeared in a blur of swabs and paperwork and mindless repetition. With Gabriel's help, she'd collected screening swabs from everyone in sight and left request forms for the night shift. If he hadn't guilt-tripped her into letting him drive her home, she might've worked all night.

Anything to block out Valerie's murder.

If only it helped. Her eyes burned with fatigue. Valerie's battered face had haunted her nightmares. Asleep or awake, it made little difference.

Back to work, Julia. Too soon to know the extent of the problem. Negative swab results would take at least forty-eight hours, and confirmed positives another twenty-four. What if Brad had caught VRSA in the hospital? From another patient, or worse, a staff member. Who knew how far it could've spread?

She blinked, aware at last that all the lab staff were staring at her. A quick glance downwards. Oh, hell. She'd meant to change before she left home. She still had one of Valerie's T-shirts on. A sheer white T-shirt that she'd spilt red wine on and left soaking at Julia's place. Shame her bra matched the red of her eyes. She grabbed a lab coat for instant protection. Better wear surgical scrubs for the day.

"Anything to report?" she asked.

Lorena gave her best evil witch cackle. "Good news or bad first?"

"Please tell me you're joking." She pulled up a chair, unconvinced her legs could bear the weight of another disaster.

"The good news is we've got most of the swabs from your list."

"Hit me with the bad." She gripped the arms of the chair and braced for a crash landing. Her arms ached, a reminder of how she'd pounded her punching bag until the point of exhaustion. She'd attacked a faceless killer. Healthier than a hangover and more satisfying, but Valerie remained dead.

"Another suspicious staph on a wound from the orthopaedics ward." Lorena handed her a request form.

"Bugger." How could it have spread from the surgical ward to the orthopaedic ward so fast? They were on different floors and didn't share any staff. It didn't make any sense.

"Shall I order some more screening plates?"

"You'd better. Expect another mountain of swabs." She checked her watch. Gabriel had stayed late yesterday, so she'd told him to sleep in.

"That's not the only bad news."

How could anything get worse? "Yes?"

"The Chief Scientist wants to see you. He didn't look happy."

"He never does." Still, she should have warned him about the impending overtime to cope with the extra workload. "I'll see him later this morning when I have a better idea of how many more screens we need."

Another task she should've taken care of yesterday. So many balls to juggle when all she wanted to do was cry and howl and scream.

———— ◄○► ————

Ten minutes later, on the orthopaedic ward, Julia rummaged through the chart rack for Edith Powell's notes. She skimmed the patient's record. When she read the admission diagnosis, her hopes plummeted. A total knee replacement.

She flagged down a resident doctor. "Is Edith Powell one of yours?"

Harried eyes met hers. "Yes." He dragged out his reply as if reluctant to admit any connection.

"Her wound swab's growing a staph, a possible vancomycin-resistant MRSA."

"Great. More bloody work."

"How deep is the infection?"

He flicked his hands palm up. "Don't have a clue. I'm covering someone on leave."

"If it's only a superficial soft tissue infection, then antibiotics are enough to treat it. If the prosthesis is infected, it'll have to come out and she'll need six weeks of IV antibiotics before they can put a new joint in."

A heartfelt groan. "I'll let the registrar know when he gets out of theatre."

"I'll order her antibiotics from pharmacy and write them on her medication chart. Get your registrar to call me later."

"Thanks for nothing." He sighed. "You really know how to spoil someone's day, don't you?"

"Sorry." She tried a sympathetic smile, but it felt artificial and stiff. Her job was on the line and her best friend was dead. Dead. She forced herself to concentrate on the patient's medical history. "Has she been in hospital anywhere else? Done any overseas travelling?"

His gaze drifted to his watch. "Not that I know of. I have to . . ."

"Fine. I'll ask her myself." She shooed him away.

The resident shuffled off to his next chore.

Julia grabbed a disposable gown from the ward storeroom on her way to the patient's room. She slipped it on, tying it loosely at the back, then pulled on a pair of gloves. If Edith Powell had VRSA, full contact precautions had to be taken.

"Hello, Mrs Powell. I'm Dr Julia Sinclair from the Infectious Diseases Department." She dragged the curtain around the bed to give an illusion of privacy. "Do you mind if I ask a few questions?"

The grey-haired woman clutched the sheet to her chest. "Why are you dressed like that?" Her voice quavered. "What's wrong with me?"

"I didn't mean to scare you. Just a precaution. You might have a bug that won't respond to our usual antibiotics."

"Really?" The elderly woman cringed, her eyes wide.

"It's okay. We've got other antibiotics that will fix it."

"Oh, dear. You scared me three-quarters of the way to death." She fanned herself with a translucent hand. "I feel like I'm already halfway there myself. So why the fancy dress?"

"If you do have this bug, I'd rather not spread it around the hospital to more patients. The other antibiotics are way more expensive." And if they stopped working, the hospital would be up shit creek without a paddle.

"That I can understand. Everything costs so much these days." Edith Powell hauled herself upright. Her eyes brightened. "Now, tell me, dear. How did I get to be so special?"

"Maybe you can help me find out. Have you been in hospital before?"

"Only this hospital, dear. I had a bowel cancer taken out—oh, let me see—five years ago, something like that. The surgeon—he was so lovely—he got it all out, too. Had no more trouble after that until my knee started playing up. The arthritis, you know. It's been such a trial. Really slowed me down on the dance floor. I hope I can foxtrot again with this new knee of mine. Very nice surgeon. Not very chatty, mind. He's always so busy, rushing off to surgery."

Julia took advantage of the patient's need to breathe. "How about travel? Anywhere overseas?"

"Oh, no, dearie. Not for fifteen years now, not since my late husband passed. He loved to travel. It wouldn't be the same without him. We went absolutely everywhere. Does that help? Do you need to know where we went? I could get my daughter to bring in my photo albums to jog my memory."

"No, thanks, that won't be necessary. I'll organise the new antibiotic for you today, so we can get you back on your feet as soon as possible."

"Thank you, dear. How much longer will I be in hospital?"

"That's tricky. I have to talk to your surgeon first." Hell, should she give her the worst possible option? "You might need another operation, but it depends on the infection."

Edith Powell's face crumpled. Her lower lip quivered. "I don't want another operation."

"Let me talk to your surgeon before we get too carried away. Oh, one more question—have you visited anyone on the surgical ward, or had any visitors from there this week?"

"No, dear. I've been stuck in bed. Some old friends came to see me. All sorts of people wander in and out at all hours of the night and day. One of them even had a mask on. Didn't say a word. Just prodded my knee with one of those cotton-bud thingies and squirted something into my drip and wandered off. I felt sorry for him working so late, but that's no excuse for being so rude. Would it have killed him to say hello?"

"Maybe he didn't want to disturb your room-mate." Wonder what that was about?

"Oh, yes, dear. That must be right. It was the middle of the night, after all. Ever since my husband died . . ."

Julia let her talk for a while longer, then made her excuses and left. A quick note in her medical chart. No mention of any middle of the night procedure. Maybe it was just a dressing change, and the injection was an antibiotic dose into her drip. Sometimes elderly patients became confused in hospital, especially post-op.

What next? She had to get the nurses to isolate Edith Powell. They could juggle beds to find a single room somewhere. If the VRSA spread any further, she'd have to close the ward to all new admissions. That would make her popular with Medical Administration. A real career killer.

On her way back to the lab, Julia's pager interrupted her thoughts about outbreak control: Go to Medical Administration ASAP. Were they reading minds now? She detoured, as requested. Manfredi must want an in-depth explanation of the VRSA situation. By the time she reached the Medical Administration reception desk, she had her speech prepared. She berated herself for not notifying him about the VRSA case sooner.

The receptionist sent her through with a smile. "Dr Manfredi's on the phone, but said you're to go straight in."

The wizened administrator gestured for her to sit down. He spoke into a blue-tooth earpiece, probably because he needed both hands free to talk. She sank into a buttery-soft black leather chair and watched the almost hypnotic movements of his hands until her head nodded. She snapped awake.

Sleeping her way to the unemployment line—a novel way to do it, but not one she intended to follow. Comfiest chair she'd ever sat in. Bet it didn't come from Hospital Supplies. Neither did the original artwork on the walls. Was that a Juniper? Shame the same amount of money wasn't lavished on security.

Or car park light globes.

His phone conversation continued for another five minutes, then he stared at her for a few moments as if wondering why she was there, cluttering up his lovely office.

"I'm very disappointed in you, Dr Sinclair." He shook his head, making his red bowtie twitch from side to side.

"I've been busy—"

"We've all been busy, but that's no excuse for harassing a poor woman in her own home."

What? Bloody Rachel must've complained. "I thought you wanted to see me about the outbreak."

"Outbreak? Did I hear you right? What outbreak?" His face purpled. "When did this start?"

"We only found out about the second potential case this morning. It hasn't been confirmed yet, so it's not really an outbreak, just a potential one." Great, Julia. Babbling under pressure will definitely win you a promotion.

"That doesn't answer my question. When did you see the first case?"

"Late Monday. Straightforward post-op wound infection, a nasty one, but nothing suspicious. We suspected MRSA on Tuesday."

Dr Manfredi ran his finger around the inside of his collar as if his bowtie choked him. "Christ. You knew about this on Tuesday, and now you tell me. Just what we need. An MRSA outbreak. Will we have to close wards? Cancel theatre? Do you have any idea how tight our budget is?"

At least she'd taken his mind off Rachel's complaint. "It's a new strain of MRSA, one that's also resistant to vancomycin. VRSA. An Australian first, maybe even the world."

His eyes brightened for a second, probably at the thought of being first in the world, then he glowered at her. "I don't want to see this hospital splashed across the evening news or on the front page of all the newspapers. You hear me?"

"Yes."

"I want frequent updates."

"Of course. If we confirm the second case tomorrow, do I have your permission to close those two wards to new admissions? Or should I call you first?"

"No, no need to call me. You have my permission to do whatever is necessary. I want this stopped and sooner rather than later." He flapped his hands in the air. "Keep a lid on it. Not a word to the press. Understand?"

"Yes." She half-expected his bowtie to spin around and his head to take off.

"The press is all over that murdered nurse already. I don't need any more aggravation."

Aggravation? His callous dismissal of Valerie's murder shocked her into open-mouthed silence. How dare he? She forced herself to stand, pulse roaring in her ears. Control. Keep your mouth shut. She had to escape before she clambered across the table and throttled the slimy little weasel.

"Thank you for your time. I've got lots of work to do." Anger tightened her voice to a whisper.

He thumped his hands on his desk. "Then how the hell do you have time to harass a surgeon's wife in her own home during the rostered working day?"

Fuck.

She spun around and strode out of his office. Didn't even slam the door. Let the miserable fucker shut it himself.

⁘

Back in her office on Friday afternoon, Julia updated Gabriel on the latest VRSA developments. She had mollified the Chief Scientist with an assurance that the Medical Superintendent had approved the cost of outbreak screening and all necessary overtime. Staying flat-out busy had bolstered her illusion of control. She thought about Valerie only with every other breath.

She scanned the list of names on their spreadsheet. Gabriel had entered most of Brad's contacts. Now they had to do the same for Edith Powell. Neither of the infected patients had been outside Western Australia in the past year, so it was unlikely they'd brought the bug with them. There must be a common source, a carrier within the hospital, someone who strolled the wards oblivious to disease and death trailing their steps. All she had to do was track that person down and keep them away from patients until they'd eradicated the bacteria from their system.

How bloody hard could it be?

Gabriel tapped his finger on the screen. "How's Brad?"

"His temp has settled. He had to go for another echo, so I didn't see him for long. The cardiothoracic surgeons aren't keen to operate."

"Why? I thought all surgeons ever wanted to do was slice people open."

"He's young, and artificial valves don't last forever. Long-term anticoagulation's a risk."

"Sounds tricky."

"It is, but sometimes they have to operate to save the patient's life. The hard part is knowing which patients and when."

She returned to the computer keyboard and entered the next name from their list, one of the ward orderlies. They moved around the hospital more freely than most staff. Did anyone keep a record of which orderlies covered which wards?

"Any news about Valerie?" Gabriel asked.

Hell. For five seconds, she hadn't thought about Valerie. Maybe if she ignored the question, he'd let her grieve in private.

She entered another name on the database. "We need the orderlies' roster."

"Does she have any family here? What about her funeral? If you need some help . . ."

Funeral? Her mind shied away from thoughts of coffins and cremations. She shifted her attention from the computer screen and focussed on Gabriel. He looked like a puppy waiting for a newspaper whack across the nose.

"Not now. There's too much work to do."

"You're running on fumes. Are you getting any sleep?" He hesitated, his head cocked to one side. "I tried calling you last night."

"I've been getting nuisance calls, so I took the phone off the hook and turned off my mobile."

"How bizarre. Have you checked the phone number?"

"Yes. Withheld, of course."

"Have you reported it to the police? Maybe they can put a trace on your phone line."

"They have more important problems to solve." Like Valerie's murder. Or an assault on Gabriel if he didn't give it a rest.

"What about the absolutely edible Detective Randall? I met him when he was looking for you yesterday. Maybe he could go undercover and stake out your house." He rubbed his fingers over his designer-stubbled chin.

If he didn't shut up, she'd scream.

"Persistent little bugger, aren't you?" She'd cross-checked the two ward lists and couldn't find any staff member or patient in common. Maybe there'd been some shift changes or staff on sick leave who'd been forgotten. "Charm someone in the HR Department to give you all the rosters for the orthopaedics and surgical wards, including orderlies, physios, students. And anyone else you can think of."

Gabriel hovered over her desk. "When I get back, why don't we knock off early, and I'll buy you a drink?"

Subtle wasn't working. Time to pull out the girl card. She opened her top drawer and slapped a box of tampons on the desk.

"Killer cramps." She narrowed her eyes and gave him her best Clint Eastwood. "Feeling lucky, punk?"

"Okay, okay." Gabriel blushed and backed out of the room. "Call me on my mobile if you need some company later."

"Good luck. Threaten them with Manfredi if HR gets stroppy."

Poor guy. Maybe he had the right idea. Only one way to obliterate pain in the short-term. Alcohol and lots of it. Just because she was a doctor, it didn't mean she had to have healthy coping mechanisms.

First, more mind-numbing work.

And another trip to the mortuary.

CHAPTER TWELVE

A TYPICAL PERTH DECEMBER afternoon. Clear blue sky. Heat shimmering off the bitumen. Everything was still, breathless, waiting for the Fremantle Doctor to resuscitate the scorching dry air with a cool sea breeze.

So why the bloody hell was she pacing outside the State Mortuary, risking heatstroke and wasting time? She could've phoned Indira, made sure she was free, but what if she'd said no? Better to confront her face to face. If only she didn't have to walk through the mortuary, past the room where Valerie had been . . . examined.

Someone approached the front door, a guy in blue overalls with "Forensics" branded across his back. Julia followed him. Eyes straight ahead, she charged down the hallway towards the pathologists' offices. Don't think about Valerie's body locked in a fridge.

Indira sat at her microscope, dictating into a digital recorder. Something about metastatic lesions in the cerebellum.

"Julia, I'm so sorry I didn't call you last night." She gestured at the stack of slides on her desk. "A busy week. How are you feeling?"

She shrugged. "I hope you didn't mind my note, asking you to look after Valerie."

"Not at all, but you must appreciate I'm working with the police in this matter." She slid a chair towards Julia. "It wouldn't be appropriate for me to discuss my autopsy findings with you."

Always so professional. Damn her.

"A detective asked me about Valerie's medical history. Perhaps if I knew more details, I could help you."

Indira leant forward and grasped Julia's hands. "I understand you want to do everything possible for your friend, but let me take care of Valerie. Please look after yourself."

"I could find out if she had any procedures or blood tests elsewhere. I have contacts in the other labs, other hospitals."

"So do I." Indira squeezed her hands, then let go. "I've already made those enquiries. You look exhausted. There's no shame in taking a sedative to help you sleep."

Sleep? No way. "When will the tox screen come back?"

Indira glanced at her in-tray. "The full toxicology report will be delayed. A major drug raid has overwhelmed their resources."

"But you have a prelim?"

"Julia, please, I cannot tell you these results. I haven't even notified the police."

"If this was a movie, you'd step out of the room for a moment, leaving me alone with the results folder."

Indira dimpled. "If this was a movie, you'd be Cary Grant, and I'd risk my career for you."

"Still a sucker for those old movies?" Her mobile buzzed. A text from the lab courier. "There's my lift."

"Back to the hospital?" Indira's dimples vanished. "Be careful with your detective work."

"You think the killer is someone at the hospital?"

"The killer's identity is for the police to determine. Just remember, Valerie was abducted from the hospital."

"It's more than that. Whatever happened to Valerie . . . Something medical?" She searched Indira's expression. "A killer with medical knowledge? Access to intravenous drugs?" Not a twitch.

Her mobile buzzed again.

"Be careful." With a shadow of a smile, Indira swivelled back to her microscope.

Great. More advice, when all she wanted was answers.

———◆———

Two hours after leaving the State Mortuary, Julia walked home in the late afternoon heat, her briefcase full of roster printouts and spreadsheets that Gabriel had left on her desk. Exhausted beyond belief, but her nervous system was on red alert. Why was she so on edge? It was broad daylight, for heaven's sake. A warped grief reaction? A belief, deep down, that she deserved to be punished by some evil stalker because she hadn't prevented Valerie's murder?

Welcome to paranoia central.

Footsteps trailed behind her. She whipped around and startled a young boy with his beagle puppy. The puppy yelped. She knew how it felt.

At last, she reached home. She emptied her mailbox and flicked through the stack of mail on her way to the front door. Only bills, by the look of it, and one medical journal. Hang on—a parcel on the doormat. She picked it up. No stamps or sender details anywhere on the brown wrapping. Hand-delivered? How curious.

"Anything exciting?"

Julia's pulse rate skyrocketed. Gabriel stepped out of the shade. "Are you trying to scare me to death?" She slapped his arm.

"Hope you like Thai food." Gabriel lifted the plastic bags.

"If you're here to gossip about Valerie, start hunting for another job."

"I'm worried about you." His voice gained strength. "At the very least, you need to eat. I'll sit outside the door if I have to and wait until you've eaten something."

When was the last time she ate? Her eyes misted. "Don't you dare be nice. If I start crying, I'll never stop."

"What's wrong with that?" He pulled a tissue box from one of the bags. "Sometimes you have to let go."

"That's exactly what Valerie would say."

"So, take her advice."

"Okay, but any out-of-order questions and I'll tape your mouth shut." She unlocked the security screen and the front door.

"Fair enough." He ran his hand over the coloured panes of glass in the front door. "I love leadlights. Is it original?"

"Mostly. I replaced some of the glass, but the design is as old as the rest of the house."

"How old?"

"A hundredish, about the same age I feel today." She shut the door behind them to keep the heat out. "The old girl needs a bit of work, but she's got character."

"Much cooler in here. Lovely high ceilings." He gazed upwards, tracking along the cornices to the arch halfway down the hall.

"Let's go to the kitchen, down the back." She pointed at the other rooms that opened onto the hallway. "Bedrooms, bathroom, lounge."

She kicked off her shoes and padded down the hallway, the timber floors cool underfoot. On her way past the hall table, she dumped the mail. A light flashed on her answer machine. Police? Press? Nothing she'd want to listen to while Gabriel lurked nearby.

He placed a bottle of wine on the kitchen table. "I hope an Eden Valley Riesling is okay."

"Is that from the bottle shop on the corner?" She handed him a couple of wineglasses. "I used to work there as a student."

"Yes." Gabriel unscrewed the lid with a flourish. "Hello, puss. Where did you spring from?" He bent down to scratch Oscar's head as the cat circled his legs.

"That's Oscar, my housemate. If I'm home, it must be food time." She poured two glasses of wine and one bowl of cat biscuits.

Unable to resist temptation and needing to escape Gabriel's concerned gaze, she returned to the hall table for the mystery parcel. She shook it on her way back to the kitchen. Something rattled inside.

"Come on, open it. I love surprise presents." Gabriel snatched the parcel off her and held it up to his ear. "It's not ticking."

She took it back and tore open the brown wrapping paper. Inside, she found a shoebox encased in plastic and sealed with an abundance of tough sticky-tape. "I'll need a knife to get through this lot."

She grabbed one from the knife-block on the kitchen bench. After cutting the tape, she freed the lid and lifted it off. An unpleasant but familiar odour emanated from the box. Gabriel stepped backwards. A sealed white envelope sat on top of a pile of shredded paper. She opened it and drew out a sheet of paper with one sentence on it in large black letters, a gothic font.

"From one bitch to another." The hand she clamped over her nose and mouth muffled her voice.

The stench overpowered the small kitchen. Unwillingly, she lifted the top layer of shredded paper with the tip of her knife.

"Gross. Is that what I think it is?" Gabriel gagged on the smell and rushed into the hallway.

A delicate stomach for a nurse.

"Dog shit. Ugh." She dropped the lid on the box.

Gabriel returned, holding his nose. "That is one sick puppy."

"Disgusting. What sicko would send me that?" She clasped the box as if it were nuclear waste and placed it in a garbage bag.

She inspected the wrapping paper. Her name and address were written in thick black ink, probably a felt-pen. She didn't recognise the handwriting. The enclosed note could have come from any computer, any printer. Anonymous, threatening.

"Made any enemies lately?" Gabriel asked, recovering his composure at last.

"No."

Could it be connected to the late-night phone calls? Valerie's murderer? The sender knew where she lived. Her heart fluttered in her chest like a trapped bird. Had Valerie's murderer been to her house?

"Pity you can't mark it 'return to sender' and send it back express post," he said. "That'd teach them."

Her panic eased a fraction. Unfortunately, the stench persisted. She dumped the garbage bag outside, then came back in and washed her hands. If only she could wash out her nose, too. She opened some windows and ushered Gabriel into the lounge room.

"Have some wine. I'll nuke the food later to warm it up." Valerie loved Thai food. If only she was here . . .

"Earth to Julia."

A hand waved in front of her face. "What?"

"Okay? You were light-years away." Gabriel frowned at her.

"If only I'd left with her instead of going back to the lab . . ."

"Don't blame yourself." He put down his wineglass and placed his hand over hers.

The coolness of his fingers sent a shiver up her arm. She snatched her hand away and picked up her wine. She drained it and slammed the empty glass down on the coffee table. The stem shattered.

A shard of glass penetrated her palm. "Shit."

Blood dripped onto the white flokati rug. She wanted to feel pain, but the emptiness inside her swallowed it whole and begged for more.

Gabriel dashed out of the room and returned with a tea-towel. He knelt on the floor beside her. With gentle hands, he removed the glass splinter and pressed the tea-towel over the wound.

"Hold this here. Keep the pressure on." He raised her hands. "Where's your first-aid kit?"

"Go home." Her voice rasped.

"First-aid kit?"

"Leave me alone."

"Don't move."

She could hear him clattering about in her bathroom cabinet. Why wouldn't he leave her alone? Fussing around, mothering her. Who the fuck did he think he was? Valerie?

Gabriel returned with her first-aid kit in one hand and a clean wineglass in the other. He placed the glass out of her reach, then sat cross-legged on the floor and attended to her wound. She welcomed the sting of the antiseptic. He used a couple of butterfly strips to hold the edges of the wound together, then covered it with an adhesive bandage.

"Good as new." He stood up with one fluid movement.

"You could do that for a living." She filled the fresh glass and gulped the wine.

"If you're going to drink at that rate, I'd better force-feed you." He grabbed the wine bottle and took it with him to the kitchen.

"Hey, I'm thirsty, not hungry." Her head sagged back against the wall.

How could she survive without Valerie?

She needed obliteration. Fast.

"Where's the wine?"

CHAPTER THIRTEEN

ON SATURDAY MORNING, A very sorry Julia hauled herself out of bed. Her head throbbed in time with her pulse. How could her heart beat so loudly when the rest of her was decomposing? Her stomach revolted. She dashed to the bathroom, one hand clasped over her mouth.

She slid sideways onto the cold bathroom floor. That only made her head pound more viciously, so she tried some deep breaths. More pain.

After a long, cool shower, she wrapped herself in a towel and wandered into the kitchen.

Gabriel handed her a large glass of water. "You'll need this."

"Holy crap." She'd forgotten he'd crashed on her sofa for the night.

Blackout or brain damage? What else had she forgotten? What had she told him? She tightened her grip on the too-small towel with her spare hand, then drained the glass in one go.

"Better?"

"Almost human. Thanks." She grabbed the jug and poured another glassful. "No more alcohol. Ever."

"Can I get you something to eat before I go?" Gabriel asked.

"Food?" She shuddered ever so cautiously. "It'll be months before I can face anything solid."

He checked his watch. "I teach a yoga class on Saturday mornings. Sure you'll be alright on your own? I can cancel . . ."

"Go, please. I promise I won't slash my wrists in the bathtub."

"Call me later if you need anything." He stepped forward, his arms outstretched for a hug.

She clung onto her towel and moved out of reach. "I'll be fine."

After seeing him out, she washed down a couple of Panadols and fed the cat. Her hunt for clean clothes reminded her to load the washing machine. Household chores underway and headache cranked down a few notches, she fetched her old photo album. She'd meant to make digital copies, but was glad now she didn't have to cope with any form of technology in her fragile state.

She loaded the coffee plunger with a double-strength dose of caffeine, then flicked through the photos. Scattered amongst some heartbreaking family snaps of her sister were a few pictures from her days sharing a house with Valerie. Carefree and oh so young. Luckily, none of them could predict the future.

Look at Valerie laughing her head off at some young hopeful. Hang on. Richard? She'd forgotten they'd met at her and Valerie's house-warming party. So happy together. What had gone wrong? Had it cost Valerie her life?

Julia grabbed a sheet of paper and made a list of suspects with points for and against alongside each one.

Richard—known to be violent; works and lives near the hospital; unexplained injury to his right hand; could have done anything during a drunken blackout, but appeared genuinely upset when told Valerie was dead.

Martin—also present in the hospital on Monday evening; recent argument with Valerie; says he was at Simon's house all night, but arrived late.

Rachel—the abandoned wife; possible drug problem; looks too pathetic to have killed anyone herself, but may have had help.

Carl Bennett—person of interest with the police for unknown reason; works at the hospital; creepy vibe.

Unknown killer—could be absolutely anyone.

Hopeless. She screwed up the list and tossed it in the corner. The police had more resources, but she had local knowledge. It wouldn't hurt to ask around. She had to do something. If she cross-checked the staff rosters first, she'd have a good excuse to haunt the wards over the weekend, collecting swabs.

Her phone rang. She answered it before the answer machine clicked on.

"Is that Julia Sinclair?" A male voice, deep and resonant.

A stranger. Was the mystery caller making contact at last?

Her chest tightened. "Who is this?" she demanded, her voice pitching higher than normal.

"Hi, I left a couple of messages about the anniversary story on your sister. I understand you know Valerie Cavanaugh too. When's a good time for your interview?"

She couldn't speak, couldn't think, couldn't breathe.

"Hello . . . Are you still there?"

Bloody journalists. She slammed the phone down.

The message light on her answer machine flashed. Were they all tabloid hacks or had an actual human being wanted to talk to her? She really needed caller ID.

Sure enough, that journalist had left the first three messages. A couple of hang-ups. Telemarketer or psychotic stalker? Another journalist wanting a quote for the Sunday paper. Nothing printable came to mind. Finally, a message from Nick Randall about meeting him at Valerie's house.

An hour later, Julia parked around the corner from Valerie's place in Claremont. Nausea threatened to overwhelm her again. It had taken an age to cover up the ravages left from last night. Red eyes and green skin were definitely not a good look. She got out of the car and blinked in the obscenely bright sunshine. Her headache had faded to a dull throb behind her right eye. Sunglasses? She rummaged in her handbag. Oh crap, she was already wearing them.

Her pulse rate rose with each step. Rapid breaths drew in more oxygen. Ready to run, ready to run. Sweat trickled down her back.

Nick met her on the front veranda of the Californian bungalow. "We've dusted for prints already, but let me know if you want anything moved or opened."

She hesitated in the doorway. Despite the crowd of overalled crime scene examiners, the house felt empty. Its heart was missing.

After a deep breath, she entered the central hallway. Polished jarrah floorboards led the eye towards the main entertaining area at the back of the house. One bedroom on either side of the hallway. Valerie's on the right, the other a guest room that doubled as a study.

Valerie's bedroom. The bed was unmade, white sheets crumpled at the bottom of the bed. A pair of faded jeans and a purple T-shirt draped over a chair in the far corner. A stack of books balanced on the bedside table, waiting to be read.

She shifted her weight from foot to foot, longing to escape. Only the solid warmth of Nick at her back blocked her flight.

"Sorry. I never paid much attention to these front rooms."

"That's okay." He stepped out of her way. "Anything out of place, anything you don't recognise as hers, anything missing?"

"Oh, her laptop. It's usually on her bedside table."

"Maybe forensics have already taken it. I'll check."

Nothing new in the guest room, as messy as ever. She moved on to the bathroom. One towel discarded on the floor; another drooped from a hook on the back of the door. A half-empty tube of toothpaste next to a bar of scented soap. Valerie's favourite perfume. Her heart ached.

Nick returned. "No sign of any laptop so far. Would she have taken it to work?"

"Don't think so."

"We'll keep looking then. Other than her bathroom cabinet, did she keep medications anywhere else? Any sleeping pills?"

"No. Valerie could fall asleep anytime, anywhere. I always envied that." She watched his expression. "What did you find on her tox screen?"

"Still waiting on the lab."

If the killer had sedated Valerie, maybe she hadn't suffered the whole time. A small mercy to clutch onto.

She walked into the open-plan kitchen and lounge room area. Rotten milk stench from a cereal-crusted bowl on the kitchen bench. A greasy frypan sat on the stove and a pile of dishes cluttered the kitchen sink. An upended wine bottle drained into the sink, ready for the recycling bin. One lip-stick-stained wineglass lingered on the bench. Valerie drank her last glass of wine alone. It broke Julia's heart.

"It's like she's just stepped out the door for a minute." Her voice cracked. She stumbled to the back door and gazed out over the jacaranda-shaded garden. A lavender carpet of flowers covered the lawn. "Can I stay in the garden for a while? To say goodbye."

"No problem. We've finished with the backyard."

"Just yell out if you need me." She walked out the back door and left them to dissect Valerie's secrets.

———◆———

Ten minutes later, Julia heard Nick calling her.

"Dr Sinclair, would you come back to the bedroom?"

She hesitated. The bedroom? Crap. She had hoped some parts of Valerie's life would stay hidden. She walked down the hallway, past a couple of crime scene examiners. Both were poker-faced, not a smirk in sight. Maybe she could get through the next few minutes with her dignity intact.

She entered Valerie's bedroom. An open metal case lay on the bed. Had she kept everything?

"So, you found Valerie's toy box." She decided to bluff it out. "You guys have your own handcuffs. Why should you have all the fun?"

Nick blinked. "You knew about this?"

"What do you think women talk about when you men are busy yakking about sports and cars and power tools?"

"This could be vital evidence. Why didn't you mention it earlier?"

"Oh, by the way, my friend got off on leather. She wanted to be Catwoman and loved being tied up." She shook her head. "When exactly is a good time to drop that into the conversation?"

"Was this what she was into with her surgeon boyfriend?"

"Come on. Can you seriously imagine Martin messing up his hair by wearing a Batman mask?" She gave a burst of laughter, then sobered up in a heartbeat. "Look, after her marriage broke up, Valerie was in a dark place. She experimented a little. It didn't last."

He picked up a black leather corset complete with nipple cut-outs and stretch lace inserts. "This feels like expensive leather to me. Too expensive for a brief experiment. Custom-made?"

"So?"

"It's hardly the sort of cheap import you'd pick up in a sex shop." A blaze of red highlighted his cheekbones. "I didn't mean you specifically."

"Really?"

"Do you know who gave her this?"

Her cheeks flamed to match his. So much for playing it cool. "Valerie takes . . . took her hobbies seriously."

"If you remember anything, it could help Valerie."

"It won't . . . I can't . . ." She swallowed. "It's not relevant to the investigation."

"We decide what's relevant. Tell me what you know."

"This is nothing to do with Valerie's murder. Trust me, please. You're wasting your time."

"Thank you, Dr Sinclair. Call me when you decide to cooperate." His voice was so cold and formal, it hit her like a cold shower.

She left the room, pulled the door shut behind her, and turned to the closest crime scene examiner. "He needs some time alone. You'd better knock before you go back in."

Julia concentrated all her energy on escaping without shattering into a million pieces. She walked out the front door, spine straight, shoulders back, wishing her external calm would spread to the quaking mess inside.

Valerie's house held too many memories, too much pain.

Back at home, Julia unpacked her groceries. She'd detoured via Coles to stock up on cat food and chocolate and other essentials. She tossed a couple of Lean Cuisines into her freezer and a pair of giant T-bones into the fridge. No point being a total single woman cliché. Without Valerie's home cooking, she had to learn to fend for herself.

Something warm brushed against her leg. A plaintive meow told her Oscar wanted his second or third breakfast of the day. She reached down and scratched the back of his neck, ruffling the grey and white fur. He butted his head against her leg, then, satisfied he'd got her attention, he trotted to his food bowl, tail carried high.

Maybe he could help with her investigation.

She phoned the Cavanaugh Veterinary Clinic and was in luck. Richard was on duty, and the surgery was quiet. She grabbed Oscar, ignored his protestations, and shut him in his carry cage. He was not amused. She reminded him he was due for his annual vaccinations, so really she was doing him a favour. He did not agree with her rationalisation and muttered ancient cat curses all the way to the vet's surgery.

After a brief sit in the waiting area, they were called through to the consulting room. Richard had his back to the door. He clattered some instruments into a metal bucket, then turned around.

He did a double-take, then checked his computer. "Annual jabs. I guess even a callous bastard like me should be able to manage that simple task."

He'd aged ten years in the past few days. Just grief? Or guilt? Feeling sorry for him wouldn't help.

She countered with a shallow smile. "Well, you're crap with people, but you're magic with animals."

"I trust animals. They don't let you down." He opened the lid of the cat cage and lifted Oscar out. The cat glared at Julia, but crouched quietly while Richard's large hand stroked his back.

"At last, we agree about something," she said to Richard, then made soothing noises to the cat while he endured the indignity of having his temperature taken.

"Heard anything about Valerie?" He prepared the cat's injection with practised ease.

"They're not giving much away. Have you remembered what you did on Monday night?" She steadied Oscar as Richard injected the vaccine into the back of the cat's neck.

"My mates backed me up. Home all night." He dropped the needle and syringe into a yellow biohazard bin.

"If your mates drink as much as you do, I'd have serious doubts about their reliability."

"I trust them. Okay, I've finished with Oscar."

She picked up Oscar and settled him into his cage. "Did Valerie ever take sleeping tablets?"

"No bloody way. Valerie could sleep for Australia. Why?"

"The police asked. I guess the killer knocked her out."

Richard scowled. "I'd knock the prick out, drug-free, strap him to my operating table, then wake him up with a castration."

"I'd fight you for the scalpel."

"You would too." His brief smile never made it to his eyes. "I spoke to her mum yesterday. They want to bury her at home in Victoria."

"We should have a few drinks for her next week. Will you promise not to attack Martin?"

He snarled.

"For Valerie?"

"I'll try."

The veterinary assistant interrupted. "Urgent call for you." She thrust the mobile phone at Richard.

He showed Julia out of the room and took the call.

She carried Oscar out to the reception desk. Richard had lived with Valerie for long enough to know her habits. Only question was, could she trust him to tell the truth? He had plenty of reasons to lie.

CHAPTER FOURTEEN

ON SUNDAY MORNING, JULIA drove to the hospital. With a forty-degree scorcher forecast, she wasn't walking anywhere. She avoided the basement level of the car park where Valerie's car had been abandoned. Plenty of empty bays on the second floor—one advantage of working on the weekend.

At the stairwell door, she paused and searched her handbag for her ID card. A muffled thump. She startled. What was that noise? Her spidey senses on full alert, she scanned the car park.

"Hello?"

A blur of movement in the far corner, but she couldn't see if anyone lurked in the gloom. She watched for a few moments, hoping they'd show themselves, but nothing happened.

"Getting paranoid in my old age."

———— ◆ ————

After checking Edith Powell's results in the lab, Julia visited the Coronary Care Unit to see Brad Delaney. He must be improving if they had transferred him out of the ICU. She watched him through the glass in the door while she put on her protective equipment. The television above the end of his bed had his full attention. More alert than last week. Another good sign.

She entered the room, closed the door behind her.

"Hi, Brad." She examined his observations chart. His temperature remained down and his blood pressure up. "Remember me?"

"The bug doctor?" He clicked the TV remote and the gentle murmuring of the cricket commentary faded.

"That's right, Julia Sinclair. Your memory's improved, and so has your appetite, judging by that empty meal tray." She replaced the chart, then sat in the chair next to his bed. "Do you remember why you're here?"

"I've been living in the twilight zone." He shrugged. "Something about bugs from my nose attacking my heart."

"That's the short version. We all have bacteria living on us," she said. "Somehow, you ended up with the nastiest one I've ever seen. It got into your surgical wound and spread into your bloodstream, then it attacked one of your heart valves."

"I've never been sick before. First time in hospital ever."

"You've made up for it. Have you travelled interstate or overseas?"

His attention drawn by a faint roar from the crowd, Brad stared at the television for a moment. "Just Bali a few years ago on a surfing trip. Didn't get sick."

"Have any of your relatives or friends been in hospital lately?"

"Nobody I can think of." He gestured at her protective gear. "Why all the fuss?"

"This is a new strain of bug that's resistant to most antibiotics. We want to stomp on it before it spreads any further."

"Buggered if I know where it came from. How much longer am I going to be stuck here?" Brad fidgeted, knocking the remote onto the floor. "I'm bored out of my skull."

"Depends if you behave yourself." She picked up the remote for him. "You'll need intravenous antibiotics for six weeks, but I can arrange for you to complete the course at home under close supervision—if the surgeons stay away from you, and your condition remains stable. No promises."

"Cool."

She checked his IV site. The last thing he needed was another infection.

"Do you remember what happened here before your operation?"

Another glance at the television. "Not really. I got poked and prodded by a couple of doctors, then one of them whisked me off to have my appendix out. Once the morphine kicked in, I didn't care."

"Okay, I know who those doctors were. Did anyone else examine you? Medical students?"

"Don't think so. A student nurse took my heart rate. She was kind of alright." He grinned. "Hey, if you find out her name, tell her I need some—what did you say before? Close supervision. Yeah, that's exactly what I need."

"Careful you don't pop your stitches." Someone in the Emergency Department must have a list of student nurses on rotation. Another potential lead "Anyone else?"

"Just the doctor who knocked me out. Don't remember her name. It's all a blur after that."

"If you think of anyone else, let me know." It had to be someone he saw in that first twenty-four hours. "Any questions?"

He laughed. "No. Get me out of here before anything else goes wrong."

"Glad the infection didn't damage your sense of humour."

Julia removed her protective gear on the way out. She watched him through the glass window while she washed her hands. He was engrossed in the cricket again. He didn't realise how lucky he was. The mortality rate for his type of infection scared the crap out of her. She couldn't let it spread to anyone else.

If only she could find the source of the outbreak. Maybe Edith Powell had the answer.

Ten minutes and another set of personal protective equipment later, Julia entered Edith Powell's room on the orthopaedics ward and did a double take. She'd aged ten years in the past forty-eight hours.

Bleary eyes turned towards the doorway. "Who's that?"

"Hi, Mrs Powell. It's Dr Julia Sinclair. I saw you on Friday about the bug in your knee. Remember?"

"Oh, yes, dear, I remember you now. You're the one that got me stuck in this lonely room like a leper." She laboured to sit up, a task made difficult by the splint that kept her leg straight. "Where's my glasses? Can you see my glasses?"

Julia found them on the bedside table and handed them over. She propped a pillow behind Edith's back. "There you go. Sorry about the single room, but it's important we don't let this bug spread."

"I know. I know. It's just so quiet in here. Nobody to talk to. Now sit yourself down and tell me what's what. You know, they took my new knee out yesterday morning. Surgeon said it was no good giving me all those antibiotics with a dodgy knee. I waited so long for that knee. Forever and ever. Now I have to lie around in this lonely old bed for another six weeks with this splint thingy on. Can you believe that?"

"I'm sorry. They're right, though. Antibiotics on their own won't fix this infection."

"It's not your fault, dear. You said there's another patient with it. Did I give it to him? I feel awful if I did. Or did he give it to me? Where did it come from? I was perfectly fine for the first week after my knee operation, then I got crook. Nearly ready to go home, I was. I wish I knew what was going on."

Julia jumped into the conversation break. "Maybe you can help me find out. Think about everyone who came to see you since you were admitted to hospital. I know your doctors and all the nurses on this ward. Who else examined you or treated you?"

"Lots of people wander in, do things, and wander out again. Sometimes in the middle of the night, they don't even bother to say hello. Just squirt something into the drip or poke at my knee. I know they don't want to wake everybody up, but they could at the very least whisper hello or good night. It's rude, don't you think? And with that cover-up garb on, it's impossible to know who's hiding underneath. Could be Jack the Ripper, for all I know. You look worn out, dear. Why don't you fetch me a notepad and pen? I'll write down everyone I can think of, and you go home and get some rest. We'll work it all out tomorrow."

"That'll be so helpful. I'll come back with my lists, and we can nut this out together."

The old woman grinned. "I'll be Miss Marple. So good to have something to keep my brain occupied. Thought I was going to go gaga in here. Oh, look. There's my good friend come to visit."

"I'll leave you to it, then." Julia glanced through the window into the hallway and blinked. Her next-door neighbour was Edith's friend?

She rushed out of the room, discarding her protective gear on the way. While she washed her hands, a nurse brought her neighbour through.

"Hello, Mrs Flannery. Fancy you two knowing each other."

"I've known Edith for years. Us old chooks have to stick together. We've outlived all the men."

"No stamina. Who says women are the weaker sex?"

"Edith had the right idea. She caught herself a younger man."

"A toy boy? Good on her." In her late seventies? Go, Edith.

"I reckon that's why she's had to have her knee replaced. They go dancing every week. Her arthritis slowed her down."

"I'm sorry it got infected." If she'd acted quicker with Brad's infection, Edith might have been spared.

"Being stuck in bed all day has turned her into an old lady before her time. Does she really have to wait another six weeks before her new knee goes in?"

"I'm afraid so." Julia helped her neighbour into a paper gown "I was going to visit you later. Did you see someone deliver a parcel to my house on Friday?"

"I don't think so. So many tradesmen coming and going with all the renovations in the street. There was a lady parked across the road for quite a long while. Now, what day was that? I'd forget my head if it wasn't screwed on." She shook her head as if to test that theory. "Why do you want to know?"

"I wondered who the parcel was from." She shuddered. "I won't ruin your day by telling you what it contained. Not pleasant at all."

"Oh, dear. I wish I'd paid more attention." Mrs Flannery raised her gloved hands. "Ready for surgery, doctor. Thanks for looking after Edith. At my age, I'm fast running out of friends."

⸻◆⸻

Ten minutes later, Julia rushed through the stairwell door to the car park and crashed into someone. She staggered back a step. Only her grip on the door handle prevented her from plummeting backwards down the stairs.

"Watch where you're going." Angelo Velutti, one of the hospital orderlies, glared at her, then he smiled. A cold, reptilian smile.

She preferred the glare.

He crowded her. The stench of nicotine mixed with unwashed male filled the air. She held her breath, tried to edge past. He blocked her exit.

"Excuse me." She stepped to the left.

Angelo mirrored her moves. Silent and focussed. Like her cat tormenting a mouse.

Her heart rate soared. She lunged to the right, followed by a quick step to the left. He grabbed the neckline of her shirt, but she pulled away. One of her buttons ricocheted off the concrete wall.

His gaze dropped to her chest.

She exaggerated her rapid breathing while, behind her back, she manoeuvred her car keys between her fingers. An extra deep inhale to keep his attention on her breasts, then she jabbed the makeshift knuckleduster at his face.

He jerked backwards, slipped, landing heavily on his backside. "Fucking bitch."

A horn blasted. The driver, a nurse, slowed down, stopped her car.

Julia raced around Angelo and darted to the other side of the car. She leant on the bonnet, regaining her breath, pulse hammering. She smiled her thanks at the driver, then hurried to her car. After fumbling with the key for endless minutes, she fell into the driver's seat, slammed the door, and locked it. She rested her head on the steering wheel, too shaky to drive.

Someone knocked on her passenger-side window. She jumped. Her rescuer, the nurse, peered at her. A quick look around. Angelo had vanished. Julia leant across and wound down the window. She didn't trust her legs to hold her up if she got out of the car.

"Have you seen your tyres?" the nurse said. "Oh, my God. Are you okay? Have you called security?"

"Wait a minute."

Julia found the strength to get out and walk around to the passenger side. Sure enough, both tyres on that side were flat. One she might manage, but not two. Her car could wait. First, she needed to get the hell out of the hospital.

"You should call the police. After what happened . . . you know . . . the murdered nurse worked here."

"I will." She glanced down at her ruined shirt and pulled it into shape. Lucky her black lace bra had mesmerised Angelo long enough for her to make a weapon out of her keys. "But I need to change first."

"I'm on my way home. Need a lift?"

"Thanks, you're a lifesaver. I don't live far." Something thumped a few metres away. A muffled curse. "Angelo?"

Silence.

"Cowardly chickenshit." She grabbed her bag, locked the door, and followed the nurse to her nearby car.

Why was all of this happening to her? The poo parcel. The mystery phone calls. Was the same dickhead responsible for both? Surely, she couldn't attract more than one nutter at a time. And now this. Didn't Valerie have a problem with Angelo Velutti? Something about him harassing a female staff member? She'd have to ask someone in HR tomorrow. Had he taken his revenge?

<hr>

Julia needed to get clean, to wash Angelo Velutti's filth off her skin, out of her mind. She perched on the edge of her bath, an old cast iron claw-foot bath, deep enough for serious wallowing. The lush scent of jasmine wafted up from the cloud of bubbles.

A quick trip to the kitchen to top up her wine before she dove in. Oscar pointed out her glass wasn't the only thing in need of a refill. She poured some biscuits into his bowl, then ran her hand down his arched back while he hoovered up his food. Lucky cat. Such an uncomplicated life.

At last, she sank into the cool water. Her glass of wine rested on the windowsill. Julia slid down until her head was submerged. How peaceful it would be to hide there for a while, but she really needed to breathe. She wriggled up a fraction and wiped her face clear of froth, then rested her head on the rim of the bath.

She tried to empty her mind of worries. Valerie's lifeless face. Another sip of wine. It didn't help. What if Angelo was the killer? A shudder rippled through her.

Her mobile chirped in the bedroom, signalling a text message. Great. Might be work. She clambered out of the bath and wrapped herself in a towel, then trailed drips of water to the bedroom.

The text was brief: Sorry. Too late to save you.

What the hell was that supposed to mean? More bloody games. She checked the sender. All the air sucked out of the room. She stumbled to her bed. Her focus narrowed to the screen. Everything else blurred to empty blackness.

Sorry. Too late to save you.

Sent by Valerie.

Chapter Fifteen

On Monday morning, Julia stared at her computer screen, her brain on autopilot. The routine work felt alien after another sleepless night. Once her initial panic had faded, she'd replied to the text message, but nobody answered. When she rang the number, it was unavailable again.

Was the same person responsible for the nuisance phone calls and the ruined tyres? Anybody could've picked up Valerie's phone and left that message, but realistically the most likely culprit was her killer. That made Julia shiver even on a hot summer's morning.

What did they mean by too late to save her?

And was it an apology or a threat?

Shove the questions aside and concentrate on work. No new disasters. A million screening swabs to process. The Chief Scientist may have been placated by the administration's agreement to cover any overtime payments, but the extra workload wasn't popular with those lab staff who had to do the actual work.

Who was she kidding? She had to tell the police about the message. Maybe they could trace the phone's location. First, a quick chat with Angelo. Somewhere crowded with lots of witnesses. She phoned the orderlies' call room.

The shift supervisor rustled some papers. "He took a patient to Radiology. Where do you want him sent?"

"I'll catch him there." See how he enjoyed being stalked for a change.

She gave the scientists an excuse about seeing a patient and escaped the lab. The Radiology Department nestled between Emergency and the Outpatients clinics. Handy. There'd be plenty of people around if he got nasty. And if she hurt him, he might need an X-ray.

There he stood, sleazing over the receptionist, who ignored him. Sensible woman. An exaggerated sense of his own desirability.

At last, Angelo gave up. He spotted Julia and swaggered over.

"Hey, babe. Looking for more action, are you?"

Angelo stood so close his rank breath overpowered her. Fighting the urge to retch, she backed into the corridor. He followed, edging her away from the Radiology waiting room.

She side-stepped to keep witnesses in sight. "What were you doing in the car park yesterday?"

"Duh. I drove to work."

"Did you slash my tyres?"

"What? Fuck, no." His brow furrowed.

Neanderthal man.

"Why are you phoning me? Texting me?"

He grinned. "Give us your phone number and I will."

Yeah, right. "Why is it too late to save me?"

"What are you crapping on about?"

"Hopeless." She half-turned.

He grabbed her wrist. "What did you tell the cops?"

"Nothing." Not yet, anyway.

"Bullshit. Why do they want to see me?"

"Let me go."

His fingers dug deeper into her flesh. With her free hand, she scrabbled in her pocket, pulled out a ballpoint pen and jabbed it into his forearm.

"Fuck." He jerked his arm back.

She stepped out of his reach. "I asked you to let go."

"Everything all right, Dr Sinclair?" Nick Randall to the rescue.

"Fine, thanks." She rubbed her wrist.

"Don't move, Velutti. I'm not chasing you all over the hospital." Nick held her wrist with one hand and ran his other up the full length of her arm, checking for injuries. "Did he hurt you?"

"Just a flesh wound." Shockwaves of electricity raced up her arm. Hell of a time for her hormones to throw a party. "A misunderstanding. Angelo thinks I dobbed him in to you."

"Hang on a bloody minute." Angelo waved his arm in Nick's face. "Psycho bitch stabbed me."

Nick stepped back as if to avoid a wave of body odour. "You'll live."

"I was going to call you this morning." She gestured towards some seats down the corridor, out of Angelo's earshot. "Got a free moment now?"

"Sure. Angelo won't mind waiting for his interview."

Angelo grunted. He leant against the wall, arms folded across his chest.

She sat, then stared at the wall opposite. Where to start? Imminent hysteria jittered through her.

"Maybe I'm paranoid, but strange things are happening. Anonymous phone calls, mystery parcel on my doormat."

"Mystery parcel?"

She wrinkled her nose. "Dog poo, all wrapped up like a Christmas present."

"Charming. Did you keep the packaging?"

"No, I had to get rid of the stench." She opened the message on her phone, then handed it to him. "Last night, I got a text from Valerie's mobile . . ." Her voice faded as her throat closed tight.

"I need to get the tech guys at forensics to look into this." A muscle in his jaw worked as if he bit back angry words. "Why didn't you call me straight away?"

"I'm sorry. It could be vital evidence. I should've . . . I couldn't . . ." The message had sent her mind straight from frozen panic to deep denial.

"Bugger evidence. This is an escalating threat. Have you got somewhere else to stay?"

"I used to run to Valerie's." Her eyes burned.

"Don't handle this on your own." His voice softened. "Anything else happens, call me. Any time."

"I promise if I find any more evidence, you'll be the first person I call." She attempted a laugh. It sounded croaky. "Right after my panic attack."

"Looking for evidence is my job. Looking after patients is yours."

"I can't help it if the evidence comes to me."

"Stay out of trouble." Tough guy tones again.

"I'm trying."

"So why are you beating up Angelo?"

She had to tell him. "I popped in to see some patients yesterday and bumped into him in the car park. He kept blocking my way, wouldn't let me through until a nurse drove by and distracted him." A close call. "I reported the incident to HR, but without the nurse's name or any security vision, it was only my word against his."

His face reddened. The scar on his forehead paled in contrast. He rubbed one hand across the scar as if to wipe it away.

"Did he hurt you?"

"No, just a torn shirt, but when I got to my car, I had two slashed tyres. That's what I was asking him about now."

"Did he admit it?"

"Of course not, but it seems a strange coincidence."

"Let's make this official. I'll ask him." He stared at Angelo, then focussed on her again. "Any history with you two?"

"Don't make me vomit."

"No, not like that. Any reason he'd hold a grudge?"

"Nothing against me, but Valerie got him kicked off her ward."

"Do you know why?"

"She suspected him of manhandling a female cleaner, but the poor woman refused to lodge a complaint. Is that why you're interviewing him now?"

"I can't go into specifics. Stay away from him. Please." He placed his hand over hers and gazed deep into her eyes, as if hypnotising her into obedience. "Leave the investigating to us."

She snatched her hand away and jumped up. "Valerie was my best friend. How can you expect me to do nothing?"

Nick stood, towering over her. "You're putting yourself in danger."

"I don't care."

"Let me do my job without worrying I'll find your body next."

"I'll be careful."

"I'm not kidding. If I find you've been snooping around . . ."

"You'll do what—arrest me?"

"If I have to," he said with a hint of quiet menace.

"Be warned. I won't come quietly."

"I can imagine." The low timbre of his voice vibrated through her.

She had to walk away before her cheeks caught fire. When she reached the corner, she couldn't help turning around. Nick stood chest to chest with Angelo, close and intimidating, hands fisted by his sides. Whatever he was saying, it made Angelo shrink and cower.

Excellent.

⎯⎯⎯◆⎯⎯⎯

Nick had commandeered a room at the hospital for informal interviews. It was more efficient than dragging everybody down to the police station. Angelo Velutti had denied having anything to do with Julia's slashed tyres and insisted he had stayed at work all evening when Valerie disappeared. Nick had to verify that with the shift supervisor and check out Valerie's complaint, but it felt like a dead end. Brute force seemed more Velutti's style.

Yet again, he waited for Martin MacDougall. Grief had not improved his punctuality. Once Nick adjusted to the antiseptic smell, he found the outpatient clinic room quite comfortable. Must be getting desensitised, as the psychs called it. An examination table sat against one wall, the vinyl mattress covered with a paper sheet. A side-table held boxes of gloves and weird metal instruments in sealed packets. What the hell were they for?

A light tap drew his attention. Martin loomed in the doorway. Dark shadows ringed his eyes.

He smothered a yawn, then sank into the patient chair. "Wake me up if I fall asleep."

"Late night?"

"And early morning. Working."

"So that's why you weren't at home yesterday?"

Martin jerked upright. "Did you talk to my wife?"

"Nobody answered the door."

He slumped again. "Any questions, call me. Leave her alone."

"Did you spend much time at Valerie's house?"

"We could hardly go back to my place, could we?"

"I'll take that as a yes." Nick tapped his pen on the table. "How would you describe your sexual relationship with Valerie?"

"I don't see what that has to do with you."

"It's relevant to our investigation. Answer the question, please."

"How can our sex-life be relevant?"

A bloodstained leather mask had been found in the sand dunes near where she was buried. DNA was still pending, but they were hopeful of a match. Maybe Valerie's death was an accident, a game that went too far. The state of her body? Someone had gone way beyond playtime. And well into psycho time.

"We found some items of interest in her bedroom."

Martin frowned. "You mean that leather gear?"

"Yes. Was that yours?"

"Never touched the stuff. A joke gift." Martin gave his best too-sexy-to-need-props smile, completely wasted on Nick. "Don't know where they came from. Before my time."

"Was Valerie seeing someone else?"

"If there was another man, I would've told you by now." The skin around his eyes tightened. "I'd have known if she was sleeping around."

"Like your wife knows about you?"

"Leave my wife out of this." An animal snarl crossed his face, gone within seconds.

"We have to talk to her. I've called several times, but she never answers the phone."

Martin's face softened. "Rachel's not well. She won't cope with you prying into our lives."

"Isn't she your alibi for the night Valerie's body was dumped?" The doctor nodded.

"Do you want to change your story?" Nick asked.

"No . . . no." He rubbed his hands over his face. "Okay, I'll talk to her about coming in."

"We'll get a female officer to interview her. Now, who was Valerie seeing before you?"

"Her ex-husband. Nobody else, so far as I know."

Richard Cavanaugh had already denied any knowledge of the leather outfits. Someone shared Valerie's interests. Who was the mystery man?

Chapter Sixteen

Back in her office, Julia filled in request forms for staff swabs until her hand ached. No new cases since Friday. The source of the VRSA remained a mystery, but maybe they'd averted an outbreak.

She sorted the request forms into batches by destination. Gabriel was collecting swabs on the orthopaedic ward, so she'd deliver the others on her way to see him. A few were for the surgical ward. She hadn't seen Martin since . . . the mortuary. Most of his patients were on Valerie's ward. Wrapped up in her own grief, she hadn't considered how he was coping.

Ten minutes later, she rounded the last corner and entered the surgical ward. Martin leant against the wall, chatting with a couple of nurses. Only five days since they'd found Valerie dead, and there he stood as if nothing had happened.

Never a blunt object around when she needed one.

She drew Martin's attention. "Can I drag you away from your harem for a few minutes?"

Up close, his smile wavered, his face a brittle mask that revealed how he'd look in twenty years' time. "Okay."

"Let's talk in the seminar room."

"I'll just phone the anaesthetist to see how long I've got."

She waited, staring out the seminar room window at the rooftop garden where a lone smoker did his best to pollute the fresh air. A couple of gardenia bushes in tubs needed urgent resuscitation. Heat shimmered off the concrete pavers.

The door opened and Martin rushed in.

"What a nightmare." He paced the room, dodging chairs. "The police are still hounding me."

"Married lover? What did you expect?"

"Yeah, I've got prime suspect tattooed on my forehead, but I was with Simon the night Valerie was abducted."

"Have you spoken to Simon?"

"Not lately. Why?"

"Maybe he wasn't convincing enough. He was vague when I spoke to him."

"Great. Now you're checking up on me." He moved to the window and stared out. "I didn't kill her."

How could she trust him when he couldn't meet her eye? "If you didn't kill her, who did?"

Silence.

"See. You can't think of anyone else, can you?"

"My brother-in-law." He turned around, rested against the windowsill.

"Why?"

"To frame me, of course."

"Please explain."

"He threatened me in the theatre change-rooms last week." At last, he looked her in the eye.

"He works here?"

"Carl Bennett. He's an anaesthetics technician."

Right. The guy Nick Randall saw on Thursday. "Anaesthetics techs spend little time on the wards. How did he know Valerie?"

"He's a regular at the Friday night drinks. Big guy. Does weights. One spray-tan away from a Mr Universe contest." Martin rubbed one hand across his chest. "He told me to stay away from her or he'd make me sorry."

"So, you told all this to the police?"

"Hell, yeah. He's a nutter."

"Runs in the family."

"What?"

Oops. "Rachel is a bit . . . tightly wound." What if Rachel had got Carl to hurt Valerie and it all went too far?

"The police want to talk to her. She'll freak out."

"They won't bully her."

He scuffed one foot along the floor. "That detective asked about Valerie's leather gear and who she got it from. Was she seeing someone else?"

"No, of course not."

Martin's pager bleeped. "Theatre's ready."

"I'm organising drinks for Valerie. Keep Thursday night free."

"If I'm not under arrest by then." A half-smile quirked his lips; his eyes still looked haunted.

She hugged him. "You'll get through this."

He left with his shoulders slumped and his gaze downcast.

Too late to save Valerie, but Martin needed rescuing. Where would an anaesthetics technician hang out?

⋅◦⋅

Julia tracked Carl Bennett down to the operating theatre tea room. He sprawled on a sofa, alone. His muscle-bulging back towards her, he watched some home improvement show on the television. There wasn't so much a neck as a pyramid of muscle attaching his head to his shoulders. Steroids? If he'd wanted to take Valerie somewhere, she couldn't have stopped him.

"Carl Bennett?"

He swivelled his whole upper body to look at her. "Yes."

She sank into the armchair opposite him. Her skirt rode up when she crossed her legs. He settled in for a good perve. The distraction might loosen his tongue, so she resisted the urge to smooth her skirt down.

"I'm Julia, a friend of Valerie Cavanaugh." She waited for his response. Not a flicker. Too busy checking out her legs. "I understand you don't get on with your brother-in-law."

He straightened up. "You were with that detective the other day. Did he send you?"

"Of course not."

He scrutinised her through half-closed eyes, his gaze scanning her from head to toe and lingering on her breasts. "Maybe I should frisk you. You could be wearing a wire."

"Don't be ridiculous." She stood up and crossed the room to turn the television off. "You watch too much TV."

"You could be right, besides . . ."

His breath touched the back of her neck. She spun around. How had he moved so quietly? "Yes?"

"With the light behind you, I can see you're not wearing a wire."

Julia raised her hand, ready to slap him into next week.

He grabbed her wrist and yanked her towards him. "You don't want to do that," he said in a quiet but menacing tone. He let go of her wrist as quickly as he'd seized it.

She stumbled backwards, then dashed to the other side of the sofa. Her heart hammered. Again. All this aggression might be shattering her nervous system, but it sure as hell was giving her a cardiac workout.

"I'm not here because of the police." She fought to control the quaver in her voice.

"You're the one." He strolled towards her.

She backed away, keeping the sofa between them. "The one?"

"The bitch who upset Rachel last week."

"Rachel was upset long before I met her."

"That's Martin's fault. He broke her spirit."

"Does he hit her?" Hard to imagine, but Rachel could've been spaced out on heavy-duty painkillers.

"No, I'd kill him if he did."

The intensity of his gaze chilled her. "How does he hurt Rachel?"

"Drugs. She denies it, but one day I'll prove it. Let him weasel his way out of that with the Medical Board. Now bugger off and let me get back to my show." He switched the television back on and dropped onto the sofa.

She fled with more questions than answers. Was Martin drugging his wife? Based on her bizarre behaviour last week, it made horrible sense.

⸻ ◆ ⸻

At home on Monday night, Julia collapsed into her favourite lounge chair. With a gin and tonic in one hand, she half-heartedly flicked through a medical journal. The VRSA outbreak had filled the rest of her day and drained her energy.

The doorbell rang. Her glass slid from her fingers. Lucky it landed on her flokati rug and didn't shatter. Unlike her nerves.

Maybe the killer had dropped by to confess. Or worse.

Her pulse pounded in her throat. Pull yourself together, Julia. She placed the glass back on the table, quietly, then grabbed her mobile, ready to speed-dial the police. A quick peek around the corner. One large body, visible through the leadlight glass, was outside her front door. Male and muscle-bound. Carl? Surely not. Another burst of the doorbell.

Curiosity drew her along the hallway. Shame she didn't have a video intercom. Or an armed bodyguard. She opened the door and stayed behind the safety of her locked security screen.

Her ex-boyfriend filled the doorway. Her heart dropped back into place.

"Leon, what the hell are you doing here?"

He glanced over his shoulder, checked the street. "Can I come in?"

She opened the screen door and ushered him inside. "You made me spill my G and T. What do you want?"

"Bourbon on the rocks?"

"Not quite what I meant, but I guess it beats drinking alone. I might have a bottle left over from the bad old days." Bad old days? Their relationship had imploded before Tess's disappearance. She'd time-travel back in a heartbeat if it meant having Tess and Valerie around. "Grab a seat in the lounge."

When she returned, she found Leon sitting with his elbows on his knees and his head cradled in his hands. He turned bloodshot eyes towards her. She poured a generous slug of Jim Beam over ice, then placed the glass in front of him, along with the bottle of bourbon.

"The way you look, one drink won't be enough."

He groaned. "Got that right."

She sponged her gin-soaked rug with a damp cloth and waited for him to unload his problems on her. In his self-obsessed world, it hadn't occurred to him she might have problems of her own. It was the main reason they'd split up. Well, that and his wandering ways. She dropped the cloth on the table and retreated to her armchair.

At last, he spoke. "I don't know what I'm doing here."

"Makes two of us." She took a generous sip of her refilled drink.

"Coming here got me into this mess in the first place."

"Your fiancée kicked you out?"

"Not yet."

He jumped up, crossed the room, and rearranged the photo frames on her mantelpiece, placing them in order of ascending size. Inability to sit still for a second. Another of his annoying habits. As was avoiding confrontation.

Julia's fingers itched to put her memories back where they belonged. Her heart raced when he picked up a framed photo of Valerie.

"Do you mind?" she asked.

Leon examined the photo. "Oh, sorry. I heard . . . I liked Valerie."

"Put Valerie down."

He replaced the photo on the mantelpiece, then returned to the sofa. "She thinks I've been unfaithful to her."

"Fair point. You've been unfaithful to every woman."

"But nothing happened this time. Remember?" He drained his glass. "Someone saw us at the Subi hotel last week, and that same person saw us having breakfast together next morning."

"Oh."

"Yes. Oh." He poured another shot of bourbon. "I told her I stayed at a mate's place and met you for breakfast the next day."

"You used to lie better than that."

He hesitated. "If anyone asked, would you back me up?"

"I won't lie for you." She glanced at Valerie's photo again. "I'm organising drinks for Valerie later this week. Bring your fiancée along and I'll tell her how little you mean to me."

"Ouch." Leon swirled the ice in his glass. "You want to meet her?"

"Scared I'll frighten her off?"

"I don't know if she'll come."

"I'll text you the details. Valerie did like you, too." Remembering Valerie's outrage over Leon's infidelity made her smile. "Most of the time."

"Thanks." He placed the now-empty glass on the coffee table, then stood up. "I should go."

She showed him to the door. Although she felt safer with him in her home, having him around wasn't worth the pain of reliving the past.

Early Tuesday afternoon, Nick walked into his fourth sex shop for the day. George's idea of light duties. After a long and trying Monday at the hospital, he had needed a change of scenery. He'd certainly found one. The sooner he traced the source of the leather gear, the sooner he could get back to some actual work.

The first two shops were remarkable only for their tackiness. No custom-made goods there. Lube by the litre and fluorescent condoms. Reminded him of a recent flasher. A glow-in-the-dark wanker. Very high tech.

The third shop had been devoted to the audiovisual end of the market. Wall-to-wall DVDs with a collection out the back for the more discerning client. Judging by the images on display, synthetic was more popular with their clientele than natural.

He hit pay dirt in the fourth shop, a much classier establishment despite the roar of traffic outside the front door. A forest of vibrators decorated the far wall. Nick sidled past, drawn to the leather goods in the back room. The Goth from behind the counter followed him.

"A little something for the mistress for Christmas?" the Goth asked in a soft Irish accent. "Or, dare I hope it, the master?"

Nick burst out laughing. He couldn't help picturing George in a leather G-string and, frankly, it was not a pretty sight. "I'm interested in the origin of some items similar to this." He pointed to a photo on the wall.

"Ah, excellent taste." He looked Nick up and down. "You'll need a fitting. Nothing off the rack about Mistress Mona's gear, in a manner of speaking."

"Police business." He took the photos out of his pocket and handed them over. "Are these Mistress Mona's work?"

The Goth made an elaborate show of examining them. "Ooh, I think you could be right. That's one of her corsets. She always does that style of stitching around the nipples. And I love her suede linings."

"Thanks. Where would I find Mistress Mona?" Nick slid the photos back into his pocket. Progress towards the identity of the mystery man at last.

"Come into my parlour." The Goth crooked his finger and led Nick behind a black velvet curtain into a well-lit office that wouldn't have looked out of place in an accountancy firm. "Bit of a culture shock back here, isn't it?"

He handed Nick two business cards, one for Mistress Mona and one for the shop.

They returned to the front, startling a couple of giggling teenagers. One snapped a photo of them with her mobile before darting out the door.

"Shame you're not in uniform. I'd snap a shot myself," the Goth said. "Now, can I tempt you with these fur-lined handcuffs with matching blindfolds? Very popular gifts for Christmas."

"I prefer the real thing."

"Naughty boy. Isn't that misuse of police property?"

"I meant for work, not pleasure."

"If you say so."

"I'm out of here before I incriminate myself." He put out his hand. "Thank you . . ."

"You can call me Angel. Anytime, and I mean, anytime." He held onto Nick's hand for longer than necessary.

Nick retrieved his hand. "Thanks again, Angel. You've been an enormous help."

"Fabulous. Just wait until I tell the boys about my undercover police work."

"This is an ongoing investigation. Keep this to yourself for now."

"Spoilsport."

CHAPTER SEVENTEEN

LATE TUESDAY AFTERNOON, JULIA rushed to the orthopaedic ward. Edith Powell had become acutely short of breath, and the orthopaedic resident called for help. On the way, a list of diagnoses tumbled through her mind. She wasn't familiar with the patient's past medical history. Were there any cardiac problems? What about a pulmonary embolus, a blood clot in the lungs? Prolonged bed rest and recent surgery were definite risk factors. Post-op pneumonia?

Her heart pounded against her rib cage. Whether the cause was exertion or anxiety about the patient, she couldn't be sure. She only hoped she'd have enough breath left to cope when she reached the ward. The thought of snatching the oxygen mask off Edith to use herself brought a giggle to her throat and suppressed the rising panic. She couldn't lose a patient.

She rounded the corner into the ward just as someone pressed the arrest button, summoning the resuscitation team. Her fingers fumbled for a disposable gown and mask from the trolley outside Edith's room. Don't get careless now. In a messy resus, blood and body fluids could spray anywhere. She snapped on a pair of latex gloves, then shoved the door open with her shoulder.

First rule—take your own pulse.

Total chaos in the patient's room. In his haste, the resident knocked over the drip stand and scrambled to right it. Edith struggled to breathe, her lips blue. One nurse attached cardiac monitor leads to her bony chest. Another wound down the head of the bed.

Julia flew into action. Every second counted. She felt for a carotid pulse with one hand and grabbed a stethoscope with the other. A rapid and faint pulse flickered under her fingertips. She listened for breath sounds. No crackles at the lung bases, so excess fluid in the lungs wasn't the problem. She tossed the stethoscope aside.

"What happened?" she asked, relieved that her voice sounded calmer out loud than it did in her head. Edith Powell had enough to worry about without the doctors panicking.

"Apparently, she was sitting up in bed, reading the newspaper, when she suddenly complained about feeling short of breath. The nurse called me in." The resident glanced at the nurse as if for approval, then carried on. "Her chest sounded clear, but she looked a bit blue. She's been fading in and out. I couldn't get much sense out of her, and my registrar is tied up in theatre, so I thought I'd better call you . . ."

She squeezed his arm, as much to reassure herself as him. "You did the right thing. Any cardiac problems?"

"Ah, hypertension, I think." He grabbed the chart off the bedside table, knocking over a glass of water as he did so.

While he flicked through the notes, Julia asked the nurse, "What's the BP now?"

"A hundred over sixty. She normally runs at about one-fifty over ninety."

"Way too low for her. Keep her flat." She scanned the ECG trace, then turned to the resident. "Can you get some blood gases off?"

"I think so." He seized the patient's wrist and groped around for the radial artery. "I can't find a pulse."

The cardiac monitor shrieked. Julia reached for the carotid pulse again. Nothing. Her stomach dropped.

"Shit. We're losing her." She thumped the patient's chest once. Sometimes that would restart the heart, but not this time. "Start compressions. I'll tube her."

She snatched a laryngoscope from the arrest trolley and asked the nurse to draw up some muscle relaxant. The other nurse pulled the bed away from the wall so Julia could stand behind the patient's head.

The resident pumped Edith's chest. One of her ribs cracked under his weight. He hesitated, but Julia nodded for him to carry on.

The old woman's eyes were half-closed. Her mouth hung open. The dreaded "o" sign. She looked dead already. Circling the drain.

The memory of Valerie dead on the mortuary table flashed into her mind. Julia blinked her eyes to clear the image. Not now.

Her hand shook. It had been a while since she'd done an intubation. Better be like riding a bike.

A clatter at the doorway signalled the arrival of the arrest team. Her shoulder muscles relaxed. She handed the laryngoscope to Simon, the anaesthetist. He winked at her over the top of his mask.

"Probable massive PE," she said. "No sign of an MI on the ECG. She's post-op revision of an infected total knee replacement."

"What's her resus status?" Simon bagged the patient via a mask, getting her oxygen levels up before inserting the endotracheal tube.

"I don't know. We didn't discuss it." The resident looked like a rabbit in the headlights. He glanced at Julia for help.

She bailed him out. "They considered her functional enough for a joint replacement. We should do what we can for her."

In one smooth move, Simon intubated the patient, then connected the bag to the tube. He showed the resident how to hand-ventilate and took over the cardiac compressions.

Julia noted the cardiac rhythm on the monitor, a jagged saw-tooth. Ventricular fibrillation. Edith's heart would be wriggling like a bag of worms. No wonder she didn't have a pulse. That heart wasn't pumping anything anywhere.

"VF. Can I have some adrenaline and bicarb?" she asked.

The nurse handed her two syringes already prepared and labelled, then slapped two gel patches on the patient's exposed chest, ready for defibrillation.

"Thanks." Julia took the syringes and squirted their contents straight into the IV line. "Charge the paddles."

"Clear." Simon had the defib paddles ready, one in each hand.

He placed them over the gel pads and fired. Edith's body jerked upwards. A glance at the monitor. No change.

Julia swore under her breath. "Charge again. Get me some lignocaine."

They ran through several more cycles of defibrillation. Cardiac compressions. More anti-arrhythmic drugs. Nothing worked. Ventricular fibrillation gave way to asystole. Flatline.

The team paused. Julia checked Edith's pupils for any reaction to light.

"Pupils fixed and dilated. We've lost her."

Simon nodded. "Time of death sixteen-thirty-eight. Thanks, everybody."

The adrenaline surge had passed and left her nauseated and shaky. Now she had time to think rather than act on reflex. Doubts flooded in. Should she have done something different? Maybe she should have taken more interest in Edith's care, not left it to an inexperienced resident. Could she have prevented her death?

How could she expect to save a stranger when she hadn't been able to save her best friend?

She left the room, yanked her mask hard enough to break the ties, then peeled off her gloves. Someone put their hands on her shoulders. She turned her head. Simon.

His mask dangled around his neck. "How about that drink?"

Warm breath tickled her ear. It would be so easy to lean back and let someone else be strong.

"Sorry, not tonight." She stepped forward and slipped away from him, determined to have her emotional meltdown in private.

Nick parked in front of a sedate Federation cottage in a leafy Mt Lawley street, complete with tuck-pointed red brick and corrugated tin roof. Did the neighbours mind living next door to a fetish-wear manufacturer? Probably not, might even be customers. The thriving inner-city suburb had many restaurants, bars and cafes. Why not dress up for a night out?

He opened the gate in the white picket fence and walked down the rustic brick path to the front door. Leadlighted, naturally. Good to see a security door even though it partly obscured the coloured glass. He pressed the brass doorbell, but had only a few moments to admire the cottage garden before the door opened.

Another surprise. Surely this petite blonde wasn't the brains behind those leather contraptions. More kindergarten teacher than bondage mistress.

"You must be Nick Randall. I'm Mona." She opened the security door. "Come on in. I promise I'll be gentle."

Nick followed her down a long hallway to an open-plan living area at the back of the house. An expanse of glass showcased a backyard full of multi-coloured roses and daisies and countless other flowers he couldn't identify.

"Lovely place."

"Disappointed I don't live in a dungeon?"

She sat at the polished jarrah dining table. Nick sat beside her. "A bit. How did you get into this line of work?"

"Everyone needs a hobby. And I'm very good with my hands."

He passed her the photos of Valerie's leather items. "Do you recognise any of these pieces?"

Mona flicked through the stack. "Yes. Catwoman's a favourite of mine. Very popular. Where did you find them?"

"Part of an ongoing investigation. A suspicious death."

"You've identified the body?"

"Yes. Valerie Cavanaugh."

"Oh, such a shame." She frowned. "Surely you've got better things to do than investigate someone's shopping."

"Her boyfriend said they were a joke gift from someone. I want to find the buyer."

"Rather expensive joke, but if she's the one I'm thinking of, she paid for it herself."

"Do you keep records of all your sales?"

"On my computer." Mona got up. "My clients appreciate my discretion, so I'll need to see a warrant before I hand over any names."

"Of course." Nick followed her to a small office. Book-lined walls revealed an eclectic taste in reading.

"Sit over there and don't peek."

He obeyed, moving aside a pile of cushions to sit on the daybed.

She sat at an antique desk and accessed a laptop. "Here we are. Valerie Cavanaugh." A few more clicks. "Yes, she definitely paid for it."

"There goes the gift idea."

"I guess she lied to her boyfriend."

Would an easy lead to a suspect be too much to hope for? "Can you remember her? What was she like?"

"Some women who see me are obviously only here because of a man. It's what he wants, not her."

"And Valerie?"

"Valerie knew what she wanted. She was in control."

"In my world, the person doing the tying up is the one in control."

"It's a matter of trust—confidence in your partner." She flashed a smile over her shoulder. "Submission can be empowering. Try it sometime. Would you like a brochure?"

Could he call it anger management research? "Back to Valerie . . ."

"If you insist."

"Did anyone come with her?"

"Have you asked her friends?"

"Yes, but nobody knows who shared this interest with her."

Her mobile rang.

"Flick through these while I deal with an impatient client. It'll distract you from raiding my computer records." She thrust some brochures at him.

Another dead end. He turned a couple of pages. And there was no definite link between her hobby and her murder, anyway. He should get back to the hospital. One more page.

He stared at the next image, speechless. Not to mention breathless and mindless, too. Her face was turned away from the camera, but he recognised the hair, that necklace.

"I filed that one under B for breasts." Mona dropped her phone on the desk.

"I can see why." His entire face was on fire. "Didn't mean to say that out loud."

She laughed. "I've got someone for a fitting in fifteen minutes. Anything else I can get you? Iced water? Cold shower?"

"No, thanks." He dragged his gaze away from the photo and handed her one of his cards.

"If you want to expand your horizons, perhaps you'll come back for a fitting one day." Mona finished with a wicked laugh.

"My horizons have been expanded enough already, but I'll take this brochure for my boss. He needs a new hobby."

"Sure. Take two."

Nick escaped to his car. He opened all the windows and blasted the air-conditioner on full to combat the afternoon heat. After one last long look at the photo, he turned it face down on the passenger seat. He needed to concentrate, and that photo didn't help. Not enough blood going to his brain.

Why hadn't Julia said anything? No wonder she'd acted so strangely at Valerie's house when he asked her about the leather gear. Had they been lovers?

CHAPTER EIGHTEEN

JULIA KNOCKED ON HER neighbour's door. The late afternoon sun scorched her back. How should she break the bad news? Blurt it out fast or build up to it slowly?

She waited, knocked again. No answer. After several more minutes, she gave up and returned home. The dreaded conversation was delayed, but she couldn't avoid it altogether. She'd never forgive herself if Mrs Flannery found out from someone else. Not when Edith had died under her care.

She fed Oscar, then stared into her fridge. The T-bone steaks stared back. Her appetite had vanished. She drank a glass of iced water. Maybe a cool shower would revive her before she staked out Mrs Flannery's front porch.

As she headed to the bathroom, her doorbell rang. Typical.

She opened the front door. Mrs Flannery. Her heart sank. The old woman looked every day of her eighty-plus years. She knew.

"Edith's dead." Her voice quavered, matching the tremor in her hands.

Julia clasped them in hers. Despite the heat they were icy. If she gripped too tightly, the old woman's fingers would snap. "I'm so sorry, Mrs Flannery. I wanted to tell you myself. I was with her when she died."

Teary eyes gazed up at her. "What happened?"

"We don't know for sure. Maybe a blood clot going to her lungs, or the infection was too much for her heart."

"Blood clot. Isn't that what people get on long plane trips?"

"Yes. Exactly the same."

"Did she suffer?"

Edith's sudden shortness of breath would've been distressing. "It happened quickly."

"Are you sure?"

"Edith was unconscious. She wouldn't have known what was happening." A little white lie. "Do you want me to stay with you for a while?"

"No, thank you, dear. One of my friends is coming over." She sighed. "Not many friends left now."

"I'm so sorry."

"Don't be silly. I'm sure you did everything you could for her."

If only Julia could make herself believe that.

A battle-scarred VW Beetle pulled up in front of Mrs Flannery's house. A grey-haired man clambered out, straightening up with visible effort. Julia helped her neighbour along the footpath. The man and Mrs Flannery blinked tears at each other, then hooked arms and went indoors.

Julia walked inside, back to the kitchen. The last time one of her patients died, Valerie invited herself over after work. She'd arrived laden with a ready-to-reheat coq au vin and homemade brownies. They'd eaten dessert first, while the casserole bubbled on the stovetop and a winter storm lashed at the kitchen windows.

A microwaved Lean Cuisine for one? On impulse, she rang Gabriel and invited him over for a barbecue and an outbreak review.

She hauled the dusty cover off the barbecue and checked for spiders and other wildlife. All clear. She placed two folding chairs under the overhanging branches of her neighbour's jacaranda tree. Purple flowers carpeted the ground—a painful reminder of

Valerie's home. A scattering of pink-tinged clouds heralded the sunset. The sea breeze helped cool the air.

What else did she need? She searched the laundry for a citronella candle to keep man-eating mosquitoes at bay. Ross River virus, she could live without. Only a stub to be found, but that fit her plans for an early night. And a sober one. Less chance of Gabriel learning her secrets.

⬤

Julia put her plate in the kitchen sink, then bent over and rubbed the itchy welt on her right ankle. "Bloodthirsty little buggers."

"You must taste better than I do." Gabriel left his plate with hers and turned to go back outside.

"Leave the rest. Coffee? Or more wine?"

He glanced at the microwave clock, then at the open wine bottle. "Got a breathalyser handy?"

"I won't let you drive home drunk." She picked up the bottle. "If you don't mind the sofa again."

He blushed. "Yeah, sure, of course."

"Sit down and drink up." She refilled their glasses, then sat at the kitchen table. "What a horrible day. Edith Powell shouldn't have died."

"She was old and frail."

"Not that old. She was still active, even had a toy boy." She stared into her wineglass. "My neighbour knew her. She's devastated. I should've kept a closer eye on her, not—"

"Give yourself a break. Your best friend was murdered."

She could sense he wanted to talk about Valerie. No chance. "But VRSA? Where the bloody hell did that come from?"

"You'll work it out."

"What about Brad? A fit young guy with no previous admissions, routine abdominal surgery. It doesn't make sense."

"Didn't his appendix burst on the table?"

"Yes, but . . ." She paused with her wineglass mid-air.

"But what?"

She sipped her wine, gave her mind time to process the idea. "He should have a Gram-negative infection. *Staph aureus* post-op infection usually comes from the skin, not from the bowel."

"Wasn't he on antibiotics to cover Gram-negatives when we saw him?"

"Yeah, that knocked off the other bowel flora and let the staph take over. I'm not saying it's impossible, but VRSA? A bug that's never been found in Australia?" She shook her head. "I've got more chance of winning the Lotto."

"Maybe you should buy a ticket."

"Brad didn't have any contact with Edith Powell, so we've been looking at staff, someone who doesn't know they're carrying VRSA. Right?"

"Yes, and we'll track them down. I have supreme confidence in your detective work."

"What if someone gave the patients VRSA deliberately?"

"Huh?" Gabriel grabbed her wineglass and held it up to the light. "What's in this wine? Must be good."

"This is driving me nuts. I have to find the carrier."

CHAPTER NINETEEN

ON WEDNESDAY MORNING, JULIA poured boiling water on the coffee grounds in her plunger. She inhaled deeply, willing the scent to snap her awake. Cool water trickled from her wet hair down her back and soaked into the towel wrapped around her body. Must be over thirty degrees outside already and it didn't feel any cooler inside.

The doorbell interrupted her thoughts.

It was Nick Randall. "Sorry to bother you so early," he said, keeping his gaze locked on hers.

"You've caught me in a state of undress." Great, Julia. State the bloody obvious. She took a tighter grip on the towel, glad it was one of her king-size Egyptian cotton ones. "Guess your detective skills already picked that up. Hang on a tick."

She ducked into her bedroom and got dressed. Back at the front door, she invited him in and led him into her kitchen.

"Coffee? There's enough for two." She held up the plunger, hoping Gabriel would remain hidden in the lounge room.

"No, thanks. I won't stay long." Nick sat at the table, his back to the hallway.

She poured herself a cup and sat opposite. He put a sheet of folded paper on the table and stared at it.

"What's happened?" she asked, drawing his eyes back to her.

He pushed the sheet of paper across the table. "Why didn't you mention this to me earlier?"

She opened it to reveal a print of herself wearing her red leather corset. If she hadn't been sitting down, she'd have fallen to the floor. Holy crap. She'd forgotten that photo. He knew. How could she wriggle her way out of this?

"Would you like me to autograph this for you?"

He gave her a flat stare. "What exactly was the nature of your relationship with Valerie?"

How could she explain her relationship with Valerie when parts of it she didn't understand herself? Please don't let Gabriel come in now.

She lowered her voice to a whisper. "It's complicated."

He tapped the print so hard his finger nearly tore through the paper. The scar on his forehead glowed white against the redness of his face. "I spent hours trying to find out more about Valerie's so-called hobby. To have this thrown in my face . . ."

"I said you'd be wasting your time."

"Why on earth didn't you tell me why?"

"How could I? It was a brief fling . . . a secret brief fling." Heat rushed up her neck and set her cheeks afire. "I can't . . ." She stared down at the table, unable to meet his eyes.

"You're the mystery man I've been searching for." He snatched the photo off the table and refolded it. "We'll need another statement."

Her head snapped up. "So I'm a suspect now?"

A sneeze echoed down the hallway. She froze. Bugger. Just when she thought it couldn't get any worse. Had Gabriel overheard their conversation?

"Hope I didn't wake your housemate," Nick said.

Gabriel strolled into the kitchen, his hair spiked more than usual and his clothes rumpled. "Any news about Valerie?"

"Dr Sinclair can fill you in." His voice clipped and businesslike, Nick stood up. "Don't forget your statement, Dr Sinclair. As soon as possible. I'll see myself out."

He couldn't escape her fast enough.

<hr>

When she reached her office, Julia found Martin pacing the corridor. His dark-shadowed eyes and gaunt cheeks shocked her. She'd never seen him look less than immaculate. Was that spilt coffee on his shirt? Or a bloodstain?

"Are you okay?" She shepherded him into her office, hoping Gabriel wouldn't interrupt them too soon. He'd given her a lift to work, then detoured to the locker rooms to shower and change.

"Every time I walk into a room, everyone shuts up and stares at me." He slumped in the chair opposite her desk. "Like I killed her."

She hesitated. He still had to be a suspect, but she trusted Valerie's good judgement.

"Have you looked in a mirror lately? Maybe they're just worried about you, but don't know what to say."

"Rachel kicked me out of our bedroom—hard to blame her for that. Finally persuaded her to talk to the police today."

"Are you sure that's a good idea? She didn't seem that stable to me."

He winced. "I may have slipped something into her orange juice to calm her down."

"Martin!" Was he drugging his wife against her will? Maybe he wasn't to be trusted after all.

"Kidding—sort of. She often has a dose of vitamin V with her breakfast. Prescribed by her doctor, I swear."

"Valium? How long's that been going on for?"

"Too bloody long, but I can hardly stop her right now." Martin scrubbed both hands through his hair, adding to his state of disarray. "The police are obsessed with me. Wish they'd put the same effort into finding Valerie's killer. What about searching for leather guy?"

Her cheeks caught fire. "Heard that was a waste of time."

"Leather guy? Tell me more." Gabriel popped around the corner. Instead of his usual bright colours, he wore drab green surgical scrubs. The colour did him no favours.

"Impersonating a surgeon?" Martin asked.

Gabriel showed them what he'd been hiding behind his back—his shirt slashed to ribbons. "Someone objected to my fashion sense." His hand trembled.

"Who?"

"I had a shower in the change-rooms out the back of Emergency. Place was deserted. I didn't hear anyone over the noise of the water." He shuddered. "Glad they didn't join me."

"Annoyed anyone lately?" Martin examined the shredded shirt. "Could be a scalpel."

"Maybe someone didn't like my swab technique. Hospitals should be safe places."

"Not here, not anymore." She thought about Valerie and her own car park incident. "Do you have to swipe your ID card to get into that change-room?"

"No, there's no security at all, not even a keypad."

"Report it. Manfredi needs to take hospital security more seriously." His comment about bad publicity from Valerie's death still rankled.

⧫

Later Wednesday morning, Rachel MacDougall slumped in a chair in the police interview room. She dragged another tissue from the box, then shredded it. Her eyes stared straight ahead, focussed on nothing.

Watching her on the video screen, George shook his head. "Not looking flash."

"As tough as that tissue," Nick said.

"Too delicate for our clumsy fists, needs a woman's touch. I'll see who's around."

They left the viewing room. George ambled down the corridor while Nick returned to the interview room. Rachel jumped, then stared at the pile of torn tissues as if wondering who put it there.

"Can I get you something to drink?" he asked.

"When can I go home?" She rubbed her hands over her upper arms as if warming herself up. Despite the summer heat, she wore a long-sleeved T-shirt and jeans.

"Soon. Just a couple of things we want to check."

She stared down at the table. Nick checked the clock on the wall. Could it go any slower? He'd rather face down a couple of drunks in a brawl any day than deal with a tightly strung woman.

At last, the door opened.

George ushered in one of the older uniformed police officers. "Mrs MacDougall, this is Senior Constable Margaret Campbell. She'll ask you a few questions, then you can go home. Is that okay with you?"

A drawn-out sigh. "I suppose so."

Margaret made herself comfortable, then patted Rachel on the hand. George left the room, leaving Nick to observe the interview.

"Thanks for helping us today, Mrs MacDougall. May I call you Rachel?" Margaret spoke in a soft, calm voice. She waited for a nod before continuing. "Rachel, what can you tell me about Monday night last week?"

"Martin didn't come home that night," Rachel said in a singsong voice. "He told me he was at another doctor's house. Simon something."

"Simon Bailey?" Nick asked. That matched what Martin had said.

Rachel shrugged. "It might've been. I don't remember." She turned her body away from Nick and directed all her attention to Margaret.

"You're doing very well." Margaret resumed the interview. "How was Martin when he got home the next morning?"

"Must've been a late night. He couldn't stop yawning."

"How has he been since then?"

Rachel closed her eyes. Her breathing slowed. Had she fallen asleep?

Her head nodded forward, then jerked back with a jolt. Her eyes snapped open, a flash of anger in their depths. "I've hardly seen him. I thought with that bitch dead, he might spend more time at home, but no, he's still Mr Bigshot at the hospital, bossing everybody around."

"Does he ever hurt you?"

A shrug.

What was wrong with her? Dozing one moment, aggressive the next, then slumbering again.

"Rachel, it's important that you tell us," he said. "If he's hurting you, we can help."

She wrapped her arms around herself and faced the wall.

Margaret got up and rested a hand on her shoulder. "It's okay, Rachel," she said, then looked at Nick. He pointed to the door, and she nodded.

⋯◆⋯

Nick joined George in the viewing room. "She won't talk with me in there. Let them talk girl to girl."

"Shouldn't that be woman to woman?"

"Of course. How politically incorrect of me. You're a bad influence." Nick rubbed the back of his neck. Tension in his muscles was torture. He needed a long, long run.

"Anything useful from your shopping trip yesterday?"

More than he'd bargained for. "Tell you later." Nick watched the interview, not ready to talk about it yet. Hell, he'd never be ready to talk about it.

"Come on, tell Uncle George every sordid detail. What did you buy?"

"I found out where Valerie got her leather gear." He approached the minefield with caution. "She and Julia bought it together."

"Holy fuck. You're kidding me?" George did his best stunned mullet impersonation.

"I'm still trying to get my head around it." He was out of practice with women, but he'd never suspected that.

"Huh, mystery man is a woman." George pulled at his left earlobe. "You know the drill. Check her whereabouts, alibis, whatever. Better still, get someone else to dig the dirt."

"I already spoke to her this morning, but she had company, so I asked her to come in for an interview later."

George grinned. "I see. You popped around there hoping for a nice cosy cuppa with the good doctor in her nightie and someone beat you to it." He slapped Nick on the back. "You poor, lonely, old thing."

"You can be a real bastard sometimes."

George grabbed his shoulders and squeezed. "You can be a real bastard sometimes, *sir*."

"Yeah, whatever you say, sir," he said with heavy emphasis on the "sir". "I've got a brochure for you. I'll leave it on your desk later."

Margaret opened the viewing room door and saved him from further questions.

"She's a mess," Margaret said. "Real screwed up—"

"What did she say?" George asked. "Does she dump him in it? Come on, spit it out, woman."

"If you'll give me a chance to get a word in, I'll tell you." She didn't look impressed by his bluster.

"Get on with it." He winked at Nick and whispered, "Women."

"You never understood the concept of foreplay," she said.

Nick looked at his boss. "Am I missing something?"

"You're a bit behind with your ancient history, Nick," George said. "Margaret here was my first wife."

"First wife?" So much for George, the long-term bachelor, married to the job.

"The second Mrs Jaworski put me off marriage for life, but that's not a story for your delicate ears." George faced Margaret again. "Where were we? Any physical abuse?"

"She denied it. No ligature marks or bruises around her wrists, but what's she hiding under those long sleeves?"

"Well spotted."

"Thank you. I'm not a total idiot, even if I was stupid enough to marry you."

"Hey, you asked me," George said.

She put her hands on her hips. "Do you want to hear the rest of this or not?"

George threw up his hands in surrender. "Go on. I'm all ears."

"Makes a pleasant change from all mouth. She's so spaced out. Drugs?"

"Her husband told me she was on some sedatives," Nick said.

"What?" George shouted at him. "If I'd known she was a junkie, I would've had a doctor check her over first. See if she could handle an interview."

"They're prescription meds, not meth."

"Same bloody difference. No wonder she's so out of it." George held up his hands as if to strangle Nick. "I hope for your sake this doesn't come back and bite me on the arse."

"Her husband's a doctor. He didn't object. Much."

"Can you prove it? Is it on tape? Got it in writing?"

"No, boss."

"Fan-fucking-tastic."

"Maybe his wife's not the only one he knocks out with drugs. Has the full tox screen come back yet?"

"Not that I've heard, but apparently I'm the last to hear everything around here. Chase it up." George strode back into the interview room. "Sorry to have bothered you, Mrs MacDougall. Thanks for all your help."

"Why don't you leave us alone?" She struggled up off the chair like an old woman, then shuffled around the table.

George helped her out of the room. "We have to chase every potential lead. You do want us to clear your husband's name, don't you?"

"Bitch got what she deserved." A flash of hatred burst through the fog in her eyes, then disappeared just as quickly.

Nick caught her changing expression. What if she was involved? With her husband away that Monday night, she didn't have an alibi. Her brother could have helped her with the heavy lifting. Brothers had committed murder together. Why not brother and sister killers?

CHAPTER TWENTY

LATE WEDNESDAY AFTERNOON, JULIA steeled her nerves for an intensive grilling. The stark white walls edged closer. Her pulse rate soared. Despite her innocence, the formality of an official police interview intimidated her. She wiped her palms on her skirt and leant back in her chair, but the backrest tilted too far for comfort.

One small mercy. Nick Randall wasn't in the interview room. She doubted he'd want to see her ever again. Detective Inspector George Jaworski and his colleague Senior Constable Margaret Campbell had been patient with her so far, but they weren't interested in how she and Valerie had met years earlier and how they ended up working together at the same hospital. She'd delayed as long as she could with inconsequential background information.

Time to bare her soul.

George Jaworski refilled her water glass. "Now, you were telling us about Valerie's marriage breakup?"

A quick sip of water. "Richard claims it was an accident, but he was probably too drunk to remember if he pushed her down the stairs or if she tripped. With one arm in a cast and the pain from her broken ribs, she couldn't manage on her own. Valerie stayed with me when she came out of hospital. It happened about this time last year . . ." Julia's voice cracked. If life had a fast-forward button, she'd skip the next bit.

"Go on." Margaret Campbell slid a box of tissues towards her.

"Valerie and I went to a hospital Christmas party. It got a bit wild and, oh, that's not relevant, but we got home late and I found my sister Tess waiting on the front porch." She closed her eyes for a moment, remembering. A band tightened around her chest. "I'd forgotten she was staying with me while our parents went away on holiday." Her voice faded to a whisper.

Someone tapped on the door and opened it. George Jaworski turned around, then got up and left the room.

She couldn't see who had interrupted and didn't care. Frozen in that moment of reliving her worst memory, Julia wanted to slide from her chair and curl into a foetal ball on the floor.

When he returned, George's expression was bleak. He loomed over her, shrinking the room. What had happened?

Nick came into the room. He gave Julia a brief nod, then sat beside Margaret in the seat George had vacated. His green eyes swept over her, colder than she remembered.

A sudden chill counteracted her flush of embarrassment.

"Are you selling tickets?" Julia asked George. "Perhaps we should move to a bigger room."

George stopped her with an impatient wave. "Can we cut to the chase?" He stepped back and leant against the door.

No escape.

Maybe getting it over with quickly would hurt less, like a bullet in the brain compared to a gut-shot. She focussed on Margaret's face.

"Tess was angry I'd forgotten her, and that she had to sleep on the sofa because Valerie had the spare bed." Her vision blurred. She blinked. "When she didn't come home from school the following afternoon, I thought she'd gone to stay with a friend to punish me. She never came home again."

"Forgive my bluntness, but I'm in a hurry here. What does that have to do with you and Valerie Cavanaugh?" George asked.

"This isn't easy. My only sister disappeared while under my care. I blamed myself. They've never admitted it, but my parents blamed me, too." She grabbed a tissue and blew her nose. "I couldn't work. Couldn't sleep. Couldn't feel anything other than a vast, hollow emptiness."

She wrapped her arms around her middle, holding herself together.

"This is crazy, boss." Nick pushed his chair back and stood up. "We know she had nothing to do with the murder."

"Try telling some smart-arse lawyer that in court," George said. "We follow the evidence and don't play favourites."

"I know that, but—"

"If this case is getting too much for you, just say the word and you're back on desk duties."

"Don't worry about me." Nick sat back down and asked her, "Okay to keep going?"

"Thanks." She took a deep breath, heartened by the warmth that had returned to his eyes. "Valerie helped me live again. We needed each other. It was intense, and frankly, it scared the hell out of us, so we chickened out and went back to being best friends." She turned her attention to George. "You want specifics? Should I draw you a diagram?"

Out of the corner of her eye, she caught Margaret shaking her head at George as if she expected him to say yes.

"We get the picture. Now, what about drugs?"

"Prescription or otherwise?"

"Either. Did Valerie take any drugs?" George asked.

"The contraceptive pill, the occasional painkiller. Never anything illegal."

"Not even a little something to relax her? All that stress. Maybe she needed help to get to sleep."

"Never. Anything on her tox screen?"

"I'm not discussing that with you," George said, his tone abrupt. "What about Martin MacDougall?"

Had the killer given her drugs to keep her quiet? Or had Valerie kept secrets of her own?

George clicked his fingers at her. "What did you think of her relationship with Martin MacDougall?"

"Was I jealous?" Julia shook her head. "Hell, no. You look at Martin and see a doctor screwing around. A willing nurse in every ward. After all, hospitals are very incestuous places. Like police stations, I should imagine."

George raised a warning finger to his colleagues. "Don't even think about it." He gestured for Julia to continue.

"Martin has a hidden superpower—the ability to dodge affairs without disappointing anyone. He's a charmer, devoted to his wife."

"Until he met Valerie, and it was love at first sight and to hell with the poor missus."

"No, nothing like that. They'd worked together for years. A great team. I think their affair caught them by surprise."

George tapped his watch and looked at his colleagues. "I have to go. Run through Julia's whereabouts on the relevant dates and times."

He barrelled out of the interview room and left them to dissect her life.

"Right, shall we start with the Monday night Valerie disappeared?" Nick asked.

"I waited for Valerie in the hospital car park after work. When she didn't appear, I walked home. Well, not straight home. I detoured to the Subiaco Hotel and bumped into an old friend, Leon. He walked me home and stayed the night."

Nick rubbed the scar over his eyebrow. He slid a pen and piece of paper across the table. "Write down his full name and contact number."

She checked her mobile, then jotted the details down. "Do you think he helped me abduct her, and we dragged her back to my place for an orgy with a little torture on the side? What sort of person do you think I am?"

If only she could decipher his expression. Disgust? Pity? Stark raving horror? Unreadable cop look, she decided.

"Don't answer that," she said. "We were too drunk to . . . ah, to do anything that night. My sister had been missing for a year and I wanted to drink enough to forget it. I don't know what Leon's excuse was. I didn't want to be alone . . ."

The clock on the wall ticked the seconds away.

"When you're ready, tell us what you did the next day." Nick's voice revealed nothing.

"I went out for breakfast with Leon, then on to work for the day. After that, I came here and reported Valerie missing."

"I'll interrogate myself about that later."

"Let me know if you want any help with that. I can be very persuasive." She relaxed for the first time since entering the interview room. "After that, I had some things to tidy up at work, then I went home . . ." Shit. No, she hadn't. "Sorry, first I drove to City Beach to visit someone, then I went home and stayed home alone all night."

"City Beach?" Nick frowned. "Who did you visit?"

"I wanted to ask Martin about Valerie, but he wasn't home, only his wife, Rachel. She didn't appreciate my visit."

He watched her without responding, his green eyes guarded, his thoughts hidden behind his cop mask.

"Time to do your bad cop routine and tell me to butt out again?"

"Would it work this time?" The hint of a smile softened his eyes.

The door flew open. George came in and stared at Julia, his gaze more chilling than a cold shower.

"You can go, Margaret. I have a couple more questions for Dr Sinclair." He waited for the policewoman to leave the room, then took her seat. "Perth's just a big country town—seems like everybody knows everybody else's business. Carmela Luciano."

"Is that a question?"

"That name familiar?"

She shook her head. "Should it be?"

"Let me give you a few more clues." George glanced at a sheet of paper, then slid it across to Nick. "Twenty-five-year-old Italian-American woman, travelling around Australia a few months ago. Saw a local GP for her sore arm. Any bells?"

What was this about? "No."

"I spoke to the doctor a few minutes ago. He discussed the case with you."

She dredged her memory. Nothing. "Maybe he didn't mention her by name. I could check the hospital computer."

"You do that, and before you get carried away with patient confidentiality and medical ethics, I want you to consider two questions. How did she get from a GP's surgery to a shallow grave in Kings Park? And what's your involvement?"

⸺◈⸺

After another night of disturbed sleep, Julia hit the lab early. How could the murdered woman found in Kings Park have been one of her patients? A bloody unlikely coincidence. By the time the police had finished interviewing her, she'd half-expected to be arrested. When she'd wanted them to stop wasting time on Martin, she'd never contemplated offering up herself as prime suspect.

First step, prove Carmela Luciano wasn't her patient, then find out who treated her. How hard could it be to find one patient in the system?

She skimmed her consult diary and found no trace of any remotely similar name in the past year. The GP surgery didn't open until nine, so she tackled the lab and hospital databases with the sparse information available. She tried every spelling variation imaginable. It would be easier if she had a date of birth. Hell, it'd be easier if she had a crystal ball.

Zilch. Still too early to call the GP. Try another angle.

What if the patient came to the Emergency Department, but got sick of waiting and stormed out without seeing anyone? Must be a daily occurrence. She phoned the triage desk.

"If a patient leaves without being seen, is their name left on the computer?"

"Is this one of those if a tree falls in the forest questions?" The triage nurse's burst of laughter ended in a coughing fit.

"Slow day?"

"Catatonic. You want to know what happens to walkouts?"

"Yes. A patient was sent here, but I can't find any record of her on the system. How soon do their details hit the computer? And are they deleted if they leave?"

"Honey, everything that goes on the computer stays on the computer. We've got protocols coming out of our ears. Ambo or walking wounded?"

Sore arm from a GP's surgery? No ambulance. "Walking wounded."

"Someone comes to the triage desk. We enter their info on the computer. Urgent problems go straight out the back. Otherwise, they sit in the waiting room until they reach the top of the queue."

"What if there's a long wait when they arrive?"

"Sure, if it's really busy and a minor problem, we'll gently suggest they see a GP. If they leave then, we're still meant to keep a record—in case they drop dead on the way home."

"Thanks, I'll find out when the GP sent her in. You could tell me if that was a busy time?"

"Trust me. Everything is on the computer. Gotta go. Next victim's here."

Julia checked the time. Almost nine, so she rang the surgery. After five minutes of hold music, they put her through to the doctor. She'd never met him in person, but recognised his voice from several previous phone calls for advice.

"Do you have time to talk about Carmela Luciano? You called the police about her."

"Of course. Such a tragedy. They emailed via the Health Department, asking if anyone remembered a patient fitting her description. I've been away on holidays or I would've called sooner."

"When did you see her?"

A computer keyboard clattered. "Here we go. September fifteenth. American tourist, pain related to fractured arm, recent pin and plate, travelling so reluctant to be admitted to hospital, discussed with your good self, concern about possible MRSA from op in USA, trial of high-dose oral antibiotics, referral letter for hospital in case of poor response."

"Did you see her again?"

"No, I assumed she carried on with her trip. Did she come to the hospital?"

"I wish I knew. I never saw her, and she's not on our computer system. Maybe she hit a busy day in ED and left without being seen."

"I told her to go to Emergency, but she overheard your name." He hesitated. "She was rather pushy, the type who'd come straight to your office and demand instant attention."

Great, the patient could've bumped into anyone on her way to Pathology. So much for her brilliant idea to clear her name and rule out any connection with the hospital.

After getting a brief description of Carmela, she thanked the GP. Would anyone remember a woman who fitted the description wandering around the hospital three months ago? If she even came to the hospital. Security cameras might've picked her up, but even if the hospital kept recordings from a few months ago, they'd hardly let Julia look at them. Not after her recent complaints about security.

A stack of request forms on her desk caught her eye. Better get some work done if she wanted to leave early for Valerie's memorial service.

Chapter Twenty-One

Julia forced herself to smile, lonely in the middle of a crowd. Nod and smile, air kiss and handshake. For a Thursday afternoon, there'd been a good turnout for the memorial service. Some people she hadn't seen since Valerie's wedding day.

Creating the slideshow of Valerie's life had been heartbreaking, but even so, she'd really needed to see it again. Each time she remembered Valerie, it was her bruised, lifeless face she saw, not the vibrant, happy one of the past. She needed to focus on Valerie's life, not her death.

The old pub on the highway had been one of their favourite student haunts. Much yuppified now, but remnants of the past remained. The high ceilings with their ornate roses and cornices. The polished jarrah woodwork that glowed red under the soft-lit chandeliers. Talk about remnants from the past. Leon stretched over the pool table, concentrating on a difficult shot. His fiancée had missed the memorial service, but he'd said she might come later. Perhaps she was one of the statuesque blondes admiring his expertise with the cue. Or were they more interested in his physique?

Raucous chatter ricocheted around her. The after-work crowd had arrived. Was that Rachel's brother, Carl what's-his-name, lurking in the far corner with a bunch of bodybuilders? She hadn't invited him. Maybe the pub was his local. Better keep him away from Martin.

She fronted the bar for another gin and tonic. She'd lost count of how many she'd had so far. Who cared? It was a wake, her closest friend's wake.

While the barman prepared her drink, another urgent need distracted her. She threw a twenty-dollar note on the bar and dashed to the toilets. That problem relieved, she returned to the bar for her drink and change.

She drained a quarter of the glass in one swallow. The gin slammed into her brain at high speed.

"Whoa, must be a double."

Sprawled against the bar, she surveyed the room for signs of intelligent life. Richard had planted himself at the other end of the bar with a jug of beer and a tirade of abuse for anyone who ventured near. Even Martin was still there, telling anyone who'd listen and several who didn't that he'd lost the best thing that had happened to him in a long time. If she heard one more cliché about death, she vowed to punch the person responsible. Bugger nonviolence.

Hang on a minute. Had the bar slipped sideways? The polished timber floor tilted again, tipping her away from the bar and towards the middle of the overcrowded room. She bounced off Gabriel and into Simon, who grabbed her arms and straightened her up.

"Careful," he said. She pressed her hands to his shoulders to keep her balance. "I think you've had too much to drink."

Her head dropped forward, her forehead resting on his chest, his white linen shirt soft against her skin. She felt the rumble of his voice, but couldn't understand a word.

Gabriel dragged her away from Simon and onto the crowded dance floor. Her legs were having none of it. They wanted to go in the opposite direction to the rest of her body, a disconcerting feeling, but maybe they had the right idea. A surgical nurse from

Valerie's ward butted in, eager to dance with Gabriel, the only guy on the dance floor. Julia shoved him at the nurse and escaped to a vacant corner.

She closed her eyes. The room swirled around her, making her stomach spiral and spin. Her eyes snapped open. Bed spins? That didn't make any sense at all because she wasn't even in bed.

A jaw-stretching yawn overwhelmed her. All she wanted to do was sleep. So, so tired. Dead tired. No, that wasn't right. Valerie was the dead one.

Why did Valerie die and leave her alone?

Fresh air. That would wake her up. She couldn't quit and go home so early. Valerie deserved a better send-off. Stumble towards the closest door. Fresh air, that's all she really needed.

Julia staggered outside into the hotel car park. The double doors swung shut behind her with a thud, muffling the sounds of revelry. Warm air blanketed her bare arms. Her knees buckled. She slumped to the ground and leant back against the rough brickwork of the external wall.

Traffic hummed on the highway. A lullaby.

Gravel burrowed into the back of her legs, so she drew her knees up and hugged them to her chest. Rest a few moments, then she'd get up and walk around, clear the fog from her brain. Her head drooped. Heavy eyelids. So, so heavy.

A sudden downpour interrupted her dreamless oblivion and zapped her heart rate into the danger zone. Her head jerked backwards; her skull smacked against the wall. A scream cut short by a mouthful of cold, bitter liquid.

Beer? She spluttered. Wet hair obscured her vision, so she dragged both hands across her face, then glared up at her assailant.

A tall, furious blonde loomed over her, an empty beer jug in one hand.

"Keep your fucking hands off my man." The blonde punctuated her statement by kicking Julia's thigh.

"Ouch." That'd bruise. She rubbed the pain away.

Noise levels escalated. Her scream had drawn a fascinated crowd, but no one did anything to help. Maybe they thought a catfight was part of the night's entertainments. Did they expect her and the blonde to tear their clothes off and go for it in the car park?

She slowly stood up, then straightened her clothes in a feeble attempt to regain some dignity. Icy beer trickled down her back. A flash of clarity sparked through the haze. Bloody Leon and his tomcatting ways.

"Leon?" she asked.

"Scum-sucking, sheep-shagging, muscle-bound meathead."

The way she was waving that beer jug around, it'd be safer to steer the blonde's rage towards Leon. His fault, after all. Let him defend himself.

"Sums up Leon perfectly, but you left out two-timing . . . oh, crap, my brain won't work."

"Fornicating philanderer," Gabriel called out.

The Amazon glared at him, then turned her knife-wielding gaze back to Julia and snarled.

"If it's any consolation, he did the same to me." Julia watched for any hint of impending attack. She'd run if she could, but her legs had no intention of moving. And who could run in high heels, anyway? Only on TV. "Look what he's done to you. Is he worth it?"

"Yes, he is. Aren't I pathetic?" The warrior woman deflated and sank to the ground, seemingly oblivious to the puddle of beer she'd landed in. Black mascara trailed down her cheeks.

"The middle-of-the-night phone calls? The dog poo parcel?"

"Guilty." She rubbed her eyes, smearing mascara across her face. "You make me sound like some kind of psycho bitch from hell, a real bunny-boiler."

Gabriel said, "If the hat fits . . ."

Julia held up a hand to silence him. Throwing petrol on the fire was never a bright idea. "So that explains the bitch reference in the note. It had nothing to do with the dog being female."

"That backfired on me." She shuddered and wrinkled her nose. "I'm sure it stunk worse when I wrapped it up than when you opened it."

"I'm so glad to hear it." The woman tensed up. Julia tried to avert another onslaught. "Nothing happened between us. I have absolutely no interest in Leon. Do you believe me?"

A mournful sigh. "He grovelled. And why would he invite me to meet you tonight if you were having an affair?"

"Exactly." Julia gave her a hand and helped her up, nearly falling over again herself. "If he's making you this miserable . . ."

"I keep thinking he'll grow out of it."

"Yeah, like that'll ever happen." Her words slurred together. "I thought a psychotic killer was stalking me."

"Sorry."

"Hey, what about slashing my tyres? You owe me for two new ones."

"Tyres?" A hint of a frown. "I never touched your car. You must've annoyed someone else."

"The hospital car park on Sunday?"

"I was at a weekend retreat down south." She sneered at Julia. "You should try it sometime. Detox all that poison out of your body."

"A weekend wasn't long enough for you."

"Bitch. No wonder someone slashed your tyres."

Julia clenched her hands. One punch and she'd feel so much better. For a heartbeat, but then remorse would crash the party.

Gabriel stepped between them. "Come on, Julia. Let's get you home and out of those wet things."

Leon emerged from the depths of the crowd and approached his fiancée, caution in every step. She scorched him with one glance, then stalked off into the car park. Shoulders slumped, he followed. The crowd dispersed.

Julia retrieved her bag from a pool of beer. As the adrenaline surge ebbed, fog took over her brain again. No more booze. One thought drifted through her mind, but she couldn't grasp any plausible answers. If Leon's fiancée hadn't slashed her tyres, who did?

Chapter Twenty-Two

Julia slumped at her desk on Friday morning, her head cradled in her hands. If only she could soak her brain in a bucket of water for a year or two. Why had she drunk so much? A soft groan echoed through her head.

Bloody Leon and his psycho blonde.

Eyes tightly scrunched to repel bright light, she massaged her temples with her fingertips. At least the beer had left her hair silky soft. And far better a jealous girlfriend stalking her than a crazed killer.

But who slashed her tyres? Angelo? Right place, right time.

And those texts from Valerie's phone? Innocent messages with sinister double-meanings. Leon's girlfriend didn't know her mobile number, only the landline. And how could she have sent a message from Valerie's phone?

Don't panic. Leave it to the police.

She stretched gingerly. A twinge in the crease of her left arm reminded her to remove the dinosaur Band-Aid from her venepuncture site. Her impaired state at the wake had made her wonder if someone had spiked her drink, so she'd had blood taken for a toxicology screen. At last, something useful she could do.

Why bother the police with every problem when she could find out the answer herself?

Her phone rang. The pain in her head intensified. She grabbed the receiver to stop the racket. A consult from ICU. Just what she needed to distract her from her misery—someone in worse physical condition than herself.

⸻ ⬥ ⸻

While she waited for the ICU registrar to finish consoling a grieving relative, Julia noticed Martin sitting by one of the corner beds. At first, she thought he was examining the patient's hand, but he didn't let go. How odd. She checked the whiteboard for the patient's name. Rachel MacDougall, his wife. What on earth was wrong with her?

Before she could sneak a look at the ward census, the registrar thrust a bulky chart at her and launched into a long, complicated story about multiple fractures and head injuries from a motor vehicle accident followed by a prolonged stay in the unit. Now the patient had signs of sepsis without an obvious source.

In her fragile state, she found it hard enough to concentrate without the added intrigue of Rachel's admission to ICU.

She nodded towards the corner cubicle. "What's wrong with Rachel MacDougall?"

He scanned the unit for prying ears. "Well, it'll be all over the hospital soon, anyway." Another furtive peek over his shoulder. "OD," he mouthed.

An overdose? No wonder Martin looked shattered. "How is she?"

"Too early to know for sure. Still unconscious. She meant business. Tricyclics, benzoes and booze."

Antidepressants and sedatives explained her spaced-out behaviour. "Poor Martin."

"Not poor Rachel?" Without waiting for an answer, the registrar carried on with the patient's case history.

Her mind drifted. What had triggered Rachel's overdose? Did she know something about Valerie's murder? Guilt over her own involvement?

"Anybody home?" The registrar waved his hand in front of her face.

"Sorry, terminal hangover. Did I miss anything important?"

"Yeah, but I have to go on a ward round now. Mind flicking through the rest of the notes on your own?"

"Think I can manage."

"Leave a message if you have any bright ideas." He hurried away.

Her gaze fixed on the corner cubicle again. Martin hadn't noticed her. He stared out the window, absently stroking his wife's hand.

Why had Rachel overdosed? And why now? She couldn't stop thinking about it, even as she reviewed the chart, examined the patient, recommended a change of antibiotics, and ordered some extra investigations.

Rachel's brother, Carl, had said something about Martin and drugs. What if the overdose wasn't her fault? Maybe Martin gave her too much. Accidentally? Deliberately?

Conspiracies and stalkers and murderers. Get a grip.

She could hardly ask him about his marital relationship while his wife lay comatose in ICU. What about Simon? He'd mentioned Martin talking about his wife when they got drunk together last week. Would he break the sacred code of mateship and spill some gossip?

Instead of returning to the lab, Julia detoured to the operating suite and approached the theatre clerk.

"Hi, I'm chasing some doctors for VRSA screening swabs. Can I sneak a look at the theatre list?" Julia smiled her most sisterly smile. "Some of them are hiding from me."

The clerk sighed and handed over the list. "I wonder how they dress themselves in the morning. Go for it."

"Thanks." She scanned the list. "Gotcha. Do you know how theatre three is going?"

"On their last case, I think." The clerk buzzed theatre three on the intercom. After a brief chat with the theatre nurse, she turned back to Julia. "They're closing up now, so it shouldn't be too long."

"I'll ambush them outside the change-rooms."

"Good luck. Do you have a stun gun?"

"I wish."

Ten minutes of pacing the hospital-green corridor before the change-room door opened.

Simon draped his stethoscope around his neck and sauntered over. "Hanging around the men's room again?"

"Only to catch doctors who haven't had their VRSA screening swabs."

"Guilty." He shoved his hands in his pockets and leant against the wall opposite her. "I'm on Augmentin for a sinus infection. Don't I have to be off antibiotics before being swabbed?"

"No, VRSA is resistant to Augmentin so it won't make any difference." She reached into her pocket for a swab, but she'd used her last one in ICU. "Crap, forgot to refill my stash. Can I trust you to swab yourself? Today?"

"I'll drop them in later. Okay?"

"Don't make me chase you again. While I've got you, do you know anything about Martin's wife's admission to ICU?"

He shrugged. "Only what I've heard in the theatre tea room. An overdose. I'm on my way there now to see another patient. If I hear anything, I'll let you know."

"Thanks. I didn't get much chance to talk to him after the memorial service and now he's busy with Rachel. I'm worried about how he's coping. Or not."

"We spoke briefly last night." He hesitated. "I'm sure it was just the booze talking."

"What did he say?"

"It didn't make sense. Something about blaming Rachel for Valerie's death."

"Rachel?"

"Yeah, crazy, right? I asked what he meant and . . ." He shook his head. "It was very noisy."

"Simon." She grabbed the neck of his scrubs and dragged him closer. "Tell me or I will hurt you."

"Promise?"

She shoved him away. "Just tell me."

"He said he'd fix it."

"Fix it how?"

Simon left without answering. She stared after him, her heart racing. Had Martin given Rachel the overdose?

⸻◆⸻

Back in the Pathology Department, Julia called Gabriel into her office. So much work to do before the boss returned from his holidays next week.

"I was tied up with a patient in ICU." She mentally crossed her fingers at the slight exaggeration of the truth. "How far have you got with the VRSA database?"

"I've checked a few more names off the contact lists and updated the screening results."

She scrolled through the list and tallied the numbers. "Five patients involved from the surgical ward, six on the orthopaedics ward. All are in isolation and are following a decolonisation regime to clear the bacteria. Two infections, the rest are only carrying the bacteria on their skin or up their noses. Brad's improving. As for Edith Powell, the infected total knee replacement . . ." She closed her eyes for a moment and relived the failed resuscitation attempt. "She's dead."

"Sorry."

"No positive staff members?"

"None so far."

"Where the hell did it come from?"

"On the plus side, no new positive swabs today. We're winning. We're winning." Gabriel bounced in his chair.

"Hey, settle down. Don't go all Tom Cruise on me." Julia wished she could summon up the same level of enthusiasm. "We're not safe yet."

"But no new cases must mean we've controlled the outbreak."

"We don't know who Brad or Edith caught the VRSA from yet. It has to be someone who covers both wards and has close patient contact. Most likely medical staff."

"But most of the surgeons and nurses have been cleared." Gabriel pointed to the computer screen. "Just some stragglers left and some of those are on holidays."

"We'll catch them as soon as they come back to work. At home if we have to. I saw Simon Bailey on the way back from ICU. He's promised to drop his swabs in later today. Talking of holidays, the boss will be back on Monday."

Great job, Julia. In charge for two weeks, and the most resistant staph ever seen invades the hospital.

A sharp knock interrupted her death spiral of thoughts. Dr Manfredi loomed in the doorway. Too late to hide under her desk. He rarely left his luxurious office in the administration building. Why hadn't he waited for her appointment later in the day?

"This VRSA problem. Any good news?" he asked.

"No new cases today." She stretched to get the kinks out of her back. "No other wards involved."

"Any idea where it came from?"

"Working on that right now. About a dozen doctors and nurses haven't been swabbed yet," she said. "Then there are the physios, pharmacists, social workers, tea ladies, orderlies . . . practically anyone else who works or visits here."

"So, we may never know the source?"

"Exactly. We'll chase as many as we can, and hope there are no new cases. We're not accepting any new admissions to the two wards involved."

"The surgeons are jumping up and down at having to cancel elective admissions. Can we re-open any beds?"

"They'd be the first to complain if their patients caught this infection." How could she handle this without looking like a pushover or a total control freak? "I'll review the wards this afternoon and consider moving all the VRSA-colonised patients into one area so we can clean rooms and re-open some beds. How many beds will depend on how much nursing those patients need. I won't let their care be compromised."

"Good. Do it. What about the patients who've gone home and haven't been screened?"

"We've put a flag on their charts in case they're readmitted."

"I want the names of all the positive patients, in case any relatives get in touch."

"I'll email you a list now." She turned back to the computer, hoping he'd take the hint.

"I'm not finished, Dr Sinclair. The police have enquired about Carmela Luciano. A patient of yours, I believe?"

Hell. Of course, they'd notified Medical Admin. "Only a phone consult from a GP. She never turned up to see me."

"Are you sure?"

"I checked both hospital and lab databases. No record of her."

"Better be right. The police have requested our security videos. One murder associated with the hospital is enough bad publicity. If any journalists sniff around, say absolutely nothing. I don't want the hospital splashed across the front page of the newspapers again."

She bit back a sharp retort. Valerie's murder was just bad publicity, was it? Bloody, buggery, bastard administrators. If she tore
his head off, would that be bad publicity?

Chapter Twenty-Three

Late Saturday morning, Julia sweltered on the walk home from work. She'd planned to stay only an hour, but the lab had been inundated with specimens. Tempers flared and tantrums threatened, so she stayed on to help. With the boss due back on Monday, she couldn't afford a staff mutiny. A quick trip to the cake shop had aided her escape.

When she reached home, she stared at the funeral wreath of white lilies propped against her front door. It must've been delivered by mistake. Or the sender expected her to pass it on to Valerie's family. She checked the attached envelope. No florist's label. Addressed to her, no mention of Valerie. Creepy.

She ripped open the thick white envelope and pulled out a sympathy card.

"My dear Julia, wish you were here" it said in bold, black printing.

Her pulse rate rocketed. She jammed the card back into its envelope and carried the unwelcome gift inside. If Leon's psycho girlfriend was responsible, she'd gone light-years too far.

In the hallway, her answer machine blinked for attention. Eight messages. She listened to them, hoping for a distraction from the ghoulish wreath. More bloody reporters after an interview.

Delete. Two anonymous heavy-breathers. Delete. Nick Randall, asking her to call him as soon as possible. She couldn't tell from the tone of his voice whether he had good news or bad. The last message was from the duty biochemist at the hospital. Calling her at home on the weekend? That could only be bad news.

She returned Nick's call first, barely giving him time to say hello. "You've caught Valerie's killer?"

"No, but—"

"He's taken someone else."

"Can't be sure, but another woman's missing."

"Someone from the hospital?"

"No. A mother of two who didn't come home Thursday night. A girls' night out in Northbridge."

"What's her name?" She gripped the phone tight. What if she knew her, too?

"Paulette Matthews."

Her grip on the phone eased. "Never heard of her."

"Her husband's doing an appeal on the six o'clock news tonight. If she looks familiar or anything else occurs to you . . ."

"I'll call you."

She considered mentioning the wreath, but didn't want to waste his time. If it was a delayed prank from Leon's girlfriend, she'd rather keep that quiet.

"Since you're talking to me, does that mean I'm no longer a suspect?"

"Never thought you were. Leon confirmed your alibi."

"Was his girlfriend there when you saw him?" She crossed her fingers. Please say no.

"Yes. She thought you'd complained about her. Do I want to know what that's about?"

Not in this lifetime. "Let's just say she's very protective of Leon."

He laughed. "By the time I left, he needed protection from her. Hang on."

Murmuring in the background, then some creative swearing.

When Nick returned, she said, "I'll let you get back to work. Good luck finding her."

Her next phone call was to the hospital switchboard, asking for the duty biochemist. They transferred her to his mobile. He was driving on the freeway and wanted to find an exit so he could park somewhere safe before speaking to her. After a few minutes, he came back on the line.

"Is this about my drug screen?" she asked.

"Young lady, I don't know you very well, but I thought you were smarter than this. I have to tell your supervisor about these results. Most inappropriate." He sniffed down the phone.

"My results?"

"Testing yourself at work is highly irregular. What did you hope to gain by such arrant foolishness? I can only assume you were too drug-addled to know any better. This jeopardises any plans you had for a career in pathology." An intake of breath, too quick to interrupt. "A black mark on your record, an exceedingly black mark indeed. Don't you have anything to say in your defence?"

At last, a chance to speak. "So, are you ever going to tell me what they spiked my drink with? Or should I pick up the phone in half an hour when you've finished lecturing me?"

"I don't appreciate your attitude, Dr Sinclair."

"And I don't appreciate being drugged against my will, then being nagged to death when I attempt to find out what I was given." She heard a splutter and imagined his mouth half open, ready to resume his rant. Jump in quick. "My tox screen results. Please."

Bloody benzodiazepines. No wonder her memory of Thursday night was so hazy. Of all the people in the hotel bar that night, only one had attacked her.

Time to confront Leon's psycho girlfriend.

Early Saturday afternoon, Nick leant on the MacDougall home doorbell, his gaze drawn across the road. The Indian Ocean tempted him. A sliver of wave-tossed blue glinted between the houses opposite. Scorching white sand underfoot, the cool shock of that first dive through the waves.

A surly voice interrupted his reverie.

"What the hell do you want now?" His faded board shorts at half-mast, Martin dripped water onto the gleaming white tiles.

"Sorry to disturb you at home, but I need to show you some photos." Nick smiled as if he meant it. Civility made his cheeks ache.

"Better come in. Too bloody hot to stand around out here."

Martin led him into a kitchen as sterile as an operating theatre. All stainless steel and high-gloss white. He helped himself to an iced water, but didn't offer one to Nick.

"Where were you on Thursday night?"

An exaggerated sigh. "What did I do on Thursday night?" A long drink of water.

"Sometime today would be nice."

"I left work early. Got home about four."

"Was your wife here then?"

Martin paled and looked away. He didn't answer.

"Maybe if I could speak to her now, she could confirm what time you arrived home."

"That won't be possible right now. Besides, I only came home to change, then went straight back out again." He dragged one hand through his wet hair. "I went to Valerie's memorial service. Plenty of people could give me an alibi. Enough of them gave me the evil eye."

"And after the memorial service?"

"Some of us went for a few drinks. A very depressing night all round." A twisted smile, more pain than amusement. "The high point was some crazy bitch tipping a jug of beer over one of the doctors. That ended the party, so I came home. Ten . . . ten thirty."

"Can your wife verify when you got home?"

"No. I dozed off on the sofa for fuck knows how long." He gave a strangled laugh. "Here's an unbeatable alibi. Check the triple O calls. Rachel tried to kill herself." He brushed his hand across his eyes. "Nearly succeeded because I passed out on the sofa drunk after my lover's wake. Satisfied?"

Nick remembered the fragile woman who'd retreated from their questions on Wednesday, only one day before her suicide attempt. Had their interview tipped her over?

He struggled for the right words. "I'm sorry to hear about your wife. She must've been in a lot of emotional pain."

"Spare me the psychobabble. You can't imagine the pain she's endured."

"Did you stay with her the rest of Thursday night?"

"I stayed until they stabilised her in ICU, then I came home. Alone."

"Any detours? Anywhere near Northbridge?"

Martin slammed his glass down on the granite bench. "I've got a dead girlfriend and a wife who wants to kill herself, and you think I was out picking up women? Who the fuck do you think I am?"

Why mention picking up women? "No alibi for the rest of that night?"

"No. Didn't realise I needed one."

He removed the photo of Paulette Matthews from his folder and placed it on the bench. "Do you know this woman?"

Martin glanced at it, then checked the time on the microwave. "No. I have to get back to my wife."

"Take a proper look."

"No idea who she is."

"She's missing. Since Thursday night."

"And I'm the go-to guy for missing women now. A person of interest. What's your evidence?"

"Relax. We're talking to lots of people."

"Why is her disappearance connected with Valerie's murder?"

"It isn't. They're two separate cases, but Perth is a relatively small place. We're looking for any common ground."

"Knowing my luck lately, I probably went to school with her brother." Martin sighed. "Is that all?"

"One more photo." He handed over a fax of Carmela Luciano's photo. "What about this woman?"

Martin examined it for a few moments, then shook his head. "No. Is she missing too?"

"Dead. Someone buried her in Kings Park."

"Did the same bastard kill Valerie? What's the connection?"

"That's what we're investigating."

"And you wouldn't tell me, anyway. Can I visit my wife in hospital now?"

"Sure, thanks for your time."

Nick left, wondering how best to tell his boss about Rachel's suicide attempt. Would a text message do? Carrier pigeon would be safer.

Julia thumped the door again, bruising her knuckles. The only response came from the townhouse next door. A haggard woman leant out her front door and cursed her for waking the baby. So instead, she pressed the buzzer and held it down until Leon answered the door.

"Keep your hair on. I was in the shower." He adjusted the towel around his hips.

She jabbed the wreath at his chiselled abs. "Where's your psycho girlfriend?"

"Candi's out." He scanned the street. "Don't want to flash the neighbours. Better come in."

She followed his well-muscled back down a narrow hallway and into a lounge room that doubled as a gym.

"Candi? Oh, that's just perfect." She dodged dumbbells and other torture instruments on the floor. "I bet she dots the 'i' with a heart."

He grinned. "Of course. It's short for Candida, but she hates anyone calling her that."

"Where can I find Miss Fungal Disease?"

"No way." He dropped onto the sofa, dislodging his towel. "She'll kill me."

She grabbed Leon's mobile from the side-table and snapped a photo of him in all his glory. "Why don't I send her this photo and ask her to join us here for a threesome?"

He leapt off the sofa and snatched the phone back. "Don't you dare."

A key turned in the front door. Leon paled, snatched the towel from the floor and ran out of the room. She followed him into the hallway. He raced up the stairs, away from danger.

"I should be grateful one of you still has clothes on," Candi said, her voice quiet and cold. She dropped her bags of groceries on the floor. "What are you doing in my house?"

Julia held the wreath like a shield. "Oh, grow up, Candida. I interrupted his shower. I came here to see you."

Candi snarled. "You've got shit taste in flowers."

"Did you send them to me?"

"Why would I send you a funeral wreath?" She frowned a tiny I-don't-want-to-get-wrinkles frown.

Dressed in a pair of skimpy shorts, Leon crept down the stairs. "Is it safe to come out now?"

Julia ignored him. "That's rich coming from someone who sent me a parcel of dog poo. Why did you spike my drink on Thursday night?"

"No way," Candi said. "You were pretty drunk. I saw you knocking back way more than the recommended daily limit."

Leon patted his flat stomach. "Candi's a dietician. Alcohol's dead calories."

"No wonder you passed out on me," Julia said to him with just a hint of malice. "Was that why you came to see me on Monday night, too? For the booze?"

Candi gasped. She opened and shut her mouth like a gobsmacked goldfish.

"Sorry, babe." Leon dropped his voice to a soothing rumble. "It was only one drink. I did an extra half hour of weights on Tuesday."

Candi glared at him. Alcohol more threatening to their relationship than infidelity? Lucky for Leon.

"Forget his shortcomings." She dragged Candi into the lounge room and sat her on the black leather sofa. "What about the benzoes you dumped in my gin and tonic?"

"Benzoes?" Candi grimaced. "I don't even know what they are."

"Benzodiazepines are a type of sleeping tablet." She spoke calmly and clearly, as if explaining a diagnosis to a patient. "My drink was spiked. That's why I collapsed in the car park. I have the blood results to prove it. If you don't own up and apologise now, I'm taking this to the police."

Leon rushed to Candi's side and draped his arm around her shoulder.

"I swear I didn't do it." Candi gazed up at him with a Bambi-in-the-headlights expression. "I don't have any drugs in the house, do I? Nothing unnatural at all."

Apart from the hair dye. Nothing natural about that shade of blonde.

"That's true, babe." Leon brushed a strand of platinum blonde hair off Candi's forehead. He frowned at Julia as if he had read her mind. "She won't even let me take an aspirin. Search the house if you don't believe us."

If it wasn't Candi . . .

Icy fingers tickled Julia's spine. Who'd spiked her drink just before another woman disappeared? Who'd left a funeral wreath on her doormat? A funeral wreath with a "wish you were here" note.

Leon's face swam in and out of focus. She lurched towards the leather sofa; her legs were too weak to support the dead weight of her suspicions.

Was she the killer's next target?

CHAPTER TWENTY-FOUR

BACK AT HOME LATE Saturday afternoon, Julia paced the hallway and turned Nick's business card over and over. He'd told her to call anytime, but she didn't want to distract him when another woman was missing. Or dead.

Finally, she rang. When he said he was nearby, she invited him over.

Oscar rubbed his head over her bare foot. It tickled, sending goosebumps up her leg. She scooped up the cat. He must have been feeling neglected, as he didn't wriggle and squirm like he usually did. She carried him into the lounge room, then sprawled on the sofa with Oscar purring on her belly.

After a few minutes of feline bliss, he growled. The doorbell rang. His early warning system never failed.

She scratched behind his ears. "Sorry, puss."

He jumped to the floor and stalked towards the kitchen. Another quick burst on the doorbell made her jump. Her nerves weren't what they used to be.

When she opened the door, Nick held up a red manila folder. "A couple of photos to show you. What's up?"

"Let's start with the photos." She led him into the lounge room. Once settled on the sofa, she examined the first photo. Paulette

Matthews. A total stranger. Should she be disappointed or relieved? "Never seen her before."

"A long shot." Nick sat next to her, his jean-clad legs thrust out in front. "She was last seen late Thursday night. No contact with her family. No calls on her mobile. Bank account untouched."

"Bugger." The carriage clock on the mantelpiece ticked the seconds away, seconds that poor woman might not survive. "I have to help. What if I check Valerie's place for any connection with her?"

"Already doing that. Every scrap of paper, every email, every diary entry is being scrutinised." He handed her a faxed image. "What about Carmela Luciano?"

She studied the woman's face. "Sorry, another blank. She's not on the hospital computer system. I hate the thought of a killer hunting his victims in my hospital. Any luck with the security videos?"

"Nothing yet." He slid the photos back into the folder and dropped it on the coffee table. "So, have you remembered something else about Valerie?"

"No. Someone spiked my drink at Valerie's wake."

Nick turned towards her, his gaze intense. "Why didn't you report this straight away?"

"It didn't occur to me that I'd been drugged until the next morning, so I tested myself at the hospital lab. I got the result today."

"And?"

"Benzodiazepines, a type of—"

"Sedative." Nick rubbed the scar on his forehead. "If you'd reported it, we'd have a chain of custody on the lab specimens. What happened?"

"I dashed to the loo, and the barman left my drink on the bar. My first thought was Candi, but I've ruled her out."

"Candi?"

"Leon's fiancée. She misinterpreted our relationship. Total health nut. Wouldn't touch a drug if her life depended on it."

"Anyone else acting strangely?"

"Strange is normal for that lot. The bar was packed. Could've been anyone."

"Let's make this official. You can make a formal statement later." He pulled out his notebook. "Who was there?"

"I've got a list of everyone I invited to the memorial service. Quicker if I cross off the ones who didn't come to the pub afterwards." She could print another copy after he left. "Don't you have enough work to do?"

"You've poked around in a homicide investigation despite my warnings." He cast a pointed glance at her. "If the killer thinks you know too much, he could've spiked your drink to shut you up for a while. Or forever."

"Why would the killer risk drugging me in a crowded room? Everything else, he's done in the dark. Alone. I bet it was some sad bastard's idea of a joke."

"An unconscious woman is never a joke. Where's your list? I'll take it with me."

She stood up. "Kitchen."

He followed. She scrabbled through a pile of papers on her kitchen table.

"For Valerie?" He gestured at the wreath.

"Another sick joke." At last, she found her list and grabbed a pen to cross out irrelevant names.

"Strange joke. You either need new friends or round-the-clock protection." He pulled a latex glove from his back pocket, snapped it on, then examined the wreath. "Any card? What about the delivery?"

"I found it on my doormat when I got home from work this morning." She slid the sympathy card across the table. "It's only a bunch of flowers. I'm not a victim-in-waiting." Shame her hand tremor made her bravado less than convincing.

"Sure about that?" He reached into his other pocket, then slapped a pair of handcuffs on the table.

She laughed. A verging-on-hysteria cackle rather than the sexy chuckle she'd intended. "I wish Valerie was here to see this."

"I should lock you up. Protective custody wouldn't kill you."

"It's only flowers."

"A wreath with a creepy message delivered to your home, a spiked drink, slashed tyres, text messages from a murdered friend's phone. Anything else I need to know?"

"You were meant to reassure me, not feed my paranoia. I'll hide under the bed tonight."

"Hiding under someone else's bed would be safer," he said. "Why don't you stay somewhere else until this is sorted?"

"Is anywhere safe?" She stared at the list in front of her, crossed out a few names, and handed him the sheet of paper. "If I invited Valerie's killer to her memorial service, they'll be the one needing protective custody."

Nick checked the time. "Too late for florists, but I could visit the pub to see about security cameras."

Great. She pictured herself sprawled on the ground and soaked in beer. "If you need anyone identified, let me know."

Nick slid the sympathy card into an evidence bag. "I can't promise it'll be high on their priority list, but I'll give the wreath and the card to forensics."

"Smells better than their usual exhibits, I imagine."

"Now, what about your security? Alarm system with a panic button?"

"Yes, but not monitored." She watched him shake his head. "I'll make an appointment on Monday."

"Window locks? Deadlock on your doors? Or do I need to get my locksmith out this afternoon?"

"Thanks, but I had all that done after a break-in a few months ago. You have your own locksmith?"

"Kick enough doors in, you need one on speed-dial. Don't try to distract me. What about this break-in?"

"What can I say? I'm a one-woman crime wave. Someone smashed the glass in the back door and let themself in while I was at a work dinner."

She shuddered, remembering that ice-cold feeling when she'd seen the open back door and heard movement in the kitchen, the relief when Oscar raced towards her. If there'd been a stranger still in the house, he wouldn't have been so relaxed. Months later, her spidey senses still prickled the back of her neck if she walked past an open curtain at night.

"What happened?"

"I reported it, but the mystery remains unsolved. No usable fingerprints. Nothing stolen. My underwear drawer was . . . re-arranged."

Nick tensed. "Any DNA evidence?"

"The crime scene guys used their magic light. All clear for bodily fluids, but who knew what really happened? Everything felt unclean, so I threw all my underwear out and prescribed myself a shopping frenzy."

She'd also barricaded the doors every night for a few weeks. Something she planned to do as soon as Nick left.

"I'll check the crime report. Do you suspect anyone for the break-in or any of the other incidents?"

"The break-in was most likely kids mucking around. School holidays. As for the rest, I don't know who to trust."

"Good. Take your own advice. Trust no one, even at work. Especially at work." He crossed the kitchen, then jiggled the window lock.

She followed Nick around while he assessed her home security. Locks to slow an intruder down. Alarms to draw attention. What else could she do? Attack dogs and steel bars and razor wire might keep an intruder at bay, but she'd have to go outside sometime.

And none of those security measures would've helped Valerie.

Chapter Twenty-Five

On Sunday morning, Julia took advantage of a cool change to catch up with her household chores. Anything to give herself the illusion of control after a restless night plagued by nightmares and threatening shadows. She'd attacked the garden early. No more branches scratching at her windows in the middle of the night. Savage pruning demolished the scrubby grevilleas along the side of the house. The bushes outside the lounge room window had been large enough to hide any lurking psychopath.

Inside, she'd dusted and vacuumed and gassed herself with bleach fumes while cleaning the bathroom. She still had a bottle of Exit Mould in her hand when the doorbell rang.

She eased towards the bathroom door. Another burst on the bell. Impatient bugger. Please let it be someone flogging roof repairs or raffle tickets. She glanced around the doorframe and tried to work out who was so eager to disturb her Sunday morning. A lone male, no clipboard. Too much distortion from the leadlight glass to recognise her visitor.

He thumped the doorframe again. He must've seen her head poke into the hallway. The security screen was locked. Her across-the-road neighbour fired up his electric lawnmower. She could scream louder than that and she was armed with a deadly spray bottle. Toughen up, Julia.

She strode down the hallway and wrenched open the front door.

Martin stared at her through the security mesh, his usually immaculate hair spiked on one side, squished flat on the other. A crumpled and torn linen shirt added to his air of disarray. Blood-shot eyes, a man on the edge of exhaustion.

"I need your help." His voice cracked.

She reached for the security screen lock, then stopped with her hand in mid-air. Did she trust him enough to invite him inside? She wanted to, but he had been nearby at the wake and could've spiked her drink. Her conversation with Simon had left her uneasy about him. As if he'd read her mind, he stepped away from the door and leant against a veranda post.

Exit Mould at the ready, she unlocked the security screen and joined him outside.

"Too many fumes indoors." She sat on the edge of the veranda, the sun warm on her legs.

Martin sprawled on the lawn in front of her, looking harmless. He nodded at the spray bottle. "Thought you were going to shoot me."

"Best way to get rid of door-to-door salesmen. Look busy and if that doesn't work, squirt them." She put the bottle down beside her, within reach if needed. "What's wrong?"

He groaned. "What's right would be quicker. You know about Rachel's overdose? I guess it's all round the hospital by now."

"I saw she was in ICU on Friday. I'm so sorry." Did he blame her for confronting Rachel? She must bear some responsibility for driving the poor woman to despair. "Why did she do it?"

He rolled onto his back and blew out a deep breath. One arm covered his eyes, maybe to block out the sun. "No suicide note. She's refusing to talk, practically catatonic. Once she woke up and her heart rhythm stabilised, they moved her out of ICU, down to the psych ward."

"Now she's medically fit, psych sounds like the best place for her."

He jerked upright to a sitting position. "That's why I'm here. I don't think she is medically fit, but they won't let me close enough to examine her. I'm interfering with their therapeutic milieu or some such crap."

"What's wrong with her?"

"She's really flushed, like she's febrile, but they haven't even taken her temperature."

"Any other signs? Does she still have an IV line?" Could it be VRSA? Brad had already been discharged from ICU before her admission. All the other patients and staff in ICU had clear swabs.

"No, they took all the lines out before the transfer. Her arms and the central line site look okay from the doorway. She's breathing fast, looks confused, but how can I be sure when she's not talking?"

"Any cough?"

"Not that I noticed."

"When she overdosed, you were the one who found her?"

He nodded. "Unconscious. I don't know how long she'd been out."

Rachel could've vomited while heavily sedated, then inhaled stomach contents into her lungs. They'd had her on a ventilator in ICU and would've done regular chest X-rays to rule out pneumonia and check the position of her various lines. Infection could easily develop after aspiration and might take time to declare itself.

"Aspiration pneumonia would fit, but it's a long distance, second-hand diagnosis." She should examine Rachel. "I'd see her now, but I'm not her favourite person. Let me call the duty medical registrar and ask them to assess her today. Start her on antibiotics, maybe shift her to a medical ward where she can be monitored more closely. I'll check on her tomorrow."

Martin flopped back on the lawn. "Thank you. They wouldn't listen to me. Surgery and psychiatry don't mix."

"When did you last have a good night's sleep?"

"The night Valerie disappeared." He wiped one hand across his eyes. "I miss her." His voice was so quiet, she almost didn't hear him.

"So do I." How could she suspect him of murdering Valerie? But how could she not? "Did you notice anything suspicious on Thursday night?"

"Apart from you drowning in beer and my wife trying to kill herself?" A burst of harsh laughter.

"Someone spiked my gin and tonic." She kept her gaze locked on his face.

His mouth tightened a fraction. "Want me to confess?"

"Only if you did it."

"Still a bloody suspect." He jumped to his feet. "Just call the med reg to look after my wife." He bolted.

CHAPTER TWENTY-SIX

EARLY MONDAY MORNING, JULIA and Gabriel attacked the VRSA contact lists again. Her boss had returned from his holiday, so she'd left a note with his secretary for an urgent meeting. She wanted to present him with as complete a list as possible. Most staff members had provided their swabs and been cleared of carrying VRSA. A few remained outstanding, mostly people on leave or agency nurses who had moved on to other placements. Some lab tests weren't finished. Somewhere amongst that lot, the carrier lurked. She hoped.

"This is weird." She showed Gabriel a completed lab report, then pointed to the computer screen. "Martin McDougall already has a clear set of swabs, so why is there a second set from him?"

"I don't remember asking for any repeats." Gabriel shuffled through his list of names. "No comments about it here."

"Maybe there was a problem with his first set, so the lab asked for a repeat." She checked the private comment section on the computer, where the lab staff entered their test results and anything relevant to each specimen. "Collected Friday morning, some delay setting it up. No problem mentioned. Who wrote the request form?" She hit a few more keys and called up an image of the second request form. "Definitely not my writing. Can't decipher the signature. Is it yours?"

"Not me. Typical doctor scribble."

She printed a copy. "I wonder if Martin ordered it. He's been distracted with good reason. Friday must've been a shocker. I have to see his wife today, an informal consult for possible aspiration pneumonia. I'll ask him about the extra swabs later. Who are you missing?"

"I need one more nurse from the orthopaedic ward." Gabriel tapped a filled-in request form. "She's due back from leave tomorrow."

"Right, so apart from a few orderlies and some housekeeping staff, we have two doctors and three nurses with no recorded specimens. Several others need their final culture reports. Anyone else?"

"Nope."

"I'll chase the doctors if you track down the nurses. Deal?"

"Fine with me. Need a hand with Simon?" Gabriel fluttered his eyelashes.

"Bloody Simon. He promised me he'd drop his swabs in last Friday. I should've jammed a swab up his nose when I had the chance." She picked up the phone. "I'll see when he's on duty next."

After a quick conversation with the Anaesthetics Department secretary, she slammed the phone down.

"No luck?"

"Bugger. He's rostered off-duty until Thursday, then he's on nights. We won't get his swabs finished before the end of the week."

"I'm off to hunt nurses." Gabriel headed to the door. "Call me gutless, but I'd rather hide on the wards than face your boss with the bad news."

"Gee, thanks for your support. You haven't even met him yet." She glanced at her watch. "Better catch him before his coffee break. I don't want him to hear about it from one of his mates first."

As if the VRSA outbreak was her only problem.

Ten minutes later, Julia paced outside the Head of Department's office, waiting for her boss, Dr Branford, to get off the phone. Did she have time to sneak off to check on the outstanding culture reports? So much for her high-priority meeting. She'd barely opened her mouth before he took another phone call and shooed her out of the room.

At last, he put the phone down. "Get back in here. That was the Medical Superintendent. I go away for two weeks and the hospital ends up knee-deep in VRSA. VRSA? Did I hear that right?"

His face glowed red. An artery pulsed at his temple. Too fast. She could almost see his blood pressure rising. Tempting as it was to let his head explode, she should try to calm him down.

She sat on the grey chair in front of his grey desk with its pristine surface unmarred by any sign of work. "Yes, it is a VRSA outbreak, but I think we have it under control now."

"You think? I should bloody well hope so. Has the reference lab confirmed this so-called VRSA?"

"Yes, I've had a preliminary report. They're still typing and sequencing the bug." So far, so good.

"Do you have a list of positives with you?" When she nodded, he thrust out his hand. "Let's have a look."

"Just a few results pending." She handed him the folder. Her mouth dried.

He flicked through the pages, his gaze straying to his watch. "Give me the short version. I'll read it later." He put the report down, straightened the paper parallel to the edge of his desk.

She stifled a smile. Must be coffee time. "Only two wards are involved—general surgical and orthopaedic. We've found thirteen patients who are colonised with positive nasal swabs, but no symptoms of infection. There have been only two actual infections, one appendix and one total knee replacement. No staff carriers have been identified so far."

"What's this I hear about one of the patients dying?"

"Yes, Edith Powell, the woman with the infected knee replacement. She's a coroner's case, a post-op death. Preliminary autopsy report gave massive pulmonary embolus as the cause of death."

Another glance at her report. "I see some staff members haven't been tested yet. Make sure they get swabbed as soon as possible. I want no more cases, you hear me?"

"Yes, of course. Gabriel, the new Infection Control Nurse, is following up on the nurses right now. I have two doctors to go, both off-duty. I'll visit them at home if I have to."

"Whatever it takes." He slid her report into the top drawer of his desk. "Do we have any idea how this started? The source?"

"Not yet. The original patient had no risk factors for any hospital-acquired infection, let alone VRSA. No interstate or international contacts."

"It would help our publication if we identified the source of the outbreak." He pushed his chair back from the desk and stood.

"Our publication?" She knew who'd be doing all the work on that, but it'd certainly help her job prospects.

"Yes, this could be a seminal paper, quoted for years to come." He walked to the door. "Show me the first draft when you're ready. Now find the carrier and tie up all the loose ends for the hospital's sake . . . and yours."

Great. Saved by his caffeine addiction. She backed out of his room before he could add anything else, then raced to her office.

Gabriel popped in the moment she sat down. "I waited for you. Is it safe? Have we still got jobs?"

"Cross your fingers. So long as we get the last swabs done, find the carrier and prevent any more cases. Oh, and I have to whip up a seminal journal article in my spare time."

"Easy peasy." He wiped his brow in mock relief.

She scanned her overflowing in-tray. "I've got a shitload of work carried over from last week and Rachel MacDougall to check on. I'll get this morning's urgent stuff out of the way first."

She waved Gabriel out and grabbed the request form from the top of the pile. A positive blood culture in an eighty-year-old woman in one of the medical wards. Gram-negative sepsis, probably from a urinary tract infection, potentially fatal. Relieved it wasn't another VRSA, she almost cheered. She reached for the phone.

Death doesn't care about busy timetables.

———◆———

Late Monday morning, Indira shaded her eyes with one hand and examined the limestone archway that towered overhead, the gateway to the Fremantle Prison Museum. The former prison had been converted to a tourist attraction several years ago. Once home to thugs and rapists and murderers, the site was now a tourist attraction where visitors walked the deserted cell blocks and explored the dark labyrinth of manmade tunnels beneath the buildings.

What a disturbing venue to display a corpse.

She lowered her gaze and walked across the bitumen to the temporary screens in the far corner. Instead of busloads of sightseers, the car park teemed with police officers and forensic investigators.

Cleaners had found the body when they arrived early to prepare for the day's crowds. The Fremantle detectives had a headstart on the investigation. They'd contacted her during her regular Monday morning meeting with her colleagues and the coroner. On hearing the nature of the victim's injuries, she'd asked them to notify the Major Crime Squad. Too many similarities with the Valerie Cavanaugh case.

Mutilated and naked, the dead woman stared at the cloudless sky. Paulette Matthews, the horror movie version of the family photograph that she'd seen on the evening news. Blowflies crawled over her many wounds, feeding on her, laying their eggs. Indira placed her medical equipment case on the ground nearby. After donning gloves, she squatted beside the woman and waved the flies away. A futile gesture. They buzzed and hovered a short distance away, only to return seconds later with added fervour.

Someone cast a shadow over the body.

"Always a pleasure, doc. You've found our missing woman, Paulette Matthews."

She recognised the voice and straightened up. George Jaworski beamed at her, but his eyes revealed a deep weariness. Nick Randall stood beside him.

"Good morning, gentlemen."

"Thanks for alerting us," Nick said. "Looks like the same guy."

"Fancies himself a surgeon." George bent over for a closer scrutiny. "Piss artist, if you ask me. Only surface cuts again?"

She walked around to the woman's right-hand side, then crouched down. "Let me see what I can ascertain on preliminary examination."

When she inserted the thermometer into the liver to help determine the time of death, both police officers moved a few steps back. They surveyed the rest of the crime scene, perhaps a pretext to avoid observing her activities. She let their conversation wash over her while she studied the surface wounds.

"Somebody from the hospital next door might've seen something on their way to or from work last night," Nick said.

"Another bloody hospital." George shooed a fly away from his face. "The Fremantle detectives will concentrate on the local area. We'll liaise with the family and look into any connections with the Cavanaugh case."

Nick pointed towards the prison gates. "Creepy spot to visit at night. If we find out when this place closed, that'll give us the earliest time the body could've been dumped."

"Smart thinking, ninety-nine. Ever done one of these tours?"

"Excuse me." Indira interrupted. "If you gentlemen have finished your travelogue, this is something I would like you to see." She pointed to discoloured areas around the victim's wounds. "These wounds appear to be infected. It is possible an infection contributed to her death."

"Will our killer drop dead of the same infection?" Nick asked.

"This is not my area of expertise, but I don't think so. It's most likely a common microorganism from her own skin that infected her wounds."

"Shame," George said. "Good excuse to chat to your doctor friend Julia again, mate." He winked at Nick.

A budding relationship? Interesting.

"Excellent idea," she said. "I'll talk to her too." She stood up and rubbed her lower back. She'd been intending to call Julia to see how she was coping. "I'll know more once I've performed the autopsy, but the pattern of injuries is certainly similar to the Cavanaugh case."

"Thanks, doc. Let us know when you can fit her in, and I'll send my little helper along." George thumped Nick on the back. "Makes sense since he went to the last one."

"Great," Nick said with a less than enthusiastic tone, then he smiled at her. "Not that I won't enjoy your company, doctor."

"And I yours." Should she ask Julia to join them, so she could examine the infection in situ? Best talk to her first.

George moved into a patch of shade. "Right, I'll get onto the husband and arrange formal identification for later on today. Poor bastard."

"Poor kids," Nick said.

"Yeah, imagine explaining why Mum's not coming home." George scrubbed his hands over his cheeks. "Okay, what have we got from the investigation into her disappearance?"

Indira jotted down her preliminary examination notes while the police officers discussed the case. She'd dictate her findings later to include in the autopsy report so she could discreetly listen now to their discussion. If she ever lost interest in the victim's life, she knew it would be time to quit.

"I checked the file this morning," Nick said. "All the women at her girls' night out have been interviewed. A regular event. Lots of cocktails and no holds barred with picking up men."

"Anything from security cameras?"

"We've got her leaving the club on her own, but then she disappears around a corner. Pfft." Nick clicked his fingers. "No bastard with a big knife following her."

"Any link with Valerie Cavanaugh?"

"Nothing so far. I showed her photo around." Nick hesitated. "Julia Sinclair didn't recognise either Paulette or Carmela Luciano, but something's up with her."

"Apart from her name linked to two homicide investigations?"

"She's got a stalker—and, no, it's not me."

Indira interrupted her note-taking. "What's happened to Julia?"

"Someone spiked her G and T at Valerie's wake, slashed her tyres in the hospital car park and delivered a wreath to her home."

"And the text message from her dead friend's phone. Did the tech guys trace it?" George asked.

"Somewhere in or around Perth General Hospital."

"How's she coping?" Indira asked.

"Spooked, but too stubborn to stay somewhere safer." Nick frowned.

She shouldn't be alone. Another murder might persuade her to move. "I'd like to offer her sanctuary in my spare room."

George narrowed his eyes. "Think that's wise, doc?"

"I live on the top floor of an apartment building with excellent security. In my profession, as in yours, unwanted attention from someone under investigation can be deadly."

Memories swamped her. Would she ever forget the fear, that moment of sheer, animal panic? Her back still ached where the knife had penetrated. The scar was like a knotted rope under her fingers when she tried to massage away the pain.

"You'd invite a murder suspect into your home?" George asked.

"Seriously, boss?" Nick shook his head. "Haven't we cleared her?"

"Some criminals insinuate themselves into investigations. Where's your evidence for this stalker? What if she's protecting an accomplice?"

"Stop this nonsense." Her shout startled even herself. She was aware of heads swivelling towards her. A deep breath before she continued in a quieter voice. "I'll invite her to stay with me. I know Julia. She's not a murderer."

Chapter Twenty-Seven

"What have I ever done to deserve this?" Julia rubbed her hand across her eyes. Maybe she'd imagined it. She re-read the lab result on her computer screen. Nope, still there. "Fuck. Gabriel?"

He poked his head around her office doorway. "Was that an invitation to come in or an indecent proposal?"

"If it was an indecent proposal, I'd have said please. Consider it a scream for help." She turned the screen around. "Just after I finish telling the boss the outbreak is under control, we've got another one."

"Yikes."

She checked the patient's location on the current ward census. "A maternity patient. The obstetrics ward is in a separate wing."

She wrote down the room number and flicked back to the patient's lab results. They had admitted the woman last week. She'd had blood cross-matched on admission. Her next lab test was a post-operative haemoglobin level, followed three days later by a septic screen with urine culture, a swab from a caesarean section wound and the set of blood cultures.

"How'd she catch the bug on the maternity ward? Do they use the same operating theatres?" Gabriel asked.

"No, they have their own theatres next door to the birth suites, so they're close to the neonatal unit and the paediatric ward." She glanced at her watch. "Almost three. If we go now, we might catch the nurses' handover between shifts."

"Get the most bang for our buck with double the number of nurses at one time. I'll grab my trusty notebook, a bag of swabs and a fresh request pad."

"And I'll let the lab know where we're going—right after I ask them why the hell they didn't tell me this earlier."

She printed a copy of the patient's request form, then strode into the lab, ready for battle.

Lorena looked up from her microscope. "Oh, there you are. Finally got off the phone?"

"About this new VRSA on the maternity ward?"

"You found it, then." Lorena swivelled back to her microscope to review some more slides.

Julia clenched her hands, her nails digging into her palms. If she were ever to punch someone, it'd be Lorena. No contest. That passive-aggressive nonsense really got on her tits sometimes. She grabbed the back of Lorena's chair, dragged it away from the bench, then spun her around.

"You could've handed me the form while I was on the phone. The outbreak spreading to another ward didn't seem important to you?"

"Maybe if you spent more time in the lab instead of on the phone, you'd have noticed how busy we are in here." Lorena scowled at Julia, then her gaze shifted to one side and her expression morphed to sickly sweet. "Hello, Dr Branford, so nice to have you back again. How was your trip? Fiji, wasn't it?"

Julia summoned a smile and turned. How much had he heard? She replayed the conversation in her head. Nothing too inflammatory from what she could remember.

"Yes, my wife loves Fiji. Very relaxing." Dr Branford glanced down at the request form in Julia's hand. "I heard raised voices. Is there a problem I should know about, Dr Sinclair?"

"We were discussing the urgency of this case—a new patient with VRSA, a positive blood culture." Relax, another deep breath. Don't bite. "She's on the maternity ward. Looks like an infected C-section wound."

"You said you had this outbreak under control." His voice was controlled, scary-quiet.

"It was."

"A new case magically appears on another ward in a completely different building." His cheeks reddened as his voice grew louder. "Does that sound like it's under control?"

"No."

"Is that all you have to say for yourself?"

"Let's discuss this in private." She kept her voice low and her tone calm. Hard to do with her teeth gritted.

"Yes, let these good people get back to work. We'll finish this in my office." He spun around and strode out of the lab.

Julia detoured via Gabriel's room. "Slight delay while I have my attitude adjusted in the boss's office."

"Ouch. Sounds painful." Gabriel grimaced. "Scream if you need rescuing."

She rushed down the hallway to the administrative area, all plush carpet and soft lighting rather than the bleach and bacteria that dominated the laboratory. Dr Branford waited for her outside his office. He let her enter first, then shut the door behind them. No witnesses. Not a good sign.

He sat in his black leather chair and offered her the chair opposite. With his fingers steepled under his chin, he watched her in disconcerting silence. She preferred it when he shouted. What was he thinking? Whether he could manage the rest of the year without her services?

"The Head of Biochemistry had a quiet word with me a short while ago," he said after a lengthy delay.

Goodbye, promotion. "I can explain—"

He raised one hand. "Let me finish. He mentioned the toxicology screen result and told me about your response. I wish you'd left this allegation to the police, not taken it into your own hands. Not to mention abusing laboratory resources."

"Sorry. I meant to tell you earlier."

"I haven't finished yet. I hadn't realised the murdered nurse was such a good friend of yours. You've been under a lot of pressure for the past fortnight. This must be very difficult for you."

Julia's eyes burned. She blinked and swallowed hard, refusing to cry in his presence. Why did he have to be nice to her now? She deserved punishment, not sympathy. Get the shouting over with and let her get back to work.

"Add an outbreak, and no wonder your judgement has been clouded." He reached for the request form. "I'll see that patient. I want you to take another toxicology screen, then go home. No patient contact until I see a clear tox screen result."

She kept hold of the form. "What about VRSA screening the maternity ward?"

"I'm sure the new Infection Control Nurse has had plenty of practice lately. He can ask me if he has any questions." He still had his hand out for the form. "This is not a negotiation. Let me know if you need more time off. Otherwise, I'll see you in the lab tomorrow morning."

She gave him the form and left his office. Great job, Julia. If he didn't trust her to see one patient, how could she hope to get the Senior Registrar post? Her career prospects spiralled down the drain.

◆

Back in her office, after having her blood collected, Julia shut down her computer and turned off her pager, then dropped in on Gabriel.

"Dr Branford will see that new VRSA case. You're to go ahead with screening. Call him if you have any problems." She dredged up a fake smile. "I'm going home early."

"Is that about the . . . um, I heard some gossip . . ." His face flushed scarlet.

Oh, no. "If this is about the strip poker in the doctors' lounge tomorrow night, you're not invited."

His eyes brightened. "Strip poker? Seriously?"

"Of course not. What have you heard about me now?"

"A doctor's positive drug screen result was the hot topic of conversation at morning tea. They didn't mention a name, but I heard enough to work it out."

"So much for patient confidentiality. Who blabbed?" Luckily, the boss already knew.

"Sorry. I had my back to them and I don't know their names, anyway. Do you want me to find out?"

"Don't bother. When my homicidal impulse passes sometime next year, I'll take it up with the Chief Scientist in Biochemistry."

"Talking about Valerie's death might help more than sleeping pills . . ."

What an idiot. She'd created trouble by testing her blood at work. At the risk of making him flap even more, she'd have to tell him. Drug-related rumours, even about something as innocuous as sedatives, could kill her career.

"I didn't choose to take those sedatives. Someone spiked my gin and tonic on Thursday night."

His eyes widened. "You're shitting me. I just thought you were really, really drunk. Who do you think did it? Have you told your detective? Has he arrested anybody?"

"Calm down. I only told you so you'd leave the poor drug-addicted Julia angle alone. I don't know who did it. Neither does Detective Randall, who is not my detective. Did you see anyone acting suspiciously near the bar?"

"No." Gabriel sighed. "My big chance to be the hero and I completely missed it. Story of my life."

"I should escape before the boss sends security to throw me out." She picked up her bag. "The whole lab probably thinks I'm a drug addict by now."

"You've had a tough couple of weeks. I'm sure they'll understand when the truth comes out."

"Some people will never understand. Doctors and drugs? That nagging doubt will always follow me. Did she? Didn't she? Maybe I should move interstate." Would running away be such a bad idea?

"You're not a quitter."

"You don't know me."

She'd fucked everything up. Couldn't even protect her own sister. Valerie's friendship and her job had been the only commitments she'd ever stuck with. The pathetic truth weighed her down. She dropped back into the chair, engulfed by crushing, aching, soul-destroying grief.

Everything she loved, she'd lost.

"I'll give you a lift home."

"It's broad daylight. If I walk fast, I'll be home in ten minutes."

"You'll fry. It's forty million degrees out there. Let me call maternity to get that list started, then I'll escort you home. I've got a black belt in origami, or is it macramé? Always get those two mixed up." He pointed to the chair. "Stay."

"You're giving me obedience training now?"

"It's for your own protection."

"Everywhere I turn, I've got men telling me what to do. Have we time-warped back a couple of centuries?"

He hesitated. "I'm worried about you. What if you get yourself kidnapped or killed?"

"Stop fussing. It drives me crazy." Crazy? Bugger. She'd forgotten Rachel. If she snuck onto the medical ward, it'd be just her luck to bump into her boss. "Five minutes."

She dragged Gabriel's keyboard over to check Rachel's results. General medical ward, white count lower compared to Sunday's level, one set of blood cultures still negative. No other microbiology specimens. A quick call to the medical registrar confirmed Rachel was improving on the broad-spectrum antibiotics she'd recommended. Martin had spent the morning by her bedside, but left to do an afternoon theatre list.

Time to go home. If she wanted to keep her job, what else could she do?

———◦———

Somehow, Julia survived the drive home without demanding to go back to the hospital. She shouldn't have given in so easily. Gabriel checked around the house before he let her unlock the front door. He inspected inside while she waited on the front veranda. Her temper sparked. How dare some psychotic stalker turn her into a feeble, man-dependent scaredy cat?

No broken windows, no mystery presents, no funeral wreaths.

Just Oscar, demanding food, starving as always. Somebody still loved her. She forced Gabriel to leave, then picked up her cat and carried him inside. He butted his head against her chin. His purrs vibrated through her chest and shook free some of her tension. She set him down in front of his food bowl, then topped up his supply of cat biscuits.

Gabriel had been right about the temperature outside. What about a long and bubbly soak in the bath? The best place to relax and think. Her heart raced as she remembered her last attempted bath. That text message. An involuntary shudder shattered her bravado.

Bastard.

After kicking off her shoes in the hallway, she checked her answer machine. No messages or missed calls. At last, the nuisance phone calls had stopped, and the reporters had moved on to harass someone else. The timber floor felt cool underfoot, contrasting with the oppressive afternoon heat.

Suck it up, princess. She had to regain control of her life, not quiver with terror at the thought of a bubble bath. There are no monsters under the bed. The doors and windows are locked. It's a stinking hot day. Have a bloody bath.

On her way to the bathroom, she unzipped her skirt. She turned on the taps and glanced at the frosted bathroom window. Nobody could see through it, but she felt as if someone was watching her strip. Don't be ridiculous. She slid the skirt down over her hips and let it drop to the tiles. Five buttons later, her shirt joined it. She unclipped her bra, hesitated, then flung it at the window. Take that, imaginary pervert.

She selected a fragrant bath bomb and dropped it in. Perched on the edge of the bathtub, she swished her hand through the cool water.

The phone rang. She jumped. Her pulse raced. She grabbed a towel and drew it tight around her body. As if that would protect her. Answer it or let the machine pick up? A woman's voice. She turned off the taps, then answered the phone.

Indira spoke. "Unlike you to leave work early, Julia. I'm glad I found you at your home."

"What's happened? Is it about Valerie?" She clutched the towel even tighter.

"I wish to request a favour." A brief pause. "Will you come to an autopsy tomorrow? Please. I know how difficult it will be, but it may help the investigation for Valerie."

Oh, no. "Who's dead? That missing woman?"

"Yes, Paulette Matthews. Her body was discovered today. She suffered similar injuries to Valerie's, but on gross examination, it appears she developed an infection. I need your help."

Similar injuries to Valerie's? Her legs buckled. She slid to the floor. Paulette had been abducted the same night someone spiked her drink. Coincidence or something more sinister?

"It could've been me." Her voice faded to a whisper. "It should've been me."

"Julia, are you still there? Shall I come over?"

"When's the autopsy?" Her voice gained strength.

"Tomorrow afternoon. I'll text you the exact details in the morning."

"I'll be there. Anything to catch this prick."

"One other matter I wish to discuss with you," Indira said, her voice hesitant. "I spoke to Detective Randall earlier today. He mentioned the disturbing incidents you have experienced."

"Did he now?" Couldn't anybody keep a secret?

"Would you like to stay in my spare room? My apartment is spacious and very secure. After all, I'd rather you came to my workplace alive."

"Thanks, but I'm safe enough here. Don't worry about me. See you tomorrow afternoon."

"You're welcome to come to my home anytime. Please consider my offer. I thought I was safe once." Indira ended the call.

Julia hugged her knees to her chest. Attend an autopsy? She'd do anything to find Valerie's killer. A flicker ignited deep in her soul, something dark and primitive and vengeful.

Chapter Twenty-Eight

By mid-morning Tuesday, Julia neared the bottom of her in-tray at work. She had to fight for her job. It was the one part of her life that made sense, the one aspect she could control. She still had to prepare a medical student tutorial and print some journal articles, but order threatened and chaos retreated. It was one advantage of being banned from patient care while she waited for her tox screen result.

How was Gabriel coping with the boss on the maternity ward? Biochemistry better hurry up with her result so she could battle the VRSA outbreak.

A rap on the door interrupted her thoughts.

"Do you want the bad news or the terrible news?" Lorena asked.

"Can I say neither?" No wonder she felt paranoid.

She followed Lorena into the lab.

"I'm not sure how this happened." Lorena looked down at the bench. "We had a set of negative VRSA swabs from him, but now another set has turned up positive."

"Shit. Who?"

"You won't like this."

"Spit it out."

Lorena handed her a request form and gestured at a stack of plates. Martin MacDougall. Had they missed it the first time? Or had he picked it up since then from a patient? Whatever the reason, she had to find Martin. Fast.

Dr Branford should still be on the maternity ward. She couldn't see patients until her tox screen came back clear of all drugs, but he hadn't said anything about not talking to medical staff. Besides, her test result would be negative. It wasn't her fault Biochemistry had problems with one of their analysers and results were delayed.

It would've helped if Martin answered his page or his mobile or left a bread-crumb trail of swooning nurses she could follow. According to the surgical ward clerk, he was operating all morning. When she got to the theatres, she found he'd swapped lists with one of the other surgeons. Of course, Rachel.

She found him in the general medical ward, slumped by his wife's bedside. His usually crisp baby blue shirt was creased and crumpled. Had he slept in it or dragged it unwashed from the dirty laundry basket? Either option was most un-Martin-like. Rachel lay curled up with her back to him. Hard to tell if she was asleep or comatose.

"How's Rachel?" she whispered.

"Sleeping at last. One of her room-mates screamed all night." His face softened as he gazed at his wife. "Thanks for sorting out the med reg and her antibiotics on Sunday. She's much better."

Julia scanned the four-bed room. All beds were occupied. One elderly woman hobbled towards the bathroom. The other two patients dozed. Martin couldn't stay in the ward, not while he carried VRSA. Too risky for Rachel and the others.

She kept her voice low. "Your VRSA swabs are positive. You won't be allowed to operate or see patients until I say so."

His mouth gaped. He stared at her as if she'd sprouted horns. "Are you joking?"

She dropped a piece of paper onto the bed in front of him. "Here's a script for antiseptic body washes and nasal ointment.

You'll have to wear a gown and gloves whenever you visit Rachel. I'll move her to a single room."

"What the hell are you talking about? My swabs came up clear."

"The second set didn't."

Martin frowned. "What second set? I only had one set of swabs collected and they were negative. Somebody cocked it up at your end."

"I'll double-check with the lab, but in the meantime, at least protect your wife."

"This is crazy."

"If you promise to start the decolonisation treatment today, and you put on a gown and gloves, I'll take another set now. Happy?" He rolled his eyes and muttered something under his breath, so she took that as agreement. "Do you have any idea where you might've picked it up?"

"None of my patients have it. I haven't been out of the state for a few years." He brushed a strand of Rachel's hair off her face. "Not since . . . she doesn't like me leaving her alone."

"No interstate or international patients or visitors?"

"Absolutely none."

"What was your involvement with the index case, Brad Delaney?"

"The appendix that ended up in ICU?" When she nodded, he carried on. "Nothing to do with me. Different team."

"You didn't assist in his operation? Examine him pre-op?" Maybe Martin was a heavy shedder, a person who spread more bacteria into the environment than usual. Even a minor contact could have passed on the VRSA.

He dragged his hands through his hair. "This has to be a mistake."

Julia drew the curtain around the bed. "I'll swab you now. You can watch me label it. I'll also collect a set from Rachel." She held her hands up to forestall his objection. "Okay, when she wakes up. When I get back to the lab, I'll ask someone to pull out your original swabs and the ones that came up positive. We'll check the labels on the swabs and the plates. And repeat all the tests. Satisfied?"

"Have I got a choice?" He tilted his head back. "Go on."

While she swabbed Martin, her mind raced. Had one set of his swabs come from someone else? If so, who? They'd have to backtrack and crosscheck all the staff and patient swabs, all the screening plates. Should they start again? She shuddered. What a nightmare. A career-ending nightmare.

On Tuesday afternoon, Nick stared at a dent in the wall above the autopsy table. Had somebody thrown something? And if so, what? He'd take any distraction he could get. If only he could drown out the sound effects and ignore the smell.

"Welcome back," Indira said. "You've been daydreaming, haven't you?"

"Busted. Did I miss something important?"

"I wish to draw your attention to these abscesses scattered throughout the victim's body." She waited until he came closer to the autopsy table. "See this abscess here . . . and here."

They looked like yellowish blobs to Nick, but he took her word for it. "What does that mean?"

She plunged a needle into an abscess and drew thick yellow-brown pus into a syringe. His stomach churned. He stepped back and turned his head away until the nausea eased. Blood he could handle by the bucketload, but pus or vomit? No fucking way.

"The infection from her wounds has spread throughout her body. This must have happened quickly, according to our time frame." She discarded the needle into a yellow plastic box, then squirted the contents of the syringe into a plastic jar with a yellow lid. "I'll get it cultured out of interest. It might be of assistance to you."

"Any way it could lead us to the killer?"

"It's not my area of expertise, so I wouldn't like to comment on that matter. Fortunately, Julia Sinclair should join us shortly."

The cool mortuary air crept over Julia's skin and goose-bumped her arms. Her first autopsy for several years. It smelt like the microbiology lab on a bad day. Bleach with a hint of something rotten. The eye-watering scent of formalin wafted from an open specimen jar containing who-knew-what-bit of Paulette Matthews. She had to acclimatise her brain and lock down her emotions before she dared look at the autopsy table.

"Welcome, Julia. Perfect timing." Indira gestured towards a yellow-topped jar full of pus. "How was your night?"

"I survived."

"My offer of a bed still stands. If Detective Randall and I cannot persuade you, perhaps Paulette Matthews will be more convincing."

Nick stood on the opposite side of the table, his arms crossed, his shoulders slumped as if the yellow paper gown weighed more than he could bear. Despite his faint smile, fatigue showed in his hollowed cheeks and darkened eyes. Had he lost weight since Saturday?

"Any more trouble?" he asked.

Apart from being suspended from patient care? Could be worse. She could've been reported to the Medical Board.

"Nothing new." She grabbed a pair of latex gloves and approached the autopsy table.

Her stomach heaved. Images of Valerie's body marred by the same dreadful injuries filled her mind. Don't think about her. Keep it clinical. Just another patient for an Infectious Diseases consultation.

Indira demonstrated her findings. "See these abscesses under the capsule of the liver, and over here, scattered throughout the right kidney." She drew Julia's attention to a tray on the side-table and pointed to the cut surface of a kidney.

"Certainly looks like a staph infection." Julia turned back to the table, peered closer at the woman's right forearm. "Is that an infected IV site?"

Indira grabbed a magnifying glass to examine the area. "I think you're correct. I've reviewed her medical records. She hasn't undergone any recent procedures, nor is there any history of intravenous drug use. Also, X-rays revealed rib fractures near the sternal edge, similar to injuries one would expect after vigorous cardio-pulmonary resuscitation."

"What's it all mean?" Nick asked from the other side of the table, keeping his distance.

"Bastard's been playing doctor." Julia palpated the arm near the puncture wound, feeling for thrombophlebitis, signs of infection in the vein. Nothing obvious, but then she rarely examined dead patients. "What if the killer inserted an intravenous line, but that got infected and sped up her death?"

"I bet he didn't enjoy having his playtime cut short," Nick said.

"What a cruel thought." Indira shook her head.

"Nothing kind about this killer," Julia said. "If he did CPR, I wonder if he tried to treat the infection first."

"How devious your mind is." Indira's cheek dimpled, a hint of a smile. "I'll send blood for analysis to determine if antibiotics or any other medications were given to her."

"My boss will love you two." Nick wrote in his notebook. "Anything that fits his theory of the killer having a medical background. Any other suggestions?"

"I want to find out what this bug is," Julia said. "I know you have to send your specimens to the forensics lab—chain of custody and all that legal stuff—but I'd really like to steal some of that pus."

When Indira glanced at Nick, he shrugged and said, "Don't see what harm it could do. Any reason you're so interested?"

Julia paused on an ethical knife-edge, wanting to blurt out that Martin was carrying VRSA. If it was the same rare bacteria, that could incriminate him in the murders. Her friend and Valerie's lover, a killer.

"Just curious. There's enough evidence to show you're looking for someone with medical knowledge, capable of inserting intravenous lines and, most likely, with access to intravenous drugs. Do you agree, Indira?"

"Yes. Unfortunately, a medical or nursing background doesn't prevent someone from committing homicide. It simply gives someone so inclined a more effective skill set."

Julia avoided the magnetic pull of Nick's gaze and picked up a needle and syringe to aspirate some of the pus into another specimen jar. If she cultured it straight onto a VRSA screening plate, she'd have preliminary evidence within one to two days. Confirming VRSA would throw suspicion squarely on hospital staff and could condemn Martin. For once, she hoped her diagnosis was wrong.

"Is there something you're not telling me?" Nick asked.

His voice was so soft and dangerous, she almost said yes.

"Sorry, I'm preoccupied with an outbreak at the hospital. Plenty more work to do before I quit for the day." Barely a lie at all. She glanced over at him. Did he believe her?

"Be careful."

"Don't worry." She held up the specimen jar. "I'll set this up tonight and let you know if I find anything useful. It'll take a day or two."

"Thanks for assisting me with my enquiries." Nick smiled—a glacier-melting smile that made her want to tell him everything.

She resisted the temptation. Martin had enough problems, and she couldn't imagine him killing anyone.

"Anything to help Valerie." She turned to Indira. "Call me if your tests find any antibiotics."

"Please reconsider my offer of sanctuary. I'd prefer to have your ongoing friendship and assistance than to see you . . . well, like this." Indira gestured at Paulette Matthews' corpse. "Don't you think I have enough work?"

"Interesting technique, Indira. Guilt me into hiding. If this psycho is fixated on me, why not use me as bait?"

Nick rubbed the scar over his eyebrow. "Too risky."

"The alarm guy gave me a quote on monitoring, including a personal panic button. They're setting it up tomorrow morning. I can explain the situation, ask them to call the local police if the alarm goes off."

"I applaud you for improving your home security," Indira said, "but this is madness, Julia. What if you're attacked outside your home?"

"Valerie was abducted from the hospital," Nick said. "Their security sucks. Too many dead spots. Invisible bait can't be protected."

"Stick a tracker on me. Don't mobile phones have GPS?"

"Not going to happen. I should handcuff you to this autopsy table until you see sense."

"Heaven help your girlfriend if you whip out your handcuffs at the first sign of conflict."

He flinched as if she'd slapped him. "If I'd handcuffed her to the hospital bed, she would've survived her doctor's negligence."

His face shuttered, he turned back to the autopsy table.

Oh, hell. What had she said?

Indira broke the icy silence. "Thank you for your assistance, Julia. We must all get back to work now."

Chapter Twenty-Nine

After having her home alarm system set up for monitoring, Julia rushed to work an hour late on Wednesday morning. Her drug screen result was still not available. Equipment problems. She asked the duty biochemist to page her when it was ready. Another day stuck in the lab. The lab staff had set up the culture specimens from Paulette late on Tuesday evening. Best to leave them in the incubator until the afternoon. Her follow-up swabs from Martin showed no growth so far.

All the delays and enforced inaction gnawed at her. The VRSA screening overwhelmed everyone around her. Tempers frayed. Scientists snapped and snarled as specimens mounted. Gabriel had given her a frazzled wave, then dashed off to the maternity ward.

She escaped to the bin room out the back of the lab, where bins full of completed specimens awaited disposal. While isolated from all the action on the wards, she could help Martin by finding his old VRSA swabs. If it had been dead quiet, she could've bribed a lab assistant to dumpster dive. Fat chance of that in the middle of an outbreak.

Borrowing a lab coat, she covered her clothes, then pulled on a pair of gloves and a plastic apron in case of spills. She opened the first clinical waste bin and undid the tie on the top bag. The stench singed her nose hairs and melted her eyeballs. Breakfast threatened a reappearance. She'd have to shower and change clothes when she finished or no one would let her near them. Martin better appreciate the effort.

She opened the neck of the bag and peered in. Crap, real crap. Full of faeces jars, not the swabs she needed. Different specimen types were processed at separate benches with their own bins. She shoved that bag to the side and grabbed the next one. Urine jars. Wrong bench again. Would synchronised swimmer nose-clips help? Discard that bag and try again.

Third time lucky. She emptied the bag of swabs onto a plastic sheet on the floor, then sat cross-legged and checked them one by one, searching for Martin's name. Swabs labelled with anyone else's name went back into the rubbish bag. When she finished that bag, she hauled out the next one.

After a while, she got used to the stink of days-old faeces and urine and other bodily products. Hell of a way to spend a morning.

Five rubbish bags of swabs later, she discovered a set of Martin's swabs. The negative ones, of course. Finding the disputed set first would be too much to hope for. Clearly labelled with his name and the right date, there was nothing unusual about them. She placed them in a biohazard bag, which she then tucked into the lab coat's top pocket. If she lost them, she'd scream.

Onwards.

At back-achingly long last, she unearthed the other set. Martin owed her dinner at Rockpool with an open bar tab—unless he was the killer, of course. She stretched her back and unlocked her knees so she could stand up, then examined her find.

How weird. The swab containers had stuck-on labels with clearly marked spots to fill in—name, date of birth, site of specimen, time, date, ward—but someone had written all the details upside down. Of the million swabs she'd seen that morning, none had that same handwriting method.

While she cleaned up her mess, she puzzled over the swabs. Perhaps one of the lab staff would know who typically labelled specimens that way. What if they'd written the wrong name and now someone was wandering around the hospital spreading VRSA? She should show the swabs to Martin, too. If someone had played a practical joke on him, he might recognise the handwriting. Warped sense of humour or malicious intent?

Her pager beeped. She glanced at the screen. A familiar number. Someone wanted her to call her own office. The bin room didn't have a phone, so she threw the last bag back in the bin, then removed all her protective gear and washed her hands with extreme thoroughness. In the middle of drying her hands on a paper towel, her pager alarmed again. Impatient sod.

⸎

Two hospital security guards waited outside her office. Oh no. Was her drug screen positive? How could it be? Her body should've cleared all the drugs from Thursday night. She hadn't even had a glass of wine since then. Had someone tampered with her blood sample?

Every cell in her body urged her to flee. The guards hadn't spotted her yet. Too busy looking menacing. She half-turned, intent on sneaking back into the lab to check her tox screen results on the computer.

Her bloody pager squawked for the third time. Both guards swivelled towards her. She froze, heart racing loud enough for them to hear. Mild curiosity, their only apparent response.

Okay, if she wasn't top of their most wanted list, who the hell had paged her? She strode past them and entered her office.

Martin raced around her desk and grabbed her arm. He dragged her into the room, then locked the door behind them.

"Where were you? Why didn't you answer?" He blocked her exit.

One by one, she pried his fingers off her arm. He'd gripped so tightly, the bone felt bruised. She backed away until her legs hit the desk. Her pulse hammered in her throat. He followed. Too close. His wild-eyed gaze and frantic tone made her glad the security guards were outside the door.

"I was neck-deep in rubbish, searching for your VRSA swabs." She pulled the plastic biohazard bag out of her pocket, showing him the swabs. Her hand trembled, so she dropped the bag on the desk behind her, hoping to hide her fear. "I'm here now. What's so urgent? And why are security guards involved?"

She barely kept the tremor out of her voice. He'd never scared her before. Had their friendship blinded her to considering him a threat? A killer?

"Fuck security. Rachel's dying." He gripped her shoulders and leant in, close and desperate. "Help her."

"Let me go." She kept her voice low despite the desire to shout loud enough to draw the guards' attention.

Martin jerked his hands off her shoulders and stumbled backwards until he thudded against the door. He sank to the floor.

Someone banged on the door and jostled the doorhandle.

"It's okay. Give us a minute," she called out, then asked Martin, "What's wrong with Rachel?"

"Septic shock. She's back in ICU." He avoided eye contact. "If she's got VRSA, I'll never forgive myself."

"She's young. We've caught it early and we'll cover all possibilities. She can beat it."

"What if she doesn't want to?" Martin raised his head, his eyes bloodshot. A man close to exhaustion. "She's given up. On me, on our marriage, on life."

"Because of Valerie?"

He ruffled one hand through his hair, adding to his dishevelled state. "I wish I knew. She hasn't spoken to me since last Thursday, not since . . ."

Her overdose.

Another thump on the door. Martin sighed. "I have to go. Look after her for me."

A goodbye speech? "Of course. Where are the security guards taking you?"

"Wherever they bloody well want to." He forced a laugh, then clambered to his feet. "Don't believe everything you hear about me."

He unlocked the door and left.

As the three men walked away, she overheard one guard say something about the cops downstairs. Holy crap. Had the police found new evidence in Valerie's murder investigation? Against Martin? Her heart sank.

⸻ ◆ ⸻

Before racing to the ICU, Julia checked the computer, but her tox screen remained unreported. Either they'd found something suspicious and were confirming it by another method or their analyser really was broken. She rang Biochemistry, but was told the scientist in charge of the drug lab was in a meeting. Even if her test had been completed, he had to review the results first. Bloody bureaucracy.

The drug test was a formality, really, and Rachel wasn't one of her patients. Who could stop her visiting a friend's wife? And it was in the hospital's interest for her to make sure VRSA was covered.

She grabbed Martin's swabs so she could drop them in the lab on her way to the ICU. Oh, no, she'd forgotten to show him the weird handwriting. With the police after him and Rachel in ICU, a nose swab wouldn't be his top priority. Hell, if he'd killed Valerie, she'd lose all interest in his mystery swabs, too.

Focus. Martin's mental state was out of her control. Rachel was sick.

She dashed into the lab and sweet-talked one of the lab assistants into plating Martin's swabs onto VRSA screening plates, then leaving the swabs in her office. No way was she digging through those bins again. The handwriting mystery could wait.

As she rushed to the ICU, she considered Rachel's diagnosis. Her latest specimens had arrived in the lab earlier that morning. Too early for blood culture results, but preliminary tests showed her urine wasn't infected. No endotracheal aspirate had been sent, so she wasn't on a ventilator. Yet. If the broad-spectrum antibiotics had cleared her chest infection, maybe she'd developed a fungal infection. Had her intravenous line become infected? Worst possibility of all, had she caught VRSA from Martin?

⊰✦⊱

When she reached the ICU, Julia scanned the room. The last thing she needed was to bump into her boss when she should be confined to the lab. A group of doctors in green scrubs huddled around a patient in the second cubicle from the end. Must be the morning ward round. All she could glimpse of the patient was a hairy, muscular leg. Not Rachel, then. Nurses attended to other patients, adjusting IV pumps, suctioning endotracheal tubes, and emptying catheter bags. One nurse eyed the bank of computer monitors on the main desk. No one paid any attention to Julia.

According to the whiteboard on the wall behind the desk, Rachel was in bay nine. The same room Brad had been in, so she must be in isolation. One less problem to worry about, but she'd have to stroll past the group of doctors to visit Rachel's room. Don't look at them. Keep moving.

"You're too late, Dr Sinclair."

She whipped around. Busted by eagle-eyed Phil. "Martin MacDougall asked me to look in on his wife. He's busy elsewhere."

"I bet he is." He gestured for her to join him in an empty cubicle.

Promising. The consultants gossiped just as much as the junior staff but had access to a better quality of dirt.

"Security escorted Martin out of the hospital and handed him over to the police. Something to do with the murder . . ."

"Murder? Don't know anything about that." Phil glanced around for eavesdroppers. "We had a senior staff meeting last night. The new pharmacy audit system revealed some irregularities."

"Why would Martin steal drugs when he could write a prescription?"

"Did I say Martin stole drugs?" He pulled an imaginary zipper across his lips.

"What was taken?"

"Word to the wise. Hanging around MacDougall is not a good career move, especially in your current position." He wandered back to the ward round.

She froze. Her current position? He knew about her tox screen. Hell, every consultant in the hospital probably knew by now. Did they think Martin had stolen sedatives for her?

Hope Rachel's not intubated. Julia needed her help.

She raced around the corner and smacked straight into her boss as he stepped out of Rachel's room. Bugger.

Dr Branford's nostrils flared. "Let me escort you back to the lab, Dr Sinclair. On the way, you can tell me all about the surgeon carrying VRSA. Shame you didn't mention it earlier."

He stomped towards the exit.

She spun around and fell into step beside him. "We've got two sets of swabs with discrepant results, but he swears only one set was collected. He's disputing the positive swabs are his, so I've re-swabbed him, dug out the originals and repeated everything."

"And until that's clarified?"

"The works. Started decolonisation, no patients, no operating, full contact precautions when he visits his wife." And a police interrogation should keep him out of the hospital for a while, but she couldn't take credit for that.

"Sounds thorough enough."

"When I heard they'd transferred his wife to ICU with sepsis, I had to check she was in isolation."

"Of course. With your toxicology screen still pending, I'm sure you weren't intending to see the patient in person."

He opened the ICU door for her. His arched eyebrow left her in no doubt that her cover was blown.

Early Wednesday afternoon, Nick heard scrapes and scratches overhead from one of the forensic scientists crawling through the roof space of Martin's City Beach home. He was grateful for the air-conditioned comfort of the master bedroom. Thirty-seven degrees outside, and he bet it was a lot hotter up there.

He was even more grateful to his mate, one of the Wembley Detectives, who let him know about a surgeon suspected of stealing prescription medications from Perth General Hospital. Some drugs on the list were the same as those found in Valerie Cavanaugh's autopsy specimens. Would he be interested in tagging along on the search of the suspect's house? Hell, yeah.

To date, the homicide investigation hadn't found sufficient grounds for searching Martin MacDougall's property. The discovery of stolen drugs could give them an edge. Even better if Paulette Matthews had the same drugs in her system, but the forensics lab was backed up again.

Nothing out of the ordinary so far. He returned his attention to the wardrobe's contents. From his perch on the stepladder, he spied an old metal cashbox tucked away in the far corner of the top shelf. He stepped off the ladder and moved it across so he could reach the box. As he lifted it from its hiding place, something rattled inside.

Nick placed the box on the bed. Locked, of course. He turned it upside down, but there was no key handily taped to the underside.

A quick search of the bedside tables didn't reveal any stray keys. He could smash it open or he could go downstairs and ask Martin to help. Try the less destructive approach first.

He carried the box to the downstairs lounge room. "Where's the key?"

Martin paled and shrank back into the white leather lounge. "There's nothing interesting in there. Just papers, passports, stuff like that."

"Then you won't mind opening the box, will you?"

He didn't move. "It's private."

"The more you fuss about it, the more suspicious I get. Besides, passports don't rattle."

Despite the air-conditioning, beads of sweat dotted Martin's upper lip. He wiped them away with the back of one hand.

"Look, my wife's sick. You've seen what she's like. Sometimes I have to give her a sedative to calm her nerves."

"Now I'm really interested. The key, doc. Where is it?" Nick held out his hand.

"In the study, taped underneath the bottom drawer of the desk." A hint of a quaver in his voice added to Nick's suspicions. "I'm a doctor. I can prescribe any drugs I want."

Nick went to the study and sat on the black leather swivel chair behind the desk. He found the key, unlocked the box, and lifted the lid. It was full of syringes, needles, and boxes of drugs. Half the drug names he'd never seen before, but some were recognisable to even a layperson like him. Valium, the housewife's friend. Injectable form, according to the label. That explained Rachel's long sleeves in the middle of summer.

A floorboard creaked. Martin had followed him.

"It's all legal," Martin said. "I didn't steal them from the hospital. Look. Her name's printed on the pharmacy labels."

"What are these for?"

"I told you. My wife's not well. She needs tranquillisers when life gets too much for her to bear."

How many tranquillisers did one woman need? No wonder she'd been so spaced out. "Is this where she got the drugs for her overdose?"

"Yes, but I'd moved the key. She must've copied it sometime."

Was that a tear in the doctor's eye? Nick wouldn't have thought he had it in him. Maybe he'd crack and spill his guts.

"So why haven't you thrown these out? Do you want her to make a proper job of it when she comes home?"

Martin's face crumpled, tears slipping down his cheeks. He stumbled forward and fell against the desk. His grip on the edge whitened his knuckles as he fought to stay upright. "I'm not that big a bastard. I shifted the box, and hid the key. She never comes into my study. Never, not since . . . It used to be . . ." He shuddered. "I don't know how to deal with her anymore. I'm so sorry."

"Maybe now she'll get the help she needs."

Martin's head jerked up. "Fuck. Don't you think she's been getting help for years?" He grabbed one of the Valium ampoules and thrust it under Nick's nose. "This is the only thing that stops her from remembering the death of our son . . . our only child." He threw the ampoule across the room, shattering it against the wall. Martin slid to the floor and wrapped his arms around his knees. "This was his room. I . . . I can't even say his name. What sort of father does that make me?"

Nick kept quiet, letting him talk.

"He was only eighteen months old. I was at work when she rang. He had a fever. I told her he'd be okay. Just a cold." He slowly shook his head. "I told her not to bother me at work." His voice quavered. "Three hours later, they called me from the paediatric ICU. Meningitis. They pumped him full of antibiotics, but it was too late. He died before I got there."

Martin dragged his hands across his eyes and down his cheeks. "How the fuck do you expect us to cope with that? It'll take more than a few doses of Valium. Will anything bring him back from the dead?"

He sobbed, buried under the dead weight of personal tragedy.

What if Valerie had threatened to tell Rachel about their affair? If she threatened the last link with his dead child, could that have driven him to kill?

Chapter Thirty

Early Thursday morning, Julia hung up the phone, then sagged back in her office chair, limp with relief. Her tox screen was clear. She called Gabriel into her office. He dashed in. His shirt, with its fluorescent yellow swirls, made her eyes flicker. She rummaged in her briefcase. Sunglasses.

"That's better. Do you have total colour blindness?"

"Jealous of my stunning fashion sense?"

"Oh, please. I'm bothered about permanent retinal damage. This is a hospital. We try not to make patients feel sicker than they already are."

"Meow." From his perch on the edge of her desk, he leant forward and pulled her sunglasses off. "Ooh, you do look tired. Someone keeping you up late?"

"Gabriel, I'm pleased you've settled in enough to show your true colours." His girly giggle made her smile. "I'm allowed out of the lab at last. Where are we at with the VRSA screening?"

"I thought my bright shirt might cheer you up after the hellish time you've had since I got here." He pouted. "I feel like a jinx."

"None of this is your fault. Any progress on the surgical ward?"

"Only one nurse to go, and she's on duty tonight. I will not leave the building until I've swabbed her."

"Hell, you're doing better than me. I see a house-call in my near future. Bloody Simon." So much for his promises. "What about orthopaedics?"

"As of yesterday, all their staff have clear swabs."

"Great. And no new cases on either of those wards. Fingers crossed. Too early for obstetrics?"

"Yes, I'm in the middle of checking the staff list, but several haven't even been swabbed yet. Do you think we're on top of this now?"

"If only. Rachel MacDougall, Martin's wife, has a staph in her blood culture this morning." How could she tell Martin?

"Bugger. What about Martin's mystery swabs?"

"I wish I knew. The swabs I collected from him on Tuesday have grown no staph, let alone any VRSA."

"Did you find his positive swabs?"

"Yes, in the last place I looked." After grovelling on the floor all yesterday morning, her knees would never be the same.

"Aha. That's where everything hides. Should've looked there first."

"Very amusing." She rolled her eyes. "His name's clear on the swab container, but it's written upside down and in the wrong spot."

"Strange. Who collected them?"

"Not a clue. I've never seen that variation." Why would someone write like that? Left-handed? Someone with a grudge disguising their handwriting to frame Martin as the carrier? None of the lab staff had recognised it. "If he infected Brad after only a brief contact, he must be a heavy shedder, so I can't understand why Martin's latest swabs haven't grown VRSA yet."

A knock on the door drew her attention. She glanced up. Oh, hell, no. Nick Randall. How much of their conversation had he heard?

"Sorry to disturb you at work again, doctor," he said. "My boss wants a progress report."

"Don't they all?" Gabriel stood up. "I was just leaving. I'll make sure you're not interrupted." He gave Julia an exaggerated wink, then pulled the door shut as he left the room.

"Ignore him. He has an overactive imagination." Julia watched Nick settle in the chair opposite her. The room shrank. "About the swabs from the autopsy . . ."

He leant forward, shrinking the room even more. "What have you found?"

"It's only preliminary."

"Sure. Give me the infection for dummies version."

"Paulette's swab is growing a *Staph aureus*. A common bug that lives on our skin and causes infection in open wounds. It can spread into the bloodstream and kill people."

"With you so far. That's what you thought it might be on Tuesday, right?"

"Yes. We divide *Staph aureus* into different groups according to which antibiotics kill them and which ones don't." Nick nodded, so she continued. "We currently have a hospital outbreak of a new antibiotic-resistant strain of staph, called VRSA for short. This particular staph has never been seen in Australia, but it's been isolated a few times in the US and India. Part of my job involves searching for whoever is carrying the bug so I can stop further spread around the hospital."

"What does this have to do with Paulette?"

"Paulette's infection might, and I stress the word might, be the same VRSA. I've only done a very basic screen. It's too early to be sure." She bit her lower lip. "I'm getting three steps ahead of myself here, but what if . . ." What the hell was she thinking? Talk about pole-vaulting to a conclusion.

"Hey, doc, don't leave me in suspense."

Oh, why not? Share the crazy idea. "Stop me when this sounds too off-the-planet. The skeleton found in Kings Park had evidence of a post-surgical infection. She had surgery somewhere in the US. What if that infection was due to VRSA? What if the killer caught

VRSA from the Kings Park victim, spread it into my hospital and then gave it to Paulette?"

She could picture the sequence in her head. Maybe not that crazy. If Martin really was the carrier, the conclusion froze her bone marrow.

Nick held up both hands. "Whoa. That's a whole lot of what ifs. Can you prove it? How long would it take?"

"Sensitivities take a couple of days to come through. And we can send the bugs for gene sequencing to compare the strains. That'll need even longer. If Paulette has the same bug as the hospital outbreak, it would link her killer to the hospital. As for the Kings Park victim, we won't grow anything from her now. Maybe the reference lab could do some PCR tests on her infected bone."

"Any idea who's spreading this bug in the hospital?"

"Still working on it."

His green eyes narrowed, lasered their focus onto hers. "You know who it is."

"Lab results are confidential."

"Killers don't deserve confidentiality. You keep saying you want to help find Valerie's killer. Help me now." His voice dropped to a whisper, soft and conspiratorial. "Help Valerie."

"Don't push me. I wish I could help, but apart from the strange wish to keep my job, the results aren't clear-cut. The person involved is denying the positive swabs are his . . . or hers."

"Sounds like every guilty person I've ever interviewed."

"A disputed lab result and my off-the-planet theory won't get you very far in court. Let Indira and the forensic scientists investigate the evidence. I'll call her later and send over a sample of our hospital VRSA strain. They'll prove the connection if there is one."

Was that a flash of embarrassment on his face before cop mode took over?

"I overheard something about Martin and his VRSA swabs."

"No, you wouldn't dare—"

"Relax. I won't put your private comments on record. We have enough reason to question him again, anyway."

"Promise me you won't tell him anything that leads back to me. It's sad and pathetic, but my job is all I have."

"It's not your job I'm worried about, it's your life." His eyes darkened. "Stay away from him. Please."

"Must be serious if you're questioning him two days in a row."

"Did he tell you that?"

"Security guards let slip when they dragged him away."

"That wasn't anything to do with Major Crimes. Where did they drag him away from?"

"So, what was it about?"

"Secret police business. I can't tell you. It's sad and pathetic, but my job is all I have. And you haven't answered my question."

"From here. He came to see me about a patient. I'd tell you more, but patient confidentiality and all that."

"Guess I asked for that. If you have to talk to him about a patient, do it by phone."

After she agreed, he left. She stared into space. Off-the-planet or not, her theory ricocheted around her brain and refused to be ignored. No matter how hard she tried to find another explanation, everything pointed to Martin. And what had Phil said about stolen drugs? Two men she trusted had warned her away from Martin.

But his last words to her lingered.

"Don't believe everything you hear about me."

<hr>

Julia raced through the rest of the day's work on automatic pilot. Two more VRSA cases had appeared, but her mind kept tracking back to Martin. The police were questioning him as a serious suspect. Her wild theory about the VRSA cases and the killer, combined with their own evidence, had fuelled their suspicions. How could someone she knew and trusted be capable of such evil?

She'd thought knowing who killed Valerie would come as a relief. Closure, as they say. Reality slapped her in the face. It didn't make any difference who killed her. Valerie was still dead.

Dead, dead, dead.

When she couldn't focus on work any longer, she checked Simon's address on the computer. One more set of swabs to cross off her list. She'd drop by his house on her way to give Indira the promised VRSA sample. A brief phone call to check Indira was still at the mortuary.

Simon could answer one nagging question. Had he provided Martin with a false alibi for the night of Valerie's abduction?

Late Thursday afternoon, Nick watched his boss barge across the hospital visitors' car park. George tucked his crumpled shirt in with one hand and held his mobile to his ear with the other, barking orders at some poor sod. He had taken little persuading to see Martin MacDougall as their prime suspect and couldn't wait to question him again. To hell with holding off until forensics sorted everything out.

George shoved the phone in his pocket, then scraped one hand over the top of his head. It crackled like sandpaper. Nick half-expected to see sparks fly.

"Okay, have I got this right? Some rare, deadly bug killed the last victim, and your lady doctor thinks the killer got it from that Kings Park body and has spread it willy-nilly around the hospital."

"Got it in one, boss."

"Fuck me. We're in an episode of *CSI Perth*." He charged through the front entrance of the hospital.

Nick caught up with him at the lifts. "He's visiting his wife in ICU. The ward clerk will phone me if he tries to leave before we get there."

"Hope his missus is still sedated." George pounded the lift button again as if that would make it come faster. "Last thing I need is another hysterical wife."

"You're all heart."

"Careful, mate. Remind me. Who interviewed her just before she decided to top herself?"

"Thanks for nothing." Nick had been trying to forget that incident. When he'd heard about her overdose, he couldn't help wondering if he'd triggered it. "What if she did it because she found out her husband was a killer?"

"Or maybe he gave her the overdose to shut her up."

The lift doors opened. They travelled to the fourth floor, ignoring inquisitive looks from a couple of nurses who had overheard the tail end of their conversation.

When they reached the Intensive Care Unit, they tagged along behind a group of doctors to bypass the security system.

Nick flashed his police ID card to a nurse sitting behind a row of computer screens. "Where's Rachel MacDougall? We need to speak to her husband."

"Around the corner, last room on the left," she said.

"Thanks. Is there a private room where we could chat with him?"

"Maybe one of the offices. I'll check."

A too-young-to-shave doctor blocked them at the corner. "She's in isolation, so you'll need to call her husband out of the room. The patient mustn't be disturbed. She's on a cardiac monitor for an unstable rhythm. Any excitement, and she could arrest."

George patted the ICU doctor on his shoulder. "We only need to talk to her husband. If he's got half a heart, he won't want to have this conversation in front of his wife. Trust me, we'll be out of your hair in no time." He gestured for Nick to follow him to her room.

The door was shut, but a large glass window gave an excellent view of the interior. Rachel MacDougall didn't have a breathing tube in her throat, but had lots of other tubes and wires attached to various body parts. Her eyes were closed, her cheeks flushed. Nick hoped, for all their sakes, she was heavily sedated.

Martin sat beside her with his back to them. He wore a yellow paper gown over his clothes and a glove on the one hand that was visible. Because of the bug he was carrying?

Nick rapped on the window. Martin's head jerked around, then he jumped to his feet. He strode to the door and wrenched it open.

"What do you want now?" He spoke in a harsh whisper. "Haven't you done enough damage?"

George held both hands up, palms out. "Relax, doctor. We don't want to disturb your wife. Just a few questions for you."

"Not now." Martin turned back to Rachel. Her eyes had opened, but they looked unfocussed. He rushed to her side, brushed a strand of hair off her forehead. "It's okay, babe. I'm still here."

Nick held the door open. "Come with us, please. You don't want to upset your wife, do you?"

Martin snorted. "Wish you'd thought of that last week. I'm not leaving."

"What's with all the fancy dress?" George asked. "Got something I don't want to catch?"

"Careful, boss," Nick said in a quiet voice. "Thin ice."

"Are you the Infection Control police now? Leave us alone."

Martin sat down again next to his wife's bed. He grasped her left hand like a drowning man grabbing a lifebelt.

Rachel moaned and pulled her hand from his grip. He muttered an apology. She rolled over. An alarm shrieked.

The ICU doctor approached the room.

"Back the fuck off." Martin bounded to his feet and blocked the doorway. "I'll shut this racket up if you lot bugger off and let me talk to my wife. Alone."

The ICU doctor shook his head. "I'm getting the consultant. Give us a yell if the patient goes off."

George turned to Nick. "Goes off? What is she—a piece of meat left out in the sun?"

The wailing alarm burrowed into Nick's brain, making thought difficult. "Let's give them a couple of minutes to talk."

He moved a few steps away. Moments later, George followed. Silence returned.

When Nick looked back through the open door, he saw Martin bent over the bed, whispering in his wife's ear. He helped her to a sitting position.

Rachel smiled, a sad smile with a hint of something else. Resignation, maybe. Despair? What had Martin said to make her smile that way, as if she'd never smile again?

Martin reached into the bedside cabinet, then passed her a handbag. He turned away and poured a glass of water from the jug on the bedside table.

Behind his back, Rachel fiddled with something under the bedcovers. She stopped when he held out the glass of water.

Rachel shook her head, lifted her hands above the bedcovers. "Sorry."

"No." Martin lunged towards her.

Chapter Thirty-One

Julia parked in a quiet leafy street in Nedlands, near to the University of Western Australia. She found Simon barefoot and wearing boardshorts and a faded T-shirt, hand-watering blood-red roses in his front garden. The picture of life in the western suburbs.

The between-the-wars Californian bungalow reminded her of Valerie's home, but he'd kept the small-paned windows that she'd modernised. Too bloody hard to clean, she'd always said. The deep veranda with its wide red brick pillars left the front door hidden in shadow.

"Hey, you're here at last. What a pleasant surprise." He turned off the water and dropped the hose in a snake-like coil on the red concrete path. "Come for that drink I promised you?"

"No. Remember these?" She showed him the swabs. "I'm not leaving until I've stuck one up your nose."

"Kinky." He wiped his hands on his T-shirt. "Come inside. Otherwise, the neighbours might think it's some deviant sexual practice and they'll all want to join in. You know what the western suburbs are like."

"Sure." She followed him onto the veranda.

"Come into my parlour, said the spider to the fly." He opened the front door and directed her to enter.

He pulled the door shut behind them and directed her into a lounge room at the front of the house. So cool and dark inside, she suppressed a shiver. He flicked on the light. Talk about a fifties flashback. All it needed was a little old lady knitting in the corner while listening to a show on the wireless.

"This is not at all what I imagined." She crossed the threadbare carpet, then sank into a lumpy armchair, engulfed by its chintzy depths. "I pictured you as a leather and stainless-steel sort of guy."

He chuckled. "This was my grandparents' place. Well, my home too after my parents died. I was only nine." He rubbed his right thigh. "Guess I'm still living in the past. I should redecorate."

"Losing both parents must've been tough. Car accident?" She shook her head. "Sorry, you don't have to tell me. I'm being nosy."

"I never talk about it, but somehow this feels right." He glanced at a family photo on the mantelpiece. "It was messy. Mum died in a housefire. She was in bed with dad's business partner. Dad was suspected of arson, but he . . . killed himself before the police could charge him."

"Oh, that's awful." Poor young Simon.

He shrugged. "Enough about my tragic past. How about that drink? Help cheer me up?"

How could she walk out after that? Indira had said she'd be at work for another hour, then they could grab a meal somewhere.

"A quick one." She reached for her handbag. "Swabs first?"

"Business before pleasure." He sat cross-legged on the floor in front of her and tipped his head back. "Ready when you are."

She steadied his face by cupping one side of his jaw. Maybe the setting made the routine task feel weird. Or was it his comment about deviant sexual practices? Sometimes Simon said the strangest things.

She rolled the tip of one swab around the inside of both his nostrils, then slid it back into its container.

"Do you have any wounds?" she asked.

"None that I know of. Shall I strip so you can check for yourself?" He reached for the button on his boardshorts.

"Thanks, but I'll take your word for it. Now, say ah." She wiped another swab across the back of his throat, making him gag a little.

He closed his warm hand around hers. "You're shaking. Cold or scared?"

"Neither." She pulled her hand away. Why did she feel so uneasy? "Coffee overdose."

"You work too hard. All those early starts and late finishes." He picked up a swab container and wrote his details on the label.

How did he know her routine? "I didn't know you were left-handed."

"Lots of things you don't know about me. What'll you have to drink?"

"Water's fine."

"I know exactly what you need." He dropped the container in her lap, then left the room.

She accidentally knocked the swab onto the floor. What was wrong with her? Skittish as a kitten. Must be a delayed reaction to discovering the police were interviewing Martin as their prime and only suspect. She bent over and picked up the swab.

He'd filled his name in upside down. Just like the writing on Martin's mystery swabs. The set Martin denied being collected. A chill skittered down her back. If Simon labelled the mystery positive swabs, did he contaminate them to frame Martin as the carrier? Or worse?

The obvious reason for his false alibi? Her heart stopped for endless seconds. Simon wanted to protect himself. Martin was innocent.

She fumbled in her handbag for her mobile, then froze. Footsteps approached. She slid the phone into her pocket. Simon re-entered the room, carrying two cocktails. He handed her one with a paper umbrella in it and placed the other on the coffee table.

"You'll enjoy this," he said. "A little something I invented."

"Thanks. What's in it?" She sniffed the colourful concoction, remembering the drink-spiking incident at the wake. Fuck. "Smells like rocket fuel."

Simon watched her, an expectant gleam in his eyes. The same expression her cat displayed when he stalked his prey. She didn't dare take a sip.

"It has quite a kick." A phone rang. "Sorry. I'm expecting a call from the hospital about my night off." He strode into the hallway.

The phone was just outside the lounge room. If she raced for the front door, he'd be on her like her cat on a cockroach. Quiet and careful, she switched the two drinks and swapped the umbrella to the other glass. She hoped she was overreacting, but every nerve jangled. A quick scan of the room revealed a bedraggled pot plant next to the fireplace. She tipped half her drink into the pot.

He was still talking. She snatched her mobile out of her pocket and selected Nick's name, hoping she had time for a quick text message. Send help . . . She blanked on Simon's address. Fuck. She could barely remember her own name.

Bloody touchscreens. Her trembling fingers botched several letters, but she managed a close approximation of Simon's name and address just as he finished his call. No time to explain anything. She hit send and jammed her phone back into her pocket.

When Simon returned, she took a tiny sip of her cocktail and faked a calm and unsuspecting expression.

"Sorry about that. Confirmed I don't have to work tonight." He sat in the other armchair, smiling, watching.

She babbled about inconsequential topics, while inside she wondered how long it would take the police to arrive. Why the hell had she come here alone? Her mother had always warned her about her independent streak.

"Fancy another drink?" he asked.

"Are you kidding? I have to drive. Another of these and I'll be legless."

All that nervous chatter had dried her mouth, and she'd drunk more than she'd intended. Idiot. Hurry up, guys.

A lazy smile. "I don't mind if you're legless."

She smiled back, convinced the tremor in her cheeks would give her away. If he suspected she knew the truth, her chances of survival would vanish.

"Thanks for the drink. I have to get these swabs back to the lab." She lurched out of the chair and had to grab onto his arm to stay upright. What the hell was in that cocktail? Maybe she'd taken the wrong glass. "Oops."

"I warned you it was a touch alcoholic." From behind, he wrapped an arm around her waist.

His breath warmed her cheek. Too close, too bloody close. She still felt unsteady despite his too-tight grip. Was he swaying, or was it her imagination?

She watched him in the mirror above the fireplace. His eyelids drooped, half-closed. He yawned. Thank you, thank you, thank you. As soon as he passed out, she'd dash to the door. Dutch courage gave her the strength to carry on, that and the hope that Nick was rushing to her rescue.

"Too much work makes Julia a sleepy girl." She laughed, a burst of hysteria.

"You've been very busy lately. All those outbreak cases, but everything's under control now." His voice was soft, almost hypnotic. "You should rest. Lie down for a while."

How would she act if she didn't suspect him of murder? He'd expect her to flirt. Could she do it when her strongest instincts warned her to flee?

"If I lie down now, who knows where that might lead?" She leant her head back against his shoulder and forced herself to smile into the mirror. "I'd hate to pass out on you."

"Do you think I'd take advantage of a woman who's had too much to drink?"

"I don't know. Would you?"

Was that a flash of malice in his eyes?

He spun her around, then put one hand on his heart. "I'm wounded, mortally wounded. How could you doubt me? Trust me, I'm a doctor."

"If I had a dollar for every time I've heard that, I could buy a bottle of Grange. A whole case of it."

"Grange? I've got some tucked away in my cellar."

"You're kidding. I thought only wine wankers and people with more money than sense bought Grange." She blinked at him. His face moved in and out of focus. "Which one are you?"

"Let me see—a wanker or a rich bastard? Maybe I'm both." His words slurred together. "Come and see my wine collection."

His eyes closed, and he stifled another yawn. He shook his head as if to clear it.

She felt more confident that she'd chosen the right glass. How much damage could he do while on the verge of passing out?

He led her into a study. Leaning over to lift the edge of a red and gold Persian rug, he toppled forward. She grabbed the waistband of his boardshorts, a reflex action she instantly regretted.

Simon seized her hand. "Trying to get into my pants?"

Only if she had a sharp knife handy. She snatched her hand away. "Don't flatter yourself. I don't want to play doctors if you hurt yourself."

"Still playing hard to get?"

He rolled back the rug, revealing a trapdoor. If she got him into the cellar, she could imprison him until the police arrived. Simon could hardly stand upright. It should be a doddle.

"I don't think you've got any wine collection."

"I'll show you." He entered some numbers on a keypad, then hauled open the trapdoor, placing the flap down on the timber floor with exaggerated care. "See. I told you so."

She peered past his shoulder into the dark cellar. Metal stairs disappeared into the gloom. A faint whiff of bleach and something dank and primeval. The smell triggered an image of Valerie on the mortuary table.

Nausea spiralled through her. "After you."

"Ladies first. I insist." He flicked a light switch just inside the trapdoor, straightened up, and waved her on with a flourish.

No fucking way. "I might slip."

The doorbell rang.

Relief buckled her knees. The police at last. She staggered backwards and leant on the edge of the desk.

He followed her.

"You're right. Those stairs are treacherously slippery. Why don't you wait for me in the lounge? Make yourself comfortable." His voice sounded husky. He caressed her cheek. "As soon as I get rid of whoever's at the door, I'll hunt out the Grange and bring it to you."

He wasn't slurring anymore. The hairs on the back of her neck stood on end. Every instinct begged her to scream and run.

He knew.

He clamped one hand over her mouth and nose. Turned her around, hauled her back against his chest with his other arm. Locked her arms against her sides.

Desperate, she kicked back against his shin and arched her back. Simon grunted, but his grip didn't loosen. Her chest burned as she fought to breathe.

He dragged her closer to the hole in the floor.

"I've got you now," he whispered. "I knew you'd swap the glasses, so I dosed the one without the umbrella. Relax."

Her vision tunnelled. Blood roared in her ears.

He loosened his hold on her body, bending forward to slide her down into the cellar.

Panic forced one last effort from her oxygen-starved limbs.

She broke his grip and plummeted straight to hell.

CHAPTER THIRTY-TWO

RACHEL SLID OFF THE far side of the hospital bed, evading her husband's grasp. She sagged against the wall as if she needed help to stay upright. A syringe protruded from one of her intravenous lines. Her right hand obscured its contents. Her thumb hovered over the fully extended plunger.

"Leave Martin alone or I'll kill myself." Her hands trembled, but her voice carried strong and clear.

Martin had one knee on the bed, poised to climb over it. "Don't do it, Rachel. Please. I'm not worth it."

Nick heard his boss mutter agreement, but he kept his focus on Rachel and the syringe. How the hell had a patient got hold of a syringe? Had Martin passed it to her under cover of their whispered conversation?

"Get in that corner," Rachel said to Martin. "I won't let them take you away."

"Please don't do this." Martin followed her instructions.

Nick edged closer, every sense on full alert. Time slowed down. Behind him, George called for assistance on his police radio. Someone else yelled for a crash trolley.

Concentrate. Block out the commotion and chaos.

Assess the situation. Only one way in, only one way out. Unless a tactical team could drop through the air-conditioning vent in the ceiling, or abseil from the roof and crash through the window. Yeah, right. Only in the movies.

What was in the syringe? How fast would it act?

His phone chirped. A text.

Rachel shifted her gaze to Nick. "You should turn your mobile off when you're in a hospital. Don't you know it's dangerous with all this medical equipment? Someone might get hurt."

She laughed, a crazy tinkling laugh that spiked the hairs at the base of his skull. The sort of laugh that said she'd be impossible to reason with.

"Okay." He dragged the phone out of his pocket. Without shifting his gaze from her, he turned it off. Better not be anything important.

"Toss it on the bed, close to me." The instant he did so, Rachel snatched up the phone and dropped it into the full water jug. "Always wanted to do that. Now, I've got your attention. See this syringe? Potassium chloride. See this tubing? It goes all the way into my heart." She tossed a plastic vial to Martin. "Tell them what'll happen. I'm just a crazy woman, but they'll believe you. The bigshot surgeon."

"Please don't do this." Tears dripped from Martin's chin. "I'm nothing without you."

"Tell them, or I'll give a live demonstration. Or should that be a dead one?" Another spasm of laughter.

Martin wiped his nose on the back of his sleeve. "It'll stop her heart. Kill her just like an execution." His voice caught on the last word. "Back off and let me talk to her for a few minutes."

Nick scanned the area. The ICU doctor had the resuscitation trolley open and was filling some syringes. Beside him, a nurse squirted something into a bag of clear fluid.

"Okay." Nick took a couple of steps backwards.

"I'm dead inside already, ever since . . ." Rachel shrugged, then slid down the wall as if that slight movement had drained all her energy. "The best thing we ever did . . . ever made, and neither of us can say his name. It's like he never existed."

"Don't do this to me," Martin said in a hoarse whisper. "I need you. Hand me the syringe. Please. For me, for the memory of our son."

"The police will take you away from me. I'll have nobody." Her eyelids flickered. She tightened her grip on the syringe, her knuckles white. "Nothing worth living for."

Martin turned to Nick, his face etched with anguish.

Nick stepped backwards towards George, out of Rachel's line of sight. "When I'm in position, create a diversion," he whispered to George.

He gestured to Martin to keep her talking, then dropped to the floor. So long as she stayed sitting on the floor, he'd be hidden by the bed.

"Why are you doing this, Rachel?" Martin asked. "The police are only here to ask me some more questions."

"But they know you lied."

"Lied about what?"

"Simon told me you were half an hour late getting to his house. He covered for you."

Nick commando-crawled through the doorway and headed towards the end of the bed. He glanced up at Martin, caught a flicker of disbelief at her response. There goes his rock-solid alibi.

"Simon spoke to you?" Martin asked. "When?"

"Thursday afternoon." Rachel hiccupped on a sob. "I couldn't bear the thought of losing you."

Another half a body length forward. Nick stopped. His breathing slowed. He pressed his hands to the floor.

An alarm screeched.

Nick lunged for Rachel's hands.

Julia fell. Her left ankle smashed into one of the metal rungs. Snap. Shockwaves of agony raced to her brain.

She slammed onto the concrete floor.

Oblivion beckoned.

She gasped for air, trying to drive away the blackness that blurred her vision. Her left ankle and right hand demanded her urgent attention. Tough. Until she caught her breath again, they'd have to scream in silence.

With her one good hand, she pushed herself up to a sitting position, moving gingerly, all too aware of the danger that lurked overhead. The trapdoor had crashed shut. Her left ankle throbbed. Every millimetre of movement swamped her senses with nausea and lightning bursts of pain.

Fight, Julia. Don't surrender.

She assessed her injuries. Ankle first. A glance downwards. Despite her worst imaginings, no bone poked through the skin. No spurts of arterial blood. Pedal pulses intact as far as she could tell through trembling fingertips. Could she stand on it? Did she have a choice? A quick look at her right hand. Must've caught it on something sharp. Mangled fingers dripped blood onto the floor.

Nothing fatal.

Yet.

A movement overhead. The trapdoor opened. Her heart missed a beat, then slammed against her chest wall like a wild bird trapped in a cage.

Simon descended the stairs with surprising agility for one meant to be so drunk.

"I sent the Jehovah's Witnesses packing." He ran his hand down her left leg, pausing mid-calf to gaze into her eyes. "We don't need God today."

Julia couldn't speak. Her throat had closed tight, probably to stop her heart from escaping. Her heart had the right idea.

"I told you to relax." A predatory smile. "Does it hurt?"

He grasped her left ankle and squeezed.

White-hot pain shot up her leg. She screamed. When he let go, she collapsed on the floor. Blood roared in her ears.

Oblivion won.

Nick pried Rachel's fingers off the syringe. He kept a tight grip on her hands. It gave him something to do while he got his heart rate under control. No way he'd touch that lethal weapon. Accidental execution by cop? Not an ideal end to a hostage situation.

She stared at him, wild-eyed, body trembling and fingers ice-cold. Her lips moved, but he couldn't hear what she was muttering over the wail of the alarm.

At last, the alarm stopped. Brief silence, then a cacophony of voices filled the void. George shouting orders. Martin calling his wife's name.

Rachel whispering, "Let me die, let me die, let me die."

The bed rolled sideways. A burly male nurse shoved past Nick to attend to Rachel. He detached the deadly syringe with a practised twist, then replaced it with a yellow plastic cap. Within seconds, he had lifted Rachel back into bed and was reattaching her heart monitor.

"Now then, young lady. Where the hell did you get this potassium from?" The nurse held the plastic vial in front of Rachel's face. "We keep this deadly shit locked up."

Good question. Nick waited for her response. And waited.

"Did Martin give it to you?" he asked. Who else would assist her suicide?

"No bloody way." Martin interrupted stroking his wife's forehead to shoot a glare at Nick. "Rachel, where did you get it?"

She scrunched her eyes closed, shook her head, whispered something.

Nick rested one hand on her forearm. "Rachel, we have to know. Who gave you the medicine?"

"It wasn't Martin. Leave him alone." She sobbed. Noisy, heart-wrenching, gut-twisting sobs.

The ICU doctor entered the room. He glanced at the heart-rate monitor and shook his head in that I'm-afraid-we've-got-bad-news way that doctors favour. "Rachel's had enough for one day, don't you think?"

Rachel scooted down the bed, taking refuge under the sheets.

The nurse tucked her in. "Let me get this poor woman settled before you drag her husband off in handcuffs."

Martin sat beside her again, murmuring something to her. Whatever he said, it calmed her down. A faint smile softened her face.

Nick retrieved his phone from its watery grave, then joined his boss outside the door. He pressed a few keys, tried to check his last message. Water trickled down his arm. The blank screen taunted him. Bugger. Maybe the forensic guys could resuscitate the message, but he wouldn't bet on it.

"Your phone's rooted, mate," George said. "That doc's going to knock Rachel out so we can spirit Martin away with no more hysterics."

"Shame we can't talk to her first." He glanced back into the room and watched the doctor squirt a clear liquid into her drip tubing.

Her eyelids flickered.

"Surgeon's alibi has gone tits up," George said.

"Thought you'd like that. Why did Simon dob him in to Rachel? Strange way to treat a mate."

"I'm more bloody interested in why he didn't tell us."

"Thursday's when she overdosed. Wonder what else he told her . . ."

Raised voices from the patient's room drew his attention. Martin didn't sound happy with the ICU doctor's assessment of Rachel's condition. She slept through their heated conversation.

No chance of finding out her version of events any time soon.

Martin rushed out of the room and confronted George. "If you want to talk to me, you'll have to do it here. I'm not leaving Rachel."

George stuck his hands on his hips and scanned the ICU. "This is hardly the place for a formal interview."

"She's got pneumonia, and they've had to sedate her. If her oxygen sats drop, they'll have to tube her."

George turned to Nick. "What do you reckon? Got enough to arrest him?"

"Dodgy alibi, surgical skills, relationship with one victim. No known connection to the others yet, but they're linked to this hospital. Possession of—"

"Enough." Martin shepherded them away from the ICU doctor who loitered in the doorway, listening. "Rachel didn't need sedation until you appeared. Intubation puts her at risk of more hospital-acquired infections. Infections that could kill her. Do you want to share that responsibility?"

"We could place a police guard here while we talk to Simon," Nick said. "Find out what he told Rachel."

"Ask me whatever you like. Just do it here and now." Martin tore off his paper gown. "I don't need a lawyer. I need to be near my wife when she wakes up."

"We need to talk to Rachel too, when she's medically stable." Emotionally stable was a whole other story. Nick didn't want to wait that long to find out who'd given her the deadly syringe.

Martin sighed. "When the ICU consultant says it's okay and only if I can stay with her. I want to know what lies Simon has been telling her."

"We'll discuss that after your interview." Nick turned to his boss. "On tape?"

George nodded. "Find a room and get a digital recorder sent over. I'll keep the doc company."

"And I'll call Simon to check his version, too." Nick strode to the nurses' station to commandeer an office and a phone.

Chapter Thirty-Three

Julia blinked a few times to clear the fog from her brain. How long had she been out? Simon's bare feet loomed in front of her face, close enough to see the hairs on his toes. He stood between her and the only exit, the stairs she'd fallen down. The trapdoor was shut. He'd opened a set of bi-fold doors, revealing another room. Panic froze her to the floor. She caught glimpses of metal instruments and an examination table that belonged in nightmares.

She scrambled backwards, crashed into some boxes. Glass bottles clinked together. Her heart raced. She strained to hear if the police had arrived, but silence mocked her.

In the far corner of the room, a red light flashed a few times.

"The phone's ringing. Such good soundproofing down here, I used to miss a lot of calls." He smiled. "But you're the only person I want to talk to now."

Simon stepped backwards a few paces, then leant against his torture table. He stretched and put his hands behind his head. The bottom of his T-shirt lifted, revealing a patch of shiny, discoloured skin. A burn scar? Had he been hurt in the housefire that killed his mother? She shuddered. His gaze never left her. A cat watching a terrified mouse, savouring every moment, confident of the outcome.

She fumbled behind her back, grabbed a bottle from the nearest case. Time to see how much her upper body strength had improved. Her life depended on her punching bag. If only she could stop shaking.

"This isn't Grange," she said after ungluing her tongue from the roof of her mouth. How long ago had she texted Nick? Keep talking. "Something French. Any good?"

"If you have to ask, it'd be wasted on you. Put it back, there's a good girl."

She tossed the bottle up into the air, then caught it again, glimpsing the slightest hint of anxiety in his eyes. Trust him to value a bottle of wine over a human life. Could she take advantage of that sliver of weakness?

"Does this bother you?" She faked fumbling with the bottle.

"Put it back." An icy cold order.

"Do you really think I'd ruin a perfectly good premier cru?"

She twisted as if to replace the bottle in the case. Instead, she snatched a second bottle with her mangled hand. Fear overrode the spasms of pain shooting up her arm. Aiming at his bare feet, she smashed both bottles on the floor. Glass shattered around him. An expensive wave of red wine splashed across the concrete.

As red as blood.

"Fucking bitch." He sprang at her, but slipped in the wine and crashed to his knees.

She slid to the left and dragged an open case of wine onto the concrete. Bottles exploded on impact.

Simon clambered to his feet. He winced, then hopped backwards to sit on the bottom step. A large shard of glass protruded from the ball of his right foot. He extracted the splinter. Blood mingled with wine on his fingers. Dark eyes locked on hers, he licked the redness away.

His gaze flickered towards the table on the far wall.

If he reached those instruments, she wouldn't stand a chance. He'd overpower her and . . . No. Don't think about it. Heart pounding, she tightened her grip on a champagne bottle.

Simon lunged towards the table.

She threw herself after him, screamed when her left foot hit the ground.

He stretched, his right hand reaching for a scalpel.

She pivoted and swung the champagne bottle against the base of his skull. Shock waves jarred her arm.

He collapsed to the floor, boneless. Still breathing, unfortunately.

Julia dropped the bottle, too exhausted to hold it. She sank to the cold concrete floor. Her injured ankle twisted underneath her. Pain lightning-bolted through her body. She doubled over and vomited.

She wiped her mouth on her sleeve. A burble of hysterical laughter welled up in her throat. The champagne bottle had stayed intact. Veuve Clicquot. Must be a bloody good year.

When she recovered her breath, she dared to examine the hellhole. Simon remained motionless, so she threw another bottle at him to test his conscious state.

Bastard didn't even flinch.

Could she make it up the ladder? Her ankle twinged at the idea. Not without help. She dragged herself past him. With a death-grip on the edge of the table, she hauled herself upwards until she could stand on her uninjured leg.

Obstetric forceps and other surgical instruments glinted in the light. She couldn't imagine what he used some of them for and never wanted to find out. Bags of intravenous fluids and intravenous giving sets sat side by side with a wicked array of scalpels.

A large grey cabinet in the corner caught her eye. Why on earth did he have a microbiology incubator? Next to that, a noticeboard partially blocked by a screen. Lots of photos. A chill swept through her. Photos of her, some she remembered being taken on Valerie's phone. Others were shots of her house, her bedroom. He'd been inside her home?

Her chest tightened. She needed more air.

Get out now.

She spun around, then froze. Confronted by the centrepiece of Simon's twisted home operating theatre, she stood, rooted to the ground in fascinated horror. A twisted surgeon's DIY heaven. Wrist and ankle restraints contradicted the extra padding. Dark stains on the leather screamed out to her, breaking her heart.

"Want to help me with my research into pain?"

Simon's voice paralysed her.

Breathe. Run. Escape.

If only she could move.

After his phone calls, Nick strolled towards Rachel's room. When he saw Martin rush in, he sped up. A huddle of medical staff blocked his view of the patient.

"What's up?" he asked George.

"She's awake, and she's not happy. What did Simon say?"

"No answer, so I left a message for him to call you."

"Shouldn't he be at work? Page him."

"Tried that. Off-duty for a couple of days."

"Lucky bugger. Plenty of time to talk to us then. The video recorder?"

"On its way."

The crowd had thinned in Rachel's room, so Nick could see her through the glass window. She sat up in bed, clutching her arms to her chest. Hard to believe she'd just had a dose of sedative. She shook her head at whatever Martin was saying, then pointed at Nick.

Martin nodded. He brushed a strand of hair from her cheek, tucked it behind her ear, then left the room.

The ICU doctor followed him. "Some metabolism she's got there. Thought she'd be out for hours."

"Years of practice, unfortunately," Martin said. "She's much calmer, back to normal. Okay for her to talk to the police now?"

Nick waited for the doctor's answer. She certainly looked more in control compared to every other time he'd seen her.

A thoughtful grimace. "I'd rather the psych sees her first."

"If they'd looked after her properly in the first place, she wouldn't be back in ICU." Martin crossed his arms. "I know her moods better than any psychiatrist. This is as good as she gets."

"A physical exam and a chest X-ray, then I'll decide if she's fit for interrogation." The ICU doctor crooked a finger at one of his junior doctors.

More bloody waiting.

⸺◆⸺

Fuck. Julia fumbled in her pocket for her phone. It skittered out of her sweaty palm into a puddle of wine.

"You won't get a signal down here." He sounded almost apologetic—a civilised conversation between friends about poor mobile phone reception.

She snatched it up anyway, flicked it open and found, for once, he'd told the truth.

"Bastard." The only word she could get her petrified brain around.

Simon sat on the floor, picking splinters of glass out of his feet. "Pass me a pair of artery forceps."

"Why don't you bleed to death?"

"After everything I've done for you, all you do in return is insult me and trash my wine collection." He slapped the back of his right hand, then smiled. "Where are my manners? Please excuse my ungrateful behaviour. A whole year I waited and, at last, you came to me."

A whole year? She shivered. A year ago, her sister disappeared. Must be a dreadful coincidence. What exactly had he done for her? Keep him talking until the police arrive.

"I noticed the way you labelled the swab upstairs. Did you collect Martin's swabs for me?"

"Why do you want to know?"

"Those swabs were positive for VRSA, but he's denying they were his. If you collected them from him, then he'd have to accept the result." She twisted her mouth into a smile. "You could help me prove it to him."

"Positive for VRSA? That's perfect. Didn't you want someone to blame for the outbreak?"

"So, they are Martin's swabs?" She glanced at the incubator. Had Simon swabbed one of the VRSA patients instead?

"Glad to help your research project."

Keep going. "Wonder how he caught it. He denied contact with any of the hospital cases. No travel history. Could he have examined an infected international traveller?"

"So close. Maybe someone was smart enough to use pus from an infected international traveller to design a resistant infection and use Martin as the scapegoat."

Carmela from the grave in Kings Park? She shook her head. "Why the ever-loving fuck would you do that?"

"Surgery Christmas party last year? Your lips said no, but your eyes said ravish me. Such a tease. I looked everywhere for you, but you'd disappeared with Valerie and left me alone. That's why I punished you." He grimaced. "I over-reacted at the time, so I made you an anniversary gift. Your own research project."

"Punished me? How?" That was the week Tess disappeared. A steel fist squeezed the life out of her heart.

"You and Valerie? Oh, to have been a fly on the wall." He gave an exaggerated wink. "A hidden spy camera would've been perfect."

She shuddered. "Perv. What did you do?"

"At least you didn't abandon me for a surgeon. Mindless butchers." A harsh bray of laughter echoed around the cellar.

Simon sprang to his feet and glided one feline step towards her. The hunter and his prey. "You remind me so much of my favourite nurse in the Burns Unit. The one bright memory of my time in hell, isolated from all other human contact. While surgeons carved away my burns and scarred me for life, she showed me genuine compassion. She touched my scars as if they didn't exist. Just like I know you will."

"Burns? That must've been awful. Was that from the same fire that your mother . . ." Had he tried to save her? Maybe that failure and the traumatic experience had warped his mind.

He smoothed his T-shirt over his boardshorts. "I came home early from school that day and got quite the surprise. Not that they noticed me, of course. Too busy fucking. Hadn't even bothered to close the bedroom door. In the end, the surprise was on them."

She gasped. He couldn't have, could he? "What did you do?"

"Tsk, tsk. Don't play with matches, children."

Julia recoiled. He'd killed his mother—let his father take the blame—and not a flicker of remorse showed on his face. Just a boy then, and now ... he was a monster. Nobody was safe. Had he killed Tess too?

"How did you punish me?" Her voice quaked. "Did you take my sister? And Valerie? Did you kill them to punish me for rejecting you?"

His cold, heartless smile froze her bone marrow.

"I've been watching you all year, waiting for you to come to me. I nearly got you the night of Valerie's wake. Had to make do with a poor substitute." He gestured at his torture table. "I thought you'd appreciate my research project. Pain management is part of anaesthetics training. I study how much pain the human body can tolerate."

"No," she whispered. Her throat was too tight for anything louder.

"Valerie had quite a high pain threshold." Simon advanced again; his breath was warm on her face. "Impressive."

She couldn't move, couldn't breathe, couldn't think.

"Do you know what I really want to find out?" He licked his lips.

Another step—close enough that she could see the pulse in his neck. Closer.

He gripped her upper arms and lifted her onto the table, leaning his whole bodyweight into her, forcing her legs apart.

"No." She screamed in his ear, struggled to escape, but he'd pinned her arms by her sides and her movements only increased his excitement.

"Who's stronger? You . . ." He wrapped one arm around her waist and pulled her close, trapping her. "Or your sister."

Chapter Thirty-Four

While the medical staff checked Rachel's fitness for interview, Nick ran through Martin's revised statement. He had admitted to fudging his arrival time at Simon's house the night of Valerie's abduction.

"What did you do in that missing half hour?"

"A physio overheard us and waylaid me after Simon left. She's got a bit of a crush on me, wanted to invite herself along. We chatted for five, ten minutes, then I drove to Simon's."

"Why didn't you mention her before?"

"She was going on holidays—a ski trip in Canada—and she's still there, so she can't back me up, anyway."

"Anyone see you talking to her?"

"No. Look, Valerie wasn't killed straight away, was she? I'd have to be Superman to have spirited her somewhere in that short time. Simon must be mistaken. Or Rachel got confused. Have you checked with him?"

"Not yet."

"He took a bloody long time to come to the door. Said he was on the phone and hadn't heard me knocking."

The ICU doctor entered the room. "She's ready now, but keep it short. The registrar will stay with her and has my backing to throw you out if medically necessary."

⸻ ◆ ⸻

Seconds after moving to Rachel's room, George's mobile rang, earning him a lethal glare from the ICU doctor.

"Dr Singh. Back in a tick."

Nick adjusted the digital video camera on a table at the end of Rachel's bed. He zoomed out to include Martin in the frame. The young doctor on the other side of the bed edged out of view. Paper gowns rustled and monitors beeped. Not standard interview background noise by any stretch of the imagination.

Martin dragged his chair closer to Rachel. She smiled at him and, for the first time, Nick understood why the surgeon tolerated her moods. She looked like a distant, younger relative of the crazy woman he'd faced earlier. She lit up from the inside on seeing her husband. Or maybe that came from the drugs they'd poured into her.

George returned, his face shuttered. He closed the door with exaggerated care, then faced Rachel and Martin. A muscle jumped at the angle of his jaw. He didn't speak.

Nick couldn't catch his eye. What had Indira told him?

The only sound in the room came from Rachel's heart monitor. The longer George stared at her, the higher her heart rate rose.

When the ICU doctor shuffled his feet and opened his mouth to speak, George interrupted.

"Who gave you that medicine and syringe?"

She darted a glance at Martin. "It came this morning with some other gifts."

"The box from theatre?" Martin asked.

"Yes. Wrapped up with an unsigned card. Open in case of emergency. When I saw what was inside, I hid it in my handbag."

"A couple of scrub nurses said they'd organise a collection box for the staff tea room." Martin groaned. "What sick bastard would give her a lethal drug as a gift?"

"Anybody could've put it there?" George asked.

"Anyone with access to the operating suite." Martin's eyes brightened. "I'm in the clear. Security confiscated my ID card yesterday and I haven't operated all week."

"Thanks for your time." George turned away from Rachel and faced Nick, his expression still unreadable. "Outside."

He followed his boss out of the room. "Why'd you stop the interview? We could get prints or DNA if she kept the card or wrapping paper."

"What do we know about Simon Bailey?"

"He's an anaesthetist. He gave Martin an alibi for the night of Valerie's disappearance, but that's been blown."

"And he may have upset Rachel enough to drive her to suicide. Hardly best mate material."

"Medical skills, access to the operating theatres and anywhere else in the hospital, dodgy alibi." He stepped towards Rachel's room. "Let's find out more about his visit to Rachel."

"Wait a minute." George rested his beefy hand on Nick's shoulder. "Indira's worried about Julia. She's late and isn't answering her phone."

"Why didn't Indira—oh, shit, my phone's dead." His heart leapt into his throat. "How late?"

"Only an hour, but she had to collect some swabs on the way—from Simon."

Fuck. Julia was at Simon's house?

He shoved George out of the way, ran into Rachel's room, and skidded to a halt in front of Martin.

"Where does Simon live?"

A blank response from Martin.

Screw anger management counselling. He grasped the surgeon's protective gown with both hands and hauled him off the chair. The fabric ripped, but he'd caught enough of the underlying shirt in his grip. He swung Martin around and shoved him against the wall.

"He's got Julia." Breathing hard, he pressed his forearm across Martin's chest and leant in close. "Where does that bastard Simon live?"

Martin blurted out an address. One suburb away.

So close, yet so fucking far.

"Quickest way out of here?"

"Fire stairs," the nurse said. "You'll come out on the ground floor, near the coffee shop."

"I'll get back-up sorted. No heroics." George's order echoed behind him.

Nick dashed to the fire exit, threw the door open, raced down the stairs two and three at a time. Dizzy and breathless, he burst into the open air. His heart hammered. He sprinted to the car.

He couldn't be too late. Not again.

⸺◆⸺

Simon's words slammed into Julia. Her sister? Tess?

All year, she'd searched and waited and hoped. All for nothing. Tess and Valerie gone. Dead. Her brain short-circuited. Without Simon crushing her like a vice, she'd have slumped to the floor. A desperate, aching, hollow shell.

At last, awareness filtered through her pain. A slight movement eased the pressure on her body. The sound of a zipper. A shuddering groan. Simon's hand slid under her skirt.

Her left hand slipped free, her uninjured hand. Did he realise? Millimetre by millimetre, her fingers edged across the table behind her.

Simon clamped his mouth over hers, hot and demanding.

She fought the urge to gag. Cold metal at her fingertips. So close. Twisted her shoulders, leant backwards. Almost there. Fuck. She'd given him more room to manoeuvre.

His hand slipped down between them. He ripped her pants.

Breathing hard and fast, he wrenched his head back and smiled. "Much sexier than your sister."

Rage obliterated reason.

Julia slashed the scalpel across his throat.

His eyes widened. He clutched his throat with both hands, desperate fingers slipping and sliding in frothy cascades of blood. Awful gurgling noises filled the torture chamber. He staggered, dropped to his knees, then toppled sideways.

Her vision pulsed. What the fuck happened?

Red. Too much red.

She stared at the scalpel in her left hand, then at Simon's neck. The scalpel clattered to the floor. Do something. Help him.

But she couldn't move.

Oh, God. Tess. He'd killed Tess.

Her body. Where was Tess?

She slid off the table, knelt beside him. Was he dead? She felt for a pulse on the left side of his neck. His blood pumped out between his fingers with every beat of his evil heart. She compressed his severed right carotid artery and jugular vein with her own hands.

Simon fought against her, panic deep in his eyes.

"Where's Tess?" she screamed. "Where did you bury her?"

An unintelligible gurgle, his only reply. His hands fell away from his neck. No more struggling. A look of defiance in his eyes?

Bastard had surrendered.

She grabbed a dressing off the table and jammed it into his wound, pressed down as hard as she could. If only she could stop the bleeding and keep him alive long enough to get him to an operating theatre.

Within seconds, the dressing soaked through with blood. She kept the pressure on.

"Where's Tess?"

His eyes half-closed, he didn't respond.

She searched for a pulse in the left side of his neck, her fingers slick with his blood. Nothing. No pulse, no respiratory effort. She pulled his eyelids apart, checked his pupils. No reaction to light.

Not a single fucking sign of life.

She placed her hands over his chest and started rapid cardiac compressions.

"Don't you dare die on me now."

Nick fishtailed around the corner, swerved to avoid a jet-black SUV reversing out of a concealed driveway. Couldn't the idiot driver hear his siren?

He craned forward, urging the car faster. His gaze swept from side to side, on constant watch for obstacles. Heart hammering, he tried to block the images of blood and pain and terror that slide-showed through his mind.

A lifetime later, he skidded into Simon's street and squealed into his driveway. Julia's car sat across the road, empty. He turned off the engine, grabbed a heavy Maglite torch from the glove compartment and scrambled out of the car.

Fuck waiting for back-up.

He short-cut through the rose bushes, dashed onto the veranda. He pounded on the door. No answer. A thump with the Maglite shattered the glass window next to the door. He reached in, turned the knob. Not deadlocked, so he let himself in.

"Police," he shouted.

Still silence.

All senses on full alert, straight down the hallway. Lounge room on the left. Two cocktail glasses on a coffee table. Empty. A leather handbag abandoned on the floor. Julia's? Back to the hallway.

"Simon Bailey? Julia Sinclair?"

A wailing siren from the back-up police car's arrival drowned out any reply. Footsteps thudded towards him. He turned, held up a hand to silence the two uniformed police officers who clattered down the hallway.

"Julia?" Please let her answer.

Nothing.

He gestured at the other rooms. "Search the house."

The old-fashioned kitchen was empty. "Clear."

Nick hurried to the next doorway and found a study. Embedded in the floor, a trapdoor beckoned. He lifted it, flicked on his torch. Fat lot of good a torch would do if the prick had a gun. No way. The killer liked his knives far too much. Inflicting pain and killing, close and personal.

He looked down into hell. Broken glass glinting in the light. Red, lots of red. Too much red. He staggered back a step.

"Police." His voice echoed.

"About bloody time."

So fragile, but he recognised the attitude. And the voice.

"Julia, are you hurt? Where's Simon?" He pulled on a pair of gloves. "Get an ambulance," he said to the closest police officer.

A hiccup, maybe a sob. "I'll need a hand to get out of here, but don't worry about Simon. Live by the scalpel, die by the scalpel." Her voice trailed off into peals of crazy giggles, just like Rachel's.

Shit. He scrambled down the metal stairs.

A bloodbath.

Simon sprawled on the concrete floor in the total relaxation of death. His eyes stared at oblivion. Julia hunched over him in an awkward position, her left leg jutting to the side with her skirt hitched up. Her hands pressed against his throat. Simon and Julia—both soaked in blood.

Whose blood? Nick rushed to her side, knelt down, and drew her shoulders back to straighten her up. She didn't resist. Her hands dropped away from Simon's throat to expose a gaping wound. Was that the only source of blood?

"Are you hurt?" he asked.

Her giggles subsided. She lifted her right hand, then slumped against him as if that had drained her last reserves of energy. Her eyes drooped shut. Holding her up with one arm, he scanned her body for other injuries. Swollen ankle, mangled hand. Nothing to account for all that blood. Had Simon stabbed her?

"Where's that bloody ambulance?" he yelled.

No facial or neck injuries. The front of her shirt was scarlet. He undid her top button, then the next one.

"Aren't you going to buy me a drink first?" she asked in a shaky whisper.

"Did he stab you?"

"No."

"All that blood had to come from somewhere."

"Every last drop pumped by his poisonous, murdering heart after I sliced his carotid open."

That's the spirit. "You should phrase that a little differently in your official statement. Emphasise the self-defence angle."

She shuddered. "Bastard killed my baby sister. If I'd controlled my temper, I'd have found out where he buried her first. Now, I'll never find her."

"Leave some police work for me."

An ambulance stretcher rattled overhead.

"Hey, who was playing doctors a few minutes ago?" A weak laugh, but a genuine laugh at last. "Before I go, will you do one more thing for me?"

"I'll try."

"See that metal cabinet in the corner?" She pointed with her good hand. "Open it and show me what's inside."

Nick waited until the ambulance officer reached her, then stood. He passed the medical instruments on the side-table and the evil-looking examination table. What the fuck had Simon planned to do to Julia?

He grabbed the handle on the side of the grey cabinet, pulled it down and opened the door. Inside was a glass door, and behind that, stacks of plastic plates and jars of murky liquid. He stepped to one side so Julia could see.

"This mean anything to you?" he asked.

"His own private microbiology lab." She brushed aside the ambulance officer, who was trying to slide her onto the stretcher. "Grow your own bacteria. Bet that's VRSA . . . If he wasn't already dead, I'd kill him."

Chapter Thirty-Five

THE FOLLOWING MORNING, JULIA dozed on and off in an analgesic fog. Her emotions ricocheted between remorse and grief and sheer unbridled rage. So much easier to drift off again and pretend none of it had ever happened. Maybe if she slept long enough, the scars in her heart would harden and she'd forget she was responsible for her sister's death, for Valerie's death, for Simon's death.

Bastard. He deserved to die.

She wanted to curl up in the foetal position and bury herself under the bedcovers like she had as a child, hiding from the monsters under her bed. If only the monsters didn't live in her head. If only her left foot wasn't hanging in mid-air, elevated to reduce the swelling in her sprained ankle.

So bloody uncomfortable. She twisted onto her right side, but that pulled down on her damaged right hand, also suspended in space. K-wires stuck out of her fingers at odd angles, drawing her attention to the raw, bloody meat where her middle fingernail used to be. Talk about giving him the finger.

She closed her eyes. The red glow through her eyelids reminded her of the Tarantinoesque cellar. She could feel the warm stickiness of Simon's blood spurting through her fingers, could taste the copperiness from the fountain of blood that squirted into her mouth, could smell the abattoir stench of excrement and death.

Lucky she wasn't connected to a heart monitor. The alarm would go berserk.

A tentative knock on her hospital room door interrupted her morbid thoughts.

"Come in."

Martin entered. He inspected her mangled hand, then dragged a chair over to her bedside and made himself comfortable.

"Now do you believe I didn't kill Valerie?" he asked.

"Hi, Martin. Thanks for your concern. I'm feeling much better now you're here to keep an eye on my medical care."

He laughed. "I told your orthopaedic surgeon to treat you like a privately insured Olympic gold medal prospect or you'd be after him with a scalpel. Face went as white as a plaster cast."

"Does the whole hospital know about Simon?" Was she kidding? Of course they knew. Gossip central.

"You're both on the front page of the paper. He scored the bigger photo, but he killed more people than you."

"Great. I'll add it to my scrapbook." How could she stay working in the hospital? Endless whispers, knowing looks, sharp-witted jokes. Hell, even she couldn't resist. "I'll make sure the lab corrects your VRSA results. Simon contaminated your mystery swabs. Guess he wanted to frame you for everything."

Martin's whole body tensed. "Some friend he turned out to be."

She could almost hear his teeth grind. "I heard something about a showdown in ICU yesterday afternoon while I was . . ." Killing Simon. She tried to block that memory. The sounds, the smells, the hot blood pulsing between her fingers. Focus. "How's Rachel?"

"Much better." He inhaled a deep breath, relaxed his shoulders. "I can't lose her."

"Good luck."

He glanced at his watch. "I've got to run. Our first therapist appointment together." A flash of a wry smile. "Tell anyone and I'll deny everything. Blame your delusions on post-traumatic stress disorder."

"No one would believe me."

Julia closed her eyes and drifted back into bloodstained night-mares.

Minutes or maybe hours later, another knock on her door dragged her back to consciousness.

Gabriel poked his head around the corner. "Only me, warrior woman. Wish I'd seen you take down the killer. What really happened? Tell me all the juicy details."

If only she could get a word in. Typical Gabriel. He entered the room then perched on the edge of her bed.

"Oh, before I forget. Grab my handbag for me." She gestured at the side cupboard. "It should be in there somewhere."

"I guess you want a bit of lippie and a hairbrush."

"Hardly my first priority."

"Have you looked in a mirror?"

She ignored him and rummaged in her bag with her one good hand, pulling out a couple of swabs. "Fetch me a request form from the desk."

"Anything you say, boss." He paused in the doorway. "But when I get back, I'm brushing your hair. No offence, but you look like a bag lady after a cyclone."

When he returned, she filled in the form with Simon's details and handed it to Gabriel, along with the swabs.

"This is my last staff VRSA screen. His aseptic technique while handling bacterial cultures needed work."

He read the name on the form. "Wow. You did all that just to get a set of swabs? Remind me never to disobey you."

"Hey, I asked him nicely." She closed her eyes and let Gabriel fuss over her hair.

"Dr Branford said to tell you he'll drop by later on, but you shouldn't worry about your job. It'll still be there when you're fit and well." He laughed. "I think he's scared of you now."

"Good, because he won't like hearing our outbreak was a man-made present for me."

A firm knock on the door. Her eyes snapped open, but she couldn't see who lurked behind the curtain.

"Okay to come in?"

No mistaking that deep, warm voice. Nick.

Gabriel answered. "Unfortunately she's decent, but come in anyway." He gave one last flick of the hairbrush, then stood up and waved goodbye. "I have urgent specimens to deliver to the lab, but she's tied up, so you should be safe on your own."

Nick collapsed into the chair by her bed. Fatigue shadowed his eyes.

Her mouth dried, and her heart rate kicked up a notch. Fight or flight response? Neither of which she had the strength for. Was he going to question her about Simon's death? Charge her?

"How are you feeling?" A quick glance at her skewered hand, then back to her face.

"Apart from all the metalwork sticking out of me and being strung up like a carcass in a butcher shop, you mean?" She showed him a device with a button. "One press of this and everything is fuzzy and floaty and free from . . . pain and reality and death. Hell, you look like you need some, too."

"Catnapped in the office for a couple of hours." He brushed one hand along his jawline, a rasp of stubble. "The crime scene guys have a lot of work ahead, but they'll search for any clue to where he buried your sister. From what they've discovered so far, he kept detailed records. We'll find Tess."

Tess. The dead weight of grief crushed her to the bed. She curled her one good arm across her abdomen, holding herself together, desperate to bury the anguish deep inside until she was alone.

"So, you're here to take my statement? Arrest me? Give me a medal?"

"No, no, and I would if I had one." He stretched his legs out in front of him and slid further down the chair. "Someone else will be along later for your statement. Officially, I'm not here. I'm at home, keeping a low profile while they decide what to do with me."

"Why? What did you do wrong? I was the one who killed that murdering bastard."

A weary smile creased the corners of his eyes. "I disobeyed a direct order from my superior officer. I should've waited for back-up before entering the suspect's property."

"Even though I screamed my lungs out for help?" She held his gaze. "A woman in danger? You had no choice."

"But I didn't hear you."

"All these drugs are making me hazy about the exact timing, but I know I yelled for help several times, and you came. Simon is in no position to contradict me."

He shielded his eyes with a downward glance. "Thanks, but I can't ask you to lie for me."

"You didn't ask, and it's not a lie. Everything happened so fast . . . I saw death in his eyes. Valerie's death, my sister's death, my death." Her voice drifted to a whisper. "I wanted to kill him. That makes me just as much a monster as Simon."

The memory overwhelmed her. The overpowering rage, the scalpel in her hand, the bloody aftermath.

"No, it doesn't." Nick leant forward, reached out, and turned her chin with one hand until she looked straight at him. "You fought for survival. You had no choice. He wanted to torture you and kill you. He hunted you for twelve months."

"How do you know that?"

"Evidence." A jaw-breaking yawn punctuated his statement. He sank back in the chair.

"Evidence? What sort of answer is that?"

"At this crucial stage of the investigation, it would be inappropriate to discuss evidence with a witness," he said in his flattest cop voice with his most impenetrable cop face.

"I love it when you talk dirty." That scored a faint but definite twitch from the corners of his lips. "Did he leave a to-do list on the fridge, with Kill Julia written in blood?"

"Let's just say he liked to focus on you." He tipped his head back, closed his eyes.

"Focus? I saw the photographs on his noticeboard."

"Lucky you didn't see the ones on his computer. A complete photo-diary."

"When? Where was I?"

"At work. At home. Even a few while you slept."

Icy fingers crawled down her arms. Even dead, Simon had the power to terrify.

"While I slept?" A million bugs skittered over her skin.

"And you might consider a curtain for the bathroom window."

Her cheeks flamed. "Bloody, buggery, bastard Simon. I'd kill him all over again." She clenched her hands, forgetting the K-wires for a second. "Ouch, ouch, ouch."

"Didn't I warn you against making death threats in public?"

"I'm going straight from this hospital bed to a nunnery. Somewhere safe from twisted, perverted, camera-wielding murderers."

"Shame." He opened his eyes and warmed her with a grin.

"Careful. You saw what I did to the last guy who gave me cheek."

"I should go." He smothered a yawn.

"No, stay. You're too tired to drive. If the nurses kick up a fuss, I'll tell them I'm under police guard."

And maybe Simon, for a few heartbeats, wouldn't haunt her nightmares.

AUTHOR NOTE

Want to find out what happens next in the Dr Sinclair Investigations medical thriller series? Here's where to find the second book in this series, *Lethal Infection* ...

For all of my news and updates about future books, scan the QR code below to join my newsletter and get a deleted scene from *Isolation* with insight into the killer's mind.

Thank you for reading *Isolation*. Please consider leaving a review to share with other readers who are interested in medical thrillers. I'd really appreciate it too!

ABOUT THE AUTHOR

By day, SJ Gardiner is a clinical microbiologist, a pathologist specialising in the diagnosis and treatment of infectious diseases. Not the kind of pathologist who lurks around crime scenes and slices open dead bodies. In TV terms, think Dr Greg House, but without the cane or the drug habit and with a better bedside manner ... she hopes. Oh, and she'd kill for his turnaround time on lab results. Please don't tell the lab staff she said that. They do a fabulous job, and she doesn't want to scare them away.

After hours, she has a fatal weakness for crime fiction. Always buried in a book. How hard could it be to write one of her own? What about a whole series? So she combined her medical background with her occasional homicidal impulses and decided to find out.

Join SJ Gardiner on her twisted journey but be warned. It will get as gruesome as a zombie attack. Not afraid of a little blood or pus, are you?

Check out my website at https://www.sjgardiner.com or scan the QR code below.

SJ GARDINER

ALSO BY

<u>The Dr Sinclair Investigations</u>

Isolation
Lethal Infection

www.ingramcontent.com/pod-product-compliance
Lightning Source LLC
Chambersburg PA
CBHW050808190726
48285CB00005B/1839